U0687530

# BLOOD
# And
# BUTTERFLIES
## BY
### John Charles Harman

# Blood and Butterflies

## LIMITED FIRST EDITION
## FIRST PRINTING

Copyright Oct 31, 2010
All rights reserved.

# Blood and Butterflies

## CHAPTER 1

Bored is the man alone who consumed by guilt ponders plots he may never carry out. Yet, when "never" becomes the focus and obsession of his twisted mind, he snaps.

I wonder why it is that so many books have characters that are authors. Mark Twain may have said it best: "Everyone is a moon and has a dark side which he never shows to anybody." He is, of course, talking about "selfishness." We want to build ourselves up in our own minds to be always greater than we really are. But, who is to say that one man's view of reality is any clearer than another man's view of reality? Now in our modern societies of "political correctness," subjective reality is honed in messages and morals we are bombarded with through the media and our peers.

Friday, October 25, 2002

So they caught the sniper today. I thought for sure it would be some whacked out white guy, an ex-marine or something. Can you believe it is some young black guy? He even shot a black bus driver. No, there is no way he would have shot that bus driver if he knew he was black. Actually, what I heard is that he already came out and said he hates the "white man." That means he must not have seen the bus driver was black or he was just one of those light skinned blacks!" Tony said to his friend Brent, who lived in Alabama.

The conversation went on for another few minutes or so, but Tony Salerno knew he was getting too drunk and too bored, so he ended the conversation with some lame excuse. When he hung up the phone, he stared blankly into the wall in back of the phone. It only took a few seconds for him to have a plan. He chuckled out loud to himself feeling a sense of pride at how fast his mind could work even in his in drunken state. The idea of the sniper camped out in the trunk of his car with a hole to stick the gun out of brought on his idea. Tony smiled a big grin and then laughed out loud. He felt a sense of power he had never felt before and something snapped inside of him. He no longer cared about the voice of reason and morals. He knew his life would change and he liked the feeling. There was nothing that would stop him and for some reason what in the past had been vague mental ramblings and outright anger had melted into a plan.

Tony Salerno was from Italian heritage as his name would indicate and he was proud of it. Raised in Hermosa Beach, California, he grew up loving the beach. The warm water, the flow of the waves, and the surge of adrenaline when the waves started to get big were still exciting even after twenty years of surfing. There was no other thrill like falling down the face of the wave like a leaf in the wind when only he had the power to control it. He didn't surf as often as he had when he was younger, but when the urge hit and the waves were up, Tony hit the beach. He had started surfing when he was a teenager. He had been tall and handsome and never had a problem attracting women yet he was always distant from them and always felt like an outcast. Now that he was forty-five years old, he felt lonelier than ever. His son from his only marriage was off in college in Arizona and Tony had been in and out of brief relationships since his divorce eighteen years ago. He never totally cleaned up his apartment and the mess kept his rotating girlfriends from ever wanting to move in with him. He thought maybe he would get in a more stable relationship at some point, but when that time would come was not too clear or really that much of a priority for him.

After his lengthy but valueless conversation with his friend, he looked outside and saw there was a light rain. He pursed his lips into what could be called a smile, but it was more of a smirk as he looked into the misty rain that obscured his view of the beach. He stared blankly into the wet night. Tonight would be his night to make his first kill and the rain made it perfect.

Saturday, October 26, 5 PM

Detective Sloan was sitting at his desk when the phone rang. "Some gang kid has been shot. You get the case. They found the body this morning in some bushes. His girlfriend said he left her house around 1 AM," said MacIntosh, Head of Homicide.

"I just came in today to catch up on paperwork from the last case. You know I don't usually work on Saturdays, sir." replied Sloan.

"Well, I don't usually work on Saturdays either! But since we are both here, the case is yours. I'll send Maria down with the file." MacIntosh hung up the phone abruptly.

After ten years as a beat cop, Tim Sloan had finally made detective a year ago. He sat at his desk and stared at the paperwork he had almost finished. If his boss hadn't called, he would almost be ready to go home. Now he would have to stay for another hour and go over this new case. He really did not like being a detective and planned to get out of the police department in another year or so if he could. He did not want to be a policeman in Los Angeles or anywhere else for that matter. He just wanted to get out of the human zoo they called Los Angeles and find some small city where the people acted normal and were not obsessed with fame and fortune. He wanted a simpler kind of life, but he knew he would do his job and do his best at it. That was just the way he was, plus he needed the paycheck. The only good thing about being a detective and not a beat cop was now he could ask for reports more and write them less.

The Gang Unit at the Los Angeles Police Department had their own detectives and Tony was one of them. They all had different cases, but they also shared cases and worked together on different ones. There was a gang shooting almost every weekend and a murder at least thirty times a year, so they kept busy. The Crips and the Bloods were the two main black gangs there were too many Latino gangs to name. Add in the rise of the Vietnamese, Chinese, Koreans, Russians and just about any other ethnic group you could think of, and it was clear to see that the LAPD Gang Task Force Unit was understaffed and overworked. A large percentage of the cases went unsolved, as cooperation of gang members and civilian witnesses was almost non-existent. Every once in a while, a witness would come forth and gave an account, but it usually ended at that. Often when the time came to go to court and testify, the witness did not show up; subpoena or not, fear kept them away.

Tim looked at his watch, sat back in his chair, took the briefcase, and put it back on his desk so he could throw the report in it. "Crap it's almost 6 PM. I need to get out of here. I promised Linda I would take her to dinner tonight. One more dinner, she wants to talk, but about what? The same things... at least she started doing some exercise. Tennis, wow...such great exercise. Why did they have to give me this case now?" He subconsciously got up from his desk and headed to the vending machine down the hall so he could get a Coke. He knew by the time he returned to his desk there was a possibility Maria would be waiting there with the report in her hand. It was Saturday though and Maria usually didn't work Saturdays. Any other day, she would be leaning over his desk looking at all of the paperwork on it with her back to him. She would be standing and turning nervously, revealing all her sacred curves, letting her nice cute tight rear end appear into his full view as he strolled back from the vending machine. She knew that he would be looking, but she would act like she didn't see him and would slowly rub her hand over her thigh, as she would straighten her skirt. It was their little flirting game that they had been playing for almost a year. He would come up very close to her and then casually say "Hi Maria." She would turn and act surprised, as they stood very close, face-to-face. They were both married, but still felt that wild sense of animal magnetism for each other. They wanted each other, but just flirted. They both were too scared to go any further and were both too committed to their respective spouses to take the next step that they secretly desired. So, their little game of smiles and soft niceties always lingered and carried over until they would see each other when Maria would bring down a report form MacIntosh. The LAPD was a large police force and not everyone knew each other. Maria usually brought a report down only once a week or so and Tim actually felt sort of privileged today because he knew she rarely worked on Saturdays either, but there she stood.

Tim had not seen Maria since last Tuesday, but he had thought about her. He had thought about her in the shower and he had thought about her when he made love to his wife. Sometimes he thought about her in the morning when he woke up aroused having fantasized about putting his arms around her as she stood leaning over his desk.

Maria turned just as Tim approached and as usual they stood very close, face-to-face. She smiled at Tim with her soft brown eyes gleaming. She wanted to kiss him, but instead blurted out, "Oh hi! Here is the report on that homicide last night."

"Thanks Maria. I just went to get a Coke," replied Tim, a little shy as usual. His eyes drifted down to where he could see her nipples outlined through her bra. He could feel himself getting aroused. He hurriedly moved around her and sat behind his desk. Maria remained in front of his desk leaning over now and smiling even more.

Tim Sloan liked to read and he tried to write, but he knew he would never be that good of a writer. He knew he didn't have the flare. Tim was forty-four years old and was married to his high school girlfriend. They had two lovely daughters, who were fourteen and eleven years old. By nature, he was conservative and had always kept his hair short so he wouldn't be associated with the liberal crowd. He loved his wife or better put, he forced himself to stay in love with her. He had never cheated on her, at least not in the way of having another relationship with another woman. Twice at police conventions out of town, he had slept with prostitutes. He liked to think that it was more out of peer pressure than out of desire, but either way it had torn him up inside with guilt. In a way, it had been good for his marriage. It had forced him to renew his passions for his wife when he returned home.

Tim was a handsome man. He was about six feet tall with close-cropped, slightly graying, light brown hair. He was of Irish-German background, had an LA tan, and was fairly fit. Since he had become a detective he worked out a lot less though.

Maria didn't leave. Maybe it was because it was Saturday and there were not many people around, but she lingered in front of his desk just staring at him. She put the report down on his desk and then kept her hands on his desk leaning over closer to him and smiling. Tim smiled back.

Maria Sanchez had been working for the police department for two years now. She was thirty-two years old and was married to her second husband, but had two children, one belonging to each of her husbands. Felix, who was her present husband, worked in an auto repair shop, which was owned by his uncle. Maria was a third generation Mexican-American and her husband was a second generation Guatemalan. They had married mainly because Maria had become pregnant. Felix was two years younger and at times Maria thought that was the reason he tended to act so immature. He was great with her two sons and treated them both the same even though one was her former husband's child. He took the two boys to ballgames and movies almost every weekend. Julio was Maria's first son and he was a really good athlete. Leo, Felix's son, was more of the creative type, but overall the two boys got along very well and Felix gave them both a lot of attention. The problem Maria had with Felix was not how he treated her sons, but how he treated her. The macho Latino crap was getting old. Maria made more money now than her husband and she felt she deserved more attention and respect. Felix didn't help with anything around the house. He never cooked or cleaned and Maria was annoyed when she came home tired from work and found him drinking beer and hanging out with his friends. Worse was the fact that at night he treated her like he owned her and would come to bed drunk. Sometimes he would even force himself on her. There had been no passion or happiness for Maria lately. She felt more passion and happiness now in the brief moments when she could bring the reports to Tim and devour him with her eyes, smile at him, and talk softly to him.

Tim looked down at the report and then up at Maria's breasts. Maria knew he was looking and she liked his eyes on her. Both were totally aware of the zero tolerance for workplace sexual harassment, but it was Saturday and there were not many people around. Still though they knew their words had to be soft and polite, so their looks would have deeper meanings. "Did you read the report?" asked Tim looking up from Maria's breasts to her inviting eyes.

Maria smiled even broader, thinking to herself, "I wonder if he wants me like I want him or if he's just being polite." She answered, "Well you know I am only supposed to bring the reports down to you. I wouldn't want to break the rules Mr. Sloan!" Maria enjoyed calling him Mr. Sloan because she knew exactly what he would say next.

"Maria, I've told you before just call me Tim," he replied back right on cue.

Maria felt a warm tingling sensation inside of her from the pure joy of knowing how many times they had repeated that exact interaction. "Yes, Tim (She emphasized the "Tim"), I read some of it. Black male, seventeen years old, known Crypt gang member, and the name is Jamil Johnson. He has been in out of Juvenile Hall since he was twelve. The approximate time of death was 12:30 AM. Shot with a 22-caliber bullet...most likely it was a handgun at fairly close range. That is as far as I got. Oh yeah, his girlfriend said he left her house around midnight."

"Thanks Maria. That was sweet of you. I don't want to go through the whole thing now. It has been a long day and I just want to get out of here," Tim replied.

"Yeah, it has been a long day for me too. I didn't want to come in today, but the boss said he needed me so we could catch up on things. The overtime pay helps anyway." Maria wanted to stay and talk. She liked fixing Tim's face in her mind, but she knew he was ready to leave, so she took her hands off his desk and stood getting ready to turn and leave. She started to think that her fantasy of her and Tim was just a fantasy that would never happen.

"Maria, I just wanted to say before you go that, well just seeing you today made my day. I love your smile Maria!" Tim said quickly before she turned and left.

Maria turned back and smiled from ear to ear. Her legs began to tremble a little. She wanted to touch him and kiss him so badly. "Wow, that is very nice to hear and I feel that way too!" she blurted out and then walked away making sure to sway her hips just a little bit more than usual as she left, knowing he would be watching.

**Tony**

Tony Salerno sat in his apartment watching the sixth game of the World Series. It was almost 7 PM on Saturday night. He had a pizza and a six-pack of Zima. He was getting really pissed off as the score was 5 to 0 and the Giants were winning. He had bet fifteen hundred dollars on the Angels to win the World Series and he needed them to win tonight to take it to a game seven. It didn't look good as it was going into the bottom of the sixth inning and the Angels needed a big rally. He started to feel the effect of the Zimas and tried to relax, accepting the fact that he would loose his bet. He turned the TV off and went to put on some clothes, thinking he would go out to the local bar. Just for the heck of it, after he dressed, he turned the TV back on and saw that it was now the bottom of the ninth inning and the Angles had rallied, caught up, and taken the lead 6 to 5! He sat back down and opened another Zima. He watched the last out and became ecstatic, letting out a yell at the thought that there would be a game seven and he now had a chance to win his bet! He sat back on the couch and felt very relaxed from all the alcohol. He turned the TV off and closed his eyes. He smiled and started to think about what he had done the night before.

"That was so easy and so clean. One shot to the back of the head. That stupid punk gang member was nothing but a piece of trash. Now there is one less punk out there. That means a few less pregnant teen girls and a few less drugs on the street. I guess I should feel some remorse but I don't. I feel great about it. Yes, maybe I can make a small dent in the population of idiots on the street. Los Angeles is such a decadent city. I mean there are thousands of idiots out there. Maybe one doesn't make much difference, but I am not stopping now. I can play this out as long as I want. I don't see why things couldn't be like the old cowboy times...the good guys and the bad guys. The good guys just whack off the bad guys-not all this glorification of being a rapper and drug dealer. Cops should just have free reign on getting these idiots of the street. Forget about global warming. LA is boiling with putrid humans that need to be wiped out." Tony had a few more Zimas, which made him get very drowsy and he fell asleep on his couch.

Sunday Morning, 7 AM

Maria had a dilemma. The night before her boss had given her two tickets to the World Series Game 7 at Anaheim Stadium. The game was to be at 5 PM. The Angels won the night before so the game was on for sure. She didn't know whom she should invite to the game. She could take one of her sons, but the other one would be jealous. There was no way she was going to let Felix have the tickets and decide because he just had been too much of a jerk lately and didn't deserve it. Her real problem was that she sort of had decided to try and ask Tim Sloan if he wanted to go to the game with her, but she couldn't get up the courage to do it. She knew he loved baseball and just maybe he would go with her, especially because this was Game 7 of the World Series. The problem was that she would have to call him at home and she had never done that. Plus, there was a chance his wife would answer the phone and if that happened, Maria knew she would just have to hang up. If they had caller ID, which she was sure they must, then they would know she had called and that would be a total disaster. So she sat at her kitchen table at 7 AM with a cup of coffee trying to think what to do.

She had almost picked up the phone and dialed Tim's number more than once, but each time she had chickened out and went back to sipping her coffee. She didn't know his cell phone number and thought maybe she could go into her work and get it, but that would take too much time. Felix was still in bed, drunk and smelly from the night before, but she knew he could stagger out of the bedroom anytime now, so she had to make a decision soon. Then, as she was thinking what to do, she realized she subconsciously had her hand on the phone again. "Oh just do it," she said to herself trying to get the courage, and then she dialed Tim's phone number. As the phone rang, she held the receiver away from her ear sort of grimacing at what she was about to get herself into.

Tim was curled up with his wife in bed when he heard the phone ring. He answered on the second ring. "Tim Sloan."

Maria had the phone so far away from her ear she could barely hear his voice and she started to put the receiver down to hang up, but she didn't. She answered shyly, "Mr. Sloan, this is Maria. I'm sorry I called so early at home, but I just needed to talk to you for a minute."

Tim recognized her voice right away and knew she wouldn't call him at home for any work related matter because that was not her position at the police station. He wondered what she wanted and was happy to hear her voice, but didn't want his wife, who was still half asleep next to him, to know who he was talking to. He replied, "Oh hi, can you hold on just a minute?" He put the receiver down, looked at his wife who had her back to him, quietly got of bed, and started to go to the living room to talk to Maria on the other phone.

Just as he was leaving, his wife half rolled over and mumbled, "Who is that honey?"

"It's just a call from work. Probably some new information on a case I have. I'll get it in the other room," Tim said as he scurried off to the living room. He picked up the phone in the living room. "Maria, what's going on? Is there some problem?"

Maria was shaking with nervousness and hesitation. She was sure now she had made a bad decision, but she had to go through with it. "No, no, well yes sort of. I am really sorry to call you so early. I don't want to cause any problems. It is just that I got these two tickets to the game today. Mr. MacIntosh gave them to me yesterday as I was getting ready to leave and well I if I gave them to anyone in my family someone would get jealous, so I just thought maybe you would want to go with me to the game."

"You mean the seventh game of the World Series?" Tim asked surprised.

"Yes, and he said they are pretty good seats too," Maria replied. "I thought since you really liked baseball that maybe you would want to come with me to the game. I know it is a big game." Once she had finally asked she felt relieved, but again she cringed and held the phone away from her ear not wanting to hear his reply.

"Wow, that is really a surprise and very thoughtful of you. I have never been to a game seven of a World Series. Actually I have never been to a World Series game at all. I would love to go!" Tim said with excitement. At the same time, however, he realized he would have to lie and make excuses to get out of the house. He knew if his wife or daughters ever found out they would be mad and jealous that he went to the game and didn't take them. It was a chance he wanted to take though. The thought of going to a game seven of the World Series and the thought of being there with Maria was very exciting. It was definitely crazy and risky, but worth it.

Maria thought, "He said, yes! Oh my God, I am really crazy." She had a grin ear to ear.

"Why don't we meet at a restaurant or something near the stadium and we can go from there? The game is at 5 PM right?"

"Yes it is. That sounds good. Where should we meet?" replied Maria in a bit of a daze as she now began to contemplate what she would wear. She wasn't too worried about getting away for the evening as she would just tell Felix she had to go into work to catch up on some things.

"How about El Cholos on Katella Avenue?" asked Tim.

"Ok, that sounds good. I know where it is. Why don't we meet at 4 PM?" Maria replied still a bit dazed that he had actually said yes.

"Sure I'll meet you there. This should be fun!" Tim said fully awake now and wondering if he was doing the right thing even though he was excited by the idea.

"Bye," they said in unison and hung up their respective phones. They both instantly had smiles at what they had just agreed to do. Then of course, Judeo-Christian guilt ridden minds began to amend, adjust, and ponder scenario after scenario of what would happen if their spouses ever found out about their erotic thoughts. The reality set in for both of them and they started planning their excuses and lies for going to work on a Sunday so they could meet and go to the game.

**Tony**

Tony awoke on his couch at 11 AM. He was hung-over, so he went to the small dirty kitchen, drank two glasses of water, and took some aspirin. He kept thinking of his bet. He needed the money because he had lost the week before. The fact there was going to be a game seven and there was a chance he could win excited him out of his slumber. He dressed and decided to go to Denny's and eat a big breakfast. Tony knew the location of at least ten different Denny's restaurants in the

LA area and he tried not to go to the same one twice in a row. There was no favorite and he liked the fact that they seemed to often change waitresses at the different Denny's. Today he just wanted to eat, sit, and read the Sunday paper. Tony drove a 1970 Mustang. It was a faded dark blue with grey patches where he had fixed some dents. He had thought of getting it painted someday, but never got around to doing it. It ran like a charm and he had done some modifications on his own to make it even faster. He liked it because it was an old muscle car and could beat almost anything on the road if he let it out, which he rarely did. What always humored him was when some young Asian or Latino guy pulled up alongside him in some tricked out and highly chromed Honda or Toyota and wanted to race. Usually he just looked at them, turned up his radio, and laughed, but once in a while he showed them what an old American V-8 engine could do, and blew them off the road. Today as he drove, he noticed once again some young Asian guy in back of him and when he pulled up to the next stoplight, the guy revved up his engine. The car was a Honda with big tires and a hood scoop. It looked totally ridiculous to Tony and he laughed out loud and cranked up the Led Zeppelin CD he was playing. He let the guy get a head start and then blew past him, giving him the finger on the way. It was a rush and Tony loved it. Now if he could just win the bet tonight he thought to himself.

"What can I get for you, sir?" asked the petite Asian waitress as Tony sat down in the restaurant.

Tony looked at her nametag, Susi, and thought to himself her name must be Susie and she picked it as her American name because she has some unpronounceable Asian name. She was definitely cute though. He thought she was around twenty-eight or so. She had a very nice smile and a really tight body. "Susie, right, did I pronounce your name correctly?" he asked with his best smile. She nodded. "Well, I could use some coffee to start." When she came back with his coffee, he smiled again at her and this time she smiled back. He ordered a Grand Slam breakfast and started to open his paper. When she came back with the food, he thanked her politely. He knew now was not a good time to try and engage her in a conversation as it was Sunday and the restaurant was quite busy. He acted a bit coy and shy, but let her know he was interested with his eyes and smile. He liked the way she had smiled back at him.

He put down his paper as he ate and started once again to think about the killing he had committed late Friday night. "It was sort of like the time when I was fourteen and I shot that cat at close range with my BB gun...yeah, very smooth. The 22-caliber was perfect at close range, not much blood, and his head didn't blow apart. He fell straight to the sidewalk and when I dragged him into the bushes I didn't even see any blood on the sidewalk. They will think for sure that it was just another gang shooting. I can't believe what has happened to people's morals nowadays. Drugs, freaks, gangs, gays... It is out of control and totally screwed up. Someone should just drop a bomb on the LA County jail. That would eliminate a bunch of them all at once. Better yet they should just take them out to the desert and gas them like they did the Jews in World War II. The problem is that wouldn't even put a dent in the worthless trash out there in society, but I made a difference...there is one less punk out there on the streets." Then the one thought that had kept coming into his mind since last Friday night came again. "It was so easy, so easy... wow! If I do it too many times I may get caught, so I have to be very careful each time."

Tony finished eating and sat casually as if he was reading the paper, but he was really watching Susi as she waited on the other tables. He decided to do his favorite thing to assure that she would call him. He left a five-dollar bill wrapped around a twenty-dollar bill as a tip with a little note saying that he loved her smile and that she should call him when she got off work.

On the drive back home he forgot about the waitress and started thinking again, talking out loud. "Ok, so I killed one gang member...so what? It is only one and it really makes little difference in the overall scheme of things. Maybe I should do something bigger. The thing is if anyone knew they would say I'm prejudiced and I have a thing against blacks, but I'm not prejudiced. Heck, I've dated all races and I work with all races. Some I like and some I don't. I don't hate blacks; I just hate the scum of the world that makes things harder for normal people like me."

When Tony arrived at his apartment, he saw his neighbor coming in at the same time in the hallway. Tony didn't know his name even though he must have seen him a hundred times. He just referred to him as his "fat" neighbor.

"Hi Tony. Hey, what about those Angels? Were you watching the game yesterday? They pulled off another comeback and today they are going to play game seven! I am having some people over later to watch the game and you're welcome to come if you like," said the neighbor.

Tony was not in the mood to get to know his fat neighbor, but tried to be polite. "Thanks, I'll think about it, but I really have a lot to do." As he started to put the key into the lock of his apartment, he felt the anger welling up. "Why did that fat slob have to remind me of the game? I had completely forgotten about the game. I have a big bet riding on that game and I do not want to watch it or even know the outcome until tomorrow." He went straight to his bedroom and lay down on the bed, putting the pillow over his head, and hoping he would fall asleep.

He had dozed off and was in the middle of a wild dream when the phone rang. He quickly looked at his watch and saw it was nearly 5 PM. God, he hoped it wasn't his fat neighbor calling. He waited until the fourth ring and then decided to answer the phone anyway. It wasn't his fat neighbor. "Hi, is this Tony?" she asked in a soft sweet voice. "This is Susi from Denny's. You asked me to call."

For a second, Tony wasn't sure whom he was talking to, but then he remembered.

"Yes, you gave me your number at Denny's earlier today," Susi said wondering if she had made the right decision to call the guy since he didn't even seem to remember her!

Tony's charm kicked in now that he was aware of whom it was and that she had called so soon. "Oh hi! Yes, I remember you. I'm sorry I was taking a nap and just woke up. You are the lovely Asian woman at Denny's who had such a pretty smile. How are you? I'm glad you called. I have to say I'm a little shy and that was the first time I have ever done anything like that. I just loved your smile though and have to say that you seemed really nice."

Susi was still a little hesitant and wondered if he was just a player. "Well, I have to be upfront and tell you that I am engaged. I don't want you to get the wrong idea. Really though that was very sweet of you and that was the biggest tip I have ever received."

Now Tony knew a little more about her. Instantly, he calculated his chance and knew where to go in the rest of the conversation. She had tipped her hand to him and he loved it. He knew there was no way she would have called if she wasn't having some reservations about her so-called fiancé no matter what tip he had given her. "Oh, I understand completely Susi. I'll just say I'm a bit sad though because I really like you. I'm happy that you called anyway and you really do have a voice to match your lovely smile. Maybe we can just be friends? I can be a good listener!"

Susi thought for a moment and then replied, "Sure, that might be nice. Would it be ok if I called you again sometime?"

Tony knew she wouldn't give him her phone number at this time and there was no reason to push it. He knew she would call back again, probably after the next fight with her so-called fiancé. "Yes, you can call me anytime. I'm usually up pretty late, so feel free to call back and we can talk again."

"Well, it was nice meeting you and I will call back, but I can't promise when. Like I said, I have a boyfriend," replied Susi.

Now the fiancé had been reduced to boyfriend and Tony smiled at the slip. "That would be great Susi; we can be friends and you can call me anytime. It was very nice talking with you."

"It was nice talking with you too. I will give you a call again sometime," Susi replied.

Tony wasn't sure whether she would call back or not, but the option was definitely there. He had learned long ago the differences between the friendships men and women kept. No man would ever say he had a female friend unless there was a relationship in the past or the hopes of one in the future. Men were always hopeful that one day the friendship would turn into sex. Women on the other hand felt it was their liberated right to have men as just friends, but subconsciously they knew they could take the friendship to the next level if they wanted. Women needed the safety net of knowing that they had options if things didn't work out with their husband or boyfriend.

## CHAPTER 2

El Cholos Restaurant 4 PM

Maria had arrived early and was sitting at the bar looking at her watch every few minutes wondering if Tim would really show up. She had her doubts. Maybe he would get cold feet. She had come early because she needed to change her clothes in the bathroom. She had left a note for Felix, who had taken the boys to the park. She said she had to go into work, so she had dressed in work clothes. She had changed from her black skirt to her tight red leather pants in the bathroom at the restaurant. She knew the Angels colors were red, so she thought she would look nice and fit right in at the game. The silk white blouse and black blazer would do fine with the pants. While sitting at the bar and thinking about Tim, she thought about going back into the bathroom and taking her bra off, but decided against it. She looked at her watch again and finished her margarita. It was now five after four and he was supposed to be meeting her at four, so she started to get really nervous that he wouldn't show up. She thought about calling him on his cell phone, but decided he either showed or he didn't. She asked the bartender for another margarita and then headed back to the bathroom to check how she looked one more time. She stood looking in the mirror and said out loud quietly to herself, "Oh, what the heck?" and then took off her bra and put it in her large purse. She looked at herself again in the mirror and decided she should button her blazer, so it wouldn't be too obvious she wasn't wearing her bra. She touched up her lipstick and thought, "Felix should appreciate me more! I look pretty damn good for having two kids, breastfeeding them both, and doing all the work I do." She stood back from the mirror after she finished her lipstick and looked at her profile. "Damn, I am starting to look pretty good. That trainer at the police gym was right...I just needed to firm up. As long as I go at least three times a week I'm going to be in really great shape in another month or so. This is the result after just one month." She turned sideways and put her hand on her hip and traced the outline. "I am getting pretty tight!" Then she caught herself and thought, "What am I doing? I'm acting like a teenager...not a married woman with two kids!" She took a few deep breaths and thought, "Ok, ok, I have to just keep this a friendly date. We are just going to a ballgame." She looked down at her watch and it was 4:15, so she hurried out of the bathroom and back to the bar.

Tim arrived while Maria was in the restroom. He had made the same excuse that Maria had about going to work, so he could go to the game. He had snuck his red Angels jacket into the car and put it on once he had arrived at the restaurant. He was feeling sneaky and guilty mainly because his wife had said that she felt sorry he couldn't stay and watch the game with his daughters. The oldest daughter played softball and was a big Angels fan now that they were in the World Series.

When he entered the restaurant and looked around in the bar he didn't see Maria. Since he was a bit late, he almost turned around and walked out again thinking he would just go back home because this was just completely insane. He sat down at the bar though and ordered a soda knowing he couldn't go back home smelling like alcohol. He figured if Maria didn't show up he would kill at least an hour before he went back home so he could at least say he had done some work.

Just as the bartender brought his soda, he saw Maria walking out of the restroom. Suddenly his attitude changed; he was filled with a feeling of adventure and the guilt flew away like one of those school seagulls leaving the lunch area. "Oh my God she looks good!" he thought to himself. Maria saw him immediately and almost turned around and headed back into the restroom. She was thinking to herself how crazy she was to have taken her bra off and now she felt embarrassed. She took a deep breath and smiled at him and continued over to where he was at the bar. While she walked, she pulled her blazer around her chest hoping it would hide the fact she wasn't wearing her bra.

They were both smiling at each other as she approached. Their eyes were devouring each other and making love.

'Hi Maria. Wow you look really nice. I love those pants," said Tim.

"Thanks, you look nice too," replied Maria.

Tim noticed immediately as Maria leaned over to sit down on the barstool next to him that she wasn't wearing her bra. He reached out and shook her hand softly not wanting to act like this was anything more than a friendly date, but hoping it would be something more. He stood up and looked at his watch. "I'm sorry I'm a bit late. I was stuck in traffic. I guess we had better get going. Even though the stadium is not far away there is going to be a traffic jam getting there."

All Maria could think about was how nice Tim smelled. She was so used to the horrible smell of grease and sweat that pervaded her apartment every time Felix came home from work that the fresh clean smell of Tim made her want to stay close to him. "Yes, I think we should go now. The game starts at 5:30. This is going to be fun!" she said excitedly as she got up from the barstool.

As they headed out of the restaurant, Maria walked close to Tim. She wanted to touch him, to take his hand in hers, but she restrained herself. They were both excited…excited to be going to the seventh game of the World Series and even more excited to be with each other away from work. They took Tim's car. They were only about twenty minutes from the stadium, but the cars were gridlocked. They talked about how Maria had gotten the tickets from her boss. Tim made a quick turn out of the traffic toward a hotel that had a big stadium parking sign. They were charging $20 to park, but he didn't care at this point because he just wanted to get out of the traffic.

Once out of the car they blended into a crowd of people heading to the stadium, which was still half a mile away. About halfway there, Maria who had been debating in her mind whether to or whether not, went for it and reached out and held hands with Tim. He did not resist. She had thought about it ever since they had parked the car and was hoping he would make the first move, but finally she couldn't resist anymore. He just smelled so good!

On the drive from the restaurant, Tim had been concentrating on getting them there on time because the traffic was so bad. He snuck in a few glimpses at Maria as she sat next to him in his car and he could see the outline of her breasts through her blouse as her blazer was now unbuttoned. He tried not to look too hard. He had been telling himself that this was just going to be a friendly date at the ballgame, but inside he felt the guilt of an anticipated liaison because he knew he wanted her. He didn't want to cheat on his wife, but now he had already lied about going to the game with Maria and somehow he felt he would go further. He let his mind wander and go back and forth from the excitement of going to the seventh game of the World Series for the first time in his life to the thought of being with Maria. He tried to make a vow to himself to enjoy the game and not get too close to Maria. Now that they were holding hands everything had changed and the idea of this just a friendly date evolved back into the erotic fantasies he had been having for months ever since their flirting had begun.

They had only walked about twenty or so steps when Tim stopped, turned, and pulled Maria into him, and they embraced. They came together like two magnets and they kissed fully on the lips. It was passionate yet awkward and brief. When they pulled away, Tim blurted out apologetically, "I'm sorry Maria. I just had to kiss you!"

"It's fine Tim; I wanted you to kiss me," Maria replied grinning and thinking to herself that she really wanted him now. His smell was making her weak and excited. She felt like she could do anything with him right now. Forget the game. She just wanted to devour him in some hotel or back in his car.

Then they realized they had stopped in the flow of people walking to the game. Everyone else was hurrying past them and staring as they stood there gazing at each other, so they resumed holding hands and continued walking. They were smiling and their anticipation swelled like a slow fever burning inside of them. They were both thinking the same thing as they walked: "This is so crazy!"

They continued to make their way toward the stadium, but were now caught up in the excitement all around them. Everyone was wearing red, the noise was almost deafening, and the game hadn't even started yet. As they entered the stadium, they were given "thunder sticks," two inflated plastic tubes that you banged together. As they made their way to their seats, everyone was standing and the National Anthem began to play. When they sat down, the anthem had ended but the applause and noise that followed was deafening. They were sitting in the upper deck directly behind home plate, which was a perfect spot to see the game.

"This is so exciting!" exclaimed Maria as she took her blazer off.

"Yes it is," replied Tim as he turned toward her and admired how she looked through her silk blouse. He almost wished he were somewhere else with her than at the seventh game of the World Series. "Did you see the game yesterday? They were down 5 to 0 and came back to win!"

"I saw the game with my sons. Well, at least part of it in between cooking dinner," Maria replied.

"I didn't actually see the whole game either. I listened to the first part on the radio as I drove home from work. I didn't think they had a chance to win," Tim replied not wanting to seem too much like the baseball fanatic he was.

Tim had played baseball as long as he could remember. He had gone through Little League and eventually became the star of his high school team. He had been a pitcher and a good pitcher at that. Being left handed and having a strong arm allowed him to dominate. During the last two weeks of his senior year, as his team was advancing in the state playoffs, he had injured his arm. He pitched through the pain and never told anyone, but that caused the minor injury to turn into a serious injury. The season ended and he thought he would heal on his own as long as he didn't throw. He had accepted a scholarship at a major university, but when he showed up after the summer break to start, his coach saw that his arm wasn't the same. He was examined and had to have an operation. He wasn't able to pitch the whole season and his second year he was able to pitch, but had lost his blazing speed. The coaches were trying to get him to learn different pitches, but Tim was now engaged to his high school sweetheart Linda and wasn't as focused on baseball. He was in love and all he wanted was to be with Linda and get married. They did marry the following summer and they went to Europe on their honeymoon. He skipped summer baseball even though he knew it was required as part of his scholarship. When he returned to school in the fall, the athletic department dropped his scholarship. Tim's father was livid at first, but conceded to help pay for Tim's third year at the university. He made it clear though that he would only pay for one year. Tim and Linda struggled to make ends meet. They were on their own with minimal support from their parents. They were madly in love and the fact that they didn't have the money to go out or buy things didn't seem to matter too much. What did happen though was Tim's grades began to slip. He didn't tell his parents or Linda. Before he returned to school for his final year at college, he made the decision to take some time off and work full time. Linda tried to talk him out of it, but Tim was headstrong and wouldn't listen. He really didn't know if he was making the right decision, but he convinced Linda and his parents that it was only a temporary plan and that he would finish college eventually. All he knew at the time was that he didn't want to be continually worried about money and the basic necessities of life. He wanted to work to make Linda happy and to be able to buy her nice things. He wanted a family someday. After a few dead end jobs, Tim applied for the LA Police Department. His application was accepted and he told his wife he thought it would be a good career. She was furious and told him he should finish college before he decided on a career. What if he got shot in action? She said it was just too dangerous and he had to think about her and their future. He said he was thinking about their future and that the pay was pretty good. He persisted and Linda eventually gave in. She loved him too much and she knew he was doing it so she could finish college. They settled in and she felt even more attracted to him because he was becoming a policeman.

The crowd at the ballgame stood up almost the entire time. At every pitch, there was a roar or a moan. They only sat down briefly in between innings. Maria and Tim were totally caught up in the excitement and energy of the game. When Garret Anderson from the Angels doubled down the right field line in the fifth inning to clear the bases, Maria jumped up and down with the rest of the crowd and hugged Tim. Their bodies melted into each other and the sexual excitement coupled with the excitement and noise of the crowd screaming at the top of their lungs made them experience a type of euphoria they had never felt before. From that moment on, they were arm and arm, smiling, and cheering with the rest of the fans for their home team Angels.

When the game ended, the Anaheim Angels had won the World Series for the first time in franchise history. Fireworks exploded over the fountains in center field. Fans screamed and whooped at the top of their lungs. Strangers hugged strangers while Tim and Maria kissed long and passionately at the top of the stands behind home plate. They wanted to go further, but knew they had to hurry back home to their respective spouses as quickly as possible.

"Oh my god it is 9 PM," Maria yelled to Tim over the roar of the crowd as she noticed the time on the scoreboard in center field.

"I know and it is going to be crazy getting out of here," yelled Tim back as they made their way through the people hand in hand once again. When they finally made it back to the restaurant where Maria had left her car it was nearly 10 PM. They kissed a lingering kiss goodbye and said they would talk the next day at work.

As Tim was back on the freeway heading home, the guilt worked its way into the forefront of his mind. He picked up his cell phone and called home.

"Hello," Linda answered.

"Oh. Hi honey. I'm on my way home," Tim replied now feeling the guilt sear at his heart.

"Tim, is there a problem or something? You sound concerned."

Now the guilt swept over him in a wave of intense fire. Like most people caught up with feelings of lust and desire, he appeased his guilt with partial truths to keep the guilty options open. "Linda, I have to tell you something. I went to the game. I didn't go to work."

"What did you say? You went where to what game? Don't tell me you were at the Angels game," Linda said harshly.

"Yes, the Angels game. Well actually I did go to work, but someone had an extra ticket to the game, so I bought it from him and went. I'm sorry I didn't call or anything, but I could only get one ticket," replied Tim.

"Oh, so you leave me here with the girls to go off and have fun on your own; and now you tell me when you're on the way home? Why didn't you tell me before?" Linda was angry now.

"I'm sorry. I had to rush to get to the game and I didn't even get to it on time. It was too noisy to call you from the game."

"We can talk when you get home," Linda said and quickly hung up the phone.

"Mom, who were you talking to on the phone? You slammed down the phone," said Colleen as she walked into the kitchen where Linda had been talking. Colleen was Tim and Linda's 14 year old daughter.

"It was your father and guess what he said?"

"What?"

"He lied to us about going to work today and instead he went to the seventh game of the World Series on his own," said Linda still angry.

"No way!"

"Yes he did!"

"God. That sucks big time. You know, I have asked him all season to take me to an Angels game. He kept saying he would get tickets and he never did. I just can't believe it."

"Well, I guess he just loves baseball more than he loves us," said Linda.

"That was just plain selfish of him. I am just as big a fan as him or maybe even bigger. Two of the girls on the softball team went with their dads to playoff games. That's it. I'm not talking to him ever again!"

All Tim could think about as he drove home was what kind of hot water he had put himself into. On the other hand, Maria had different thoughts all together as she drove home. She was smiling and feeling more confident than any time in her life. She was ready to make some changes and this time she was serious about it. She knew she might have acted a little too bold with Tim. She knew she wanted him, but she also knew he was married. She had decided that she was through with Felix. Whether she would divorce Felix or not, she was through with him for now. She had put up with him for too long and it was going to stop from this moment on. Yes, he was good to her sons, but the passion and romance was gone completely. He was way too macho and too complacent to ever change.

Maria was a woman who enjoyed and flourished with her sexuality. She had come from warm and caring parents. Her father was a great example to her of how a man should treat a woman, as he was still very much in love with Maria's mother. Maria had never had bad experiences of rough sexuality or violence with men except for the past year or so with Felix when he came home late drunk and smelling like grease from his job. Fortunately Felix was never violent, but he had forced himself on her in bed on more than one occasion and it had been repulsive to her. She would always say something to him in the morning, but it did no good. So after a while, she stopped talking to him about it and instead wore extra clothing to bed and wrapped herself with the sheet. Maria knew she had been pretty fortunate in her life because men had abused most of the women she knew.

Maria's first husband, Ernesto, had also been her first lover. Her older and only sister Victoria was responsible for that. Victoria, who had been fourteen, showed Maria how to touch herself when she was ten. Maria had touched herself before, but not the way Victoria explained it to her.

"Mira mi hermanita," Victoria had said to her that Saturday afternoon in the summer, as they both lay naked on their bed after bathing together. It was a very hot day and their parents were not home. "Look, you make little circles, like this, and then you put your finger inside just a little. Try it...it feels really good." Maria did try and it felt nice, but not as nice at it seemed for Victoria who was now moaning as beads of moisture gathered on her finger as she lay next to Maria.

Just before their parents came home, Victoria told her to never tell their parents what she had showed her and to always be very careful to do it alone and never let mother catch her. Maria idolized her older sister and vowed to keep the secret. As time went on, Maria learned to explore and love her body. She was amazed and was very happy that she could make herself experience feelings she didn't know she could feel. It was secret, fun, and exciting. As she got a little older, she would make eyes at Victoria's boyfriends when they came over and think about them when she was alone. She imagined romantic interludes in places she had only dreamed of or read about.

Maria had never thought of herself as attractive. Victoria was much more beautiful as far as she was concerned. Maria wore glasses until she was 16 and her mother allowed her to get contacts. Not having to wear glasses made a world of difference. Now even the older guys at her high school started to take an interest in her. Some even asked if she was new to the school, not even having noticed her before. Maria was still a virgin at 16 and her friends that were sexually active often tried to set her up with a guy. Maria didn't act prudish. She just wasn't interested in an immature guy and didn't see the need to be with just anyone like most of her friends were.

Maria met Ernesto at a party. He was 19 and a friend of one of her cousins. Ernesto was cute, but not handsome. He was obviously shyer than most of the other guys she had met. He wore glasses and they laughed about the fact that she had just gotten contacts. Maria told him he should get contacts. Maria had already decided, after having heard one too many of her girlfriends talk about how painful and bad of an experience she had after having sex for the first time, that she was going to make sure her first time was a very good experience. By the end of the party, she had decided Ernesto would be the one. She knew she could never really love someone like him, but that didn't matter. He was not aggressive and macho, so she knew she could make him do what she wanted. So even though Ernesto might not be her ideal boyfriend, he was a good enough candidate and Maria had decided she did not want to wait forever. Before she left the party, they exchanged phone numbers.

A few days later, Ernesto called her and they went to a movie. She realized right away that he was shyer than she had thought and he was also a total nerd. He did have good qualities though. He was funny, kind, and he paid for everything. From Ernesto's point of view, he was amazed that such a cute girl like Maria was interested in him so he did his best to act important.

On the second date, they again went to the movies. This time Ernesto seemed different. He was more aggressive and awkwardly tried to kiss Maria in the theater. Maria let him kiss her, but acted like she wasn't too interested. Maria could tell that Ernesto was not too experienced and she wasn't sure if she wanted him to be her first anymore though she didn't want to wait much longer. Despite being a virgin, Maria had made out and done enough of the preliminaries to know what she wanted and how to do it. She had been pleasing herself recently with a vibrator that she had found from one of her sisters, so she now wanted to try a guy. So when Ernesto drove her home from the movies, she decided to have a serious talk with him. She decided to use her sister's advice, "Remember Maria. The first time you need to tell the guy exactly how to do things. They all want to be crazy and go really fast with everything, but trust me, if you make them do things slow and the way you want them to, it's a lot better. Plus, they all think they know what to do and act like they have experience, but the truth is it may be the first time for the guy too." Ernesto had parked the car halfway down the street from Maria's house hoping he could spend time making out with her in the car. When he stopped the engine, he aggressively leaned over and tried to pull her into him.

"Wait Ernesto, I just want to talk to you now. We couldn't talk in the movie," said Maria as she pushed him away from her. Ernesto felt a little rebuffed and hurt. He had been spending a lot of money on her, but he wanted her so he complied and sat back. He took off his glasses hoping she would get the talking part over quickly so he could kiss her more. "Look Ernesto, I'm going to be honest with you. I have never had sex before. I don't know what girls you have been with, but I just want to be careful." Maria knew it didn't make any difference if she asked him about his past experiences because he would just lie like all guys did. What she didn't know was that the previous weekend Ernesto's cousin had taken him to Tijuana and Ernesto had slept with a prostitute. It had been his first time and he had really liked it. He now wanted to do it with Maria. "Anyway Ernesto, what I am trying to say is that I really like you a lot. Ok, I am just going to say it; I want you to be my first one." Maria couldn't believe she had said that to him, but she had. Ernesto smiled a broad grin and leaned over while closing his eyes to kiss her. He was excited beyond belief. Here was this beautiful girl that he really wanted and she was telling him that he was going to be the first one. He was totally ready. They kissed and immediately

Ernesto's hands went to Maria's breasts. She made out with him for a bit and let him touch some, but then she pulled away from him. "Wait, wait. Not now Ernesto. Listen, you have to promise me one thing. You have to do things exactly how I ask you to do them. I know that may sound crazy, but I want it to be really special so you have to follow whatever instructions I give you." Ernesto nodded his head and tried to dive back into kissing her. He didn't care what she said or what instructions she gave him. He wanted her right now. He was totally aroused and sure that everything would happen right now in his car. What a story he would have to tell his cousin.

"Yes, yes, oh Maria. I love you so much. I will do anything you want," he said as he leaned back into her and tried to put his hand under her dress. But, Maria grabbed his hand and stopped him. She quickly opened the car door and said causally with a big smile, "Ok, ok. I will call you and we will make plans to go to a hotel on Sunday." Ernesto tried to reach out with his arm, beckoning for her to come back into the car, but it was too late. Maria ran down the street to her house.

The following Sunday, Ernesto picked her up and they went to a hotel. After that, Maria always dictated the terms. She treated Ernesto like an extension of herself. She wasn't really deeply in love with him, but that didn't matter. She was the director in her own play of her sexuality. They continued the relationship for two years and then Maria unexpectedly became pregnant. It was the summer and she was supposed to be on her way to college in the fall. Ernesto was already in college and would graduate with an engineering degree the following year. He was polite and kind to her. Maria's family liked Ernesto so even though she wanted to have an abortion, she let everyone convince her against it and they married.

After her son Julio was born, her relationship with Ernesto changed dramatically. Ernesto turned out to be a horrible father. He seemed jealous of the baby taking time away from him and Maria being together. They could no longer go out to clubs or parties like they had in the past. He made excuses to go out with his friends and spent a lot of time away from Maria and his son. He started to sleep on the couch in their tiny apartment. Julio was getting ready to turn a year old when Ernesto graduated college. He had been working part time to support Maria and his son and now that he had graduated, his dream of getting his masters degree seemed remote. He would have to work full time if Maria wasn't going to work. Maria had gained weight during her pregnancy and had not lost it even after a year. He constantly told Maria she was fat and Maria's self image was very low. They argued almost every day and eventually Ernesto started to sleep away from Maria. He made excuses about where he had been and Maria knew he was lying to her. Maria was very depressed. One day Maria came home after she had spent some time at her parents' house and saw that Ernesto had moved out completely. She cried knowing that he had moved in with another woman. A few days later, Ernesto called and told her that he had filed for a divorce. Maria had no way to pay her rent. Her only option was to take her son and move back in with her parents. Her parents no longer liked Ernesto because they could see he was not a good husband or father. Maria was sad for her son, but not for herself. She never cried because she knew she had never really loved Ernesto. Her friends and family would talk badly about Ernesto, but Maria knew he was the father of her son so she refused to let herself feel bad about the fact that he had abandoned her.

Maria was actually very happy that she was back living with her parents. Her sister was now living up in northern California with her boyfriend so there was plenty of room. Her Mom helped her with Julio and Maria was able to start junior college and take on a part time job also. Julio had a lot of attention with the family around and Maria could see how much happier he was. Occasionally, Maria would go out with some of her girlfriends and once in a while she would go on a date with a guy. She was not really interested in getting in another relationship because she wanted to focus on raising her son and trying to better herself. Her dating experiences all seemed to be the same. The guys wanted to have sex as soon as possible. They said and did all kinds of stupid things to try to get her to bed. Romance was only pretence for wanting to have sex. The few times she did concede and sleep with a guy, she did it on her terms and made it clear to the guy that she was not interested in rushing into a long term relationship.

At first, Ernesto came almost every weekend and visited his son. He would take him out to a park for a few hours and bring him back. He never took him to spend the night with him. Maria wasn't sure if that was because of the woman he was living with or because he just did not think he had the experience to care for a young child over night. Maria didn't really care. The lawyer she had talked with had already told her that divorce laws in California were the most favorable for women of any state in the country and it was essentially certain she would be granted full custody of her son.

Julio actually started to become more attached to his grandfather. He started to call him Papa. Both of his grandparents were very attentive and doting since he was their first grandchild. After a year on his own, Ernesto started to realize what he had lost, but by then it was too late. Julio was growing and becoming a playful and happy boy. Maria had now lost most of the weight and looked almost as good as she had before she had become pregnant. Maria started to have delayed feelings of resentment and anger. The divorce was almost final with the terms very favorable for Maria. She would have full custody and also child support. Ernesto started to come by less and less on the weekends. During one stretch, he didn't see his son for over a month. One day, he showed up and announced that he was moving to New York. He had a great job offer there and he had decided to take it. Maria couldn't believe any man would leave their son and move to the other side of the country. Ernesto wasn't any man though and that hurt her. He was the father of her child and he didn't care. Reality set in and Maria accepted it with an emotional numbness. When Ernesto moved, Maria actually felt sort of pleased. It seemed like that chapter in her life was officially over. She would get the child support and if he called he would be able to talk to Julio, but that was it...no visits to New York, not now, and maybe never.

Maria finished junior college and kept working part time as a secretary. Her son had just turned four and would be starting pre-school soon. His father sent the occasional card and the monthly child support, but he never called. Maria was happy he was not involved for her sake, but wondered to herself what she would say when her son was older.

She met her present husband Felix at the park near her home on a weekend afternoon. She took Julio to the park often so he could play with the other children there. She had never seen Felix at the park before or maybe she had just never noticed him. He was watching another little boy play who she assumed was his. Her son and the little boy were playing together so Felix came over to Maria and introduced himself. They talked for a while and when Maria referred to the boy as Felix's son, Felix laughed and told her the boy was his nephew. He told her he was single and had never been married. Maria was 23 and Felix was 22, but at the time they didn't talk about their ages. They began to date and Felix was very romantic. He bought her gifts and he bought Julio gifts also. He didn't kiss her until they had gone out at least five times. When he did kiss her, he left it at that and never pressed the issue of having sex. He would surprise her with flowers or candy. After a while, she would let him take her son to the park on his own. After a few months, they started to have sexual relations. Again, unexpectedly, Maria became pregnant. She thought of having an abortion, but she liked Felix very much and he liked her. She could tell he would be a great father so they decided to get married and move in together. They had a simple wedding with friends and family and hid the fact that she was pregnant.

Felix had never gone to college. He was a first generation Guatemalan immigrant and he worked in his uncle's auto repair shop. He worked hard and made pretty good money. Maria worked part time until she was incapable due to the pregnancy. Maria was very happy and felt that everything was going to work very nicely. She was confident that she was going to have a little girl this time, but when the ultrasound showed that the fetus was a boy, she hid her disappointment. After she had her second son Leo, she became the perfect housewife. She cleaned, cooked, and enjoyed the role of mother. Felix was very loving and very gentle with her. She had gained back the weight like she had during her first pregnancy, but Felix was patient and never said a word to her about losing it. Felix was a great father. He would get up in the middle of the night, feed the baby, and change diapers. The quality of their sexual relationship declined after the baby was born, but that was fine with Maria. She reverted back to the toys she had acquired over the years and wasn't concerned because Felix was good at being a provider and a father.

When Leo was a year and half old, Maria decided she needed to do something and chose to go back to work. The extra income would be nice because they could save money and maybe buy a house someday. At first, Felix didn't like the idea of her working, but was supportive in the end. He wanted to own his own auto repair shop one day and hoped that her added income might allow his dream to materialize sooner rather that later.

Maria started working as a secretary again and went about building up her résumé. She was a cheerful and competent worker. When one of her friends told her that she should apply at the police department, she decided to give it a try. A position opened up and she beat out numerous applicants who were more qualified, landing the job with her personality and smile. The job paid a lot more than any other jobs she had before and the benefits were fantastic. She had full medical and dental benefits for her and her sons. Felix was happy for her, but at the same time was a bit envious though he kept that to himself. After two years, she was promoted to executive secretary for the chief and started making almost double the salary that Felix was making though she signed her check over to her husband every Friday. In turn, he would give her spending money for food and other things. Maria trusted that he was saving the money to start his own business and for a deposit on a house. She never realized that he was wasting money by going to the racetrack and drinking with his friends. She was too busy with work and the kids to notice much at all. Yes, Felix was a good father and took the boys lots of places, but what he did when he was supposed to be at work at the repair shop was of little concern to Maria and she never asked. She was happy with her job, the boys seemed happy, and life seemed just great. She only wished Felix was a little more attentive to her and a little more romantic like he used to be.

The first time Maria noticed the change was a night when Felix came home drunk. It was late and he climbed in bed without showering. He smelled very bad and then he forced himself on her. Maria was hurt and felt she deserved more respect than that. She told Felix the next day that he had better never do that again and he promised he wouldn't. Two days later he came home late again, but Maria was prepared. She had gone to bed with three layers of clothes and had the sheet pulled around her. She pushed him off and he fell asleep. Maria was not happy and Tim was her only source of fantasy and comfort.

It was almost 10:30 PM when Maria returned home from the game. Felix was sitting in the kitchen drinking a beer and smoking a cigarette. Maria knew he was upset because he never smoked in the house unless he was feeling very macho and very mad.

"Where have you been Maria? I know you didn't go to work," he said with a condescending tone.

Maria put her purse down and sat opposite him at the small table. She noticed her bra was still in her purse and wondered why she hadn't at least put it back on before she returned. Really though, she didn't care. She hadn't changed her clothes because she didn't care what Felix thought. She was going to make sure that things changed for her. "Where are the boys?" she asked diverting his attention.

"They're in their room asleep, of course," Felix replied tersely.

"Look Felix. I don't want to get into a big argument right now and have you yell and wake up the boys. How much have you been drinking?" Maria asked.

"I've only had a few beers," Felix replied.

Maria could see he was lying as she noticed the other empty six-pack of beer in the trash behind him. "Ok, no. I didn't go to work today. I went to the World Series game in Anaheim. It was great. Did you see the game? The Angels won."

Felix laughed loudly. "Why are you lying to me? Look at the way you're dressed...tight red pants, no bra. You lying slut, you were with some guy."

"Watch what you call me Felix. I'm not lying. I was at the game," Maria replied wondering if she should just leave and go to her parents' house because it wasn't often that Felix was this rude.

"Really, okay then. So, what was the final score?" Felix asked still not believing her.

"It was 5 to 1," Maria said quickly.

"Yeah right. You probably heard the score on the radio in your car. So you are cheating on me. I know you have been cheating on me for some time. Look at you. You have been working out at the gym after work and getting in shape for your new boyfriend," Felix said convinced she was lying to him.

"No Felix. I haven't been cheating on you and I did go to the Angels game. My boss gave me two tickets yesterday afternoon and I knew if I asked one of the boys then the other would be upset. So, I asked one of the detectives from work to go with me because I know he likes baseball. He is not my boyfriend," Maria said back with a pert smile.

"Oh, really! So why are you dressed like that? You look like one of those hookers down on Sunset Blvd," said Felix, who was now trying to hurt her and make her upset.

"That's enough Felix. You are being mean because you are jealous. I am getting in shape because I want to. Yes, I'm starting to like the way I look. I am not going to get upset if you call me a prostitute because that must mean I look like one of the best!" Maria said back.

Felix laughed. They each had a way of making each other laugh no matter how bad things were. "Well, I still don't believe you went to the game."

"I did," Maria replied.

"So who is this detective then?" Felix asked. He realized he should find out about the new boyfriend.

"Tim Sloan. He's no one special, just a detective from work. I am not interested in him." Maria looked down, knowing she was now lying.

"Yeah right…you dressed like that and you're not interested in him. I don't believe that for a second. What I do know is that you haven't been interested in me for the past few months," Felix said narrowing his eyes

That was it for Maria. She had heard enough and she was now determined to go through with the changes she wanted to see happen. "Felix, I don't care how much you've had to drink. You better sober up because I have some things to say and you better listen."

Felix wasn't fazed. "Sure. Like you are going to say anything you haven't said before."

"Well maybe I am, but this time I mean it. I do not want you to touch me anymore at all. Do you understand? You will not come into the bedroom drunk and smelly and try to touch me. You can sleep on the couch for now. Also, I am not signing my paycheck over to you anymore and I want to see the bank statements every month. I am going to open my own bank account. If you want us to stay married then you have to stop drinking. I don't care how you do that; maybe going to AA would be best. Maybe you need to change friends so you don't go out drinking and gambling and you should start going to a gym. That might help. Look Felix. You are a good father and a hard worker. You used to be a good person, but over the past year that seems to have changed. What you did last month was basically rape me. I was hurt a lot and that will never happen to me again. You had better believe me. I am dead serious this time." Maria stood up from the table, put her hands on her hips, and stared at him.

Felix stared back. He narrowed his eyes even more. His anger was starting to boil over. There was no woman on Earth that could talk to him that way. He was angry at her, at himself, and at the world. "Go then. Have fun with your new boyfriend. You're the one who's changed. Ever since you started working at the police station you've been acting like you own the world. Well let me tell you one thing. I don't really care!" He stood up and knocked his beer onto the floor. He gave her one last mean look and then headed out the door, slamming it as he went.

Before Maria went to sleep, she jotted down the things she needed to do the next day, including taking all of his things out of the bedroom and having the manager install a lock on her bedroom door. He would never come back to her bed drunk and smelly.

That night she dreamed. She dreamed of teeth, an old dog with large oversized mutated teeth. It was scary, but what was worse was she knew when she woke up that dreaming of teeth meant death. That had happened before. She, of course, worked for the police department and death happened often so dreaming of teeth didn't scare her as much anymore. She was terrified the very first time her aunt from Mexico had told her the scary stories about dreaming of teeth. Maria was only 10 and her family had visited Mexico. Her aunt was the so-called fortuneteller, as she had visions. The people near the village in Mexico knew about her powers and trusted her. Maria was young and open. Her aunt took special care of her and told everyone she had the "gift." It was precious and nice, but old-fashioned for people that were now living in the U.S.

Maria realized she was running late for work so she hurried the boys into the car. As she was driving them to school and looking around the streets, she noticed two stray dogs. They both looked upset, as they ran down the road. Maria's dream came back to her and for a split second she forgot that she was driving her kids to school and made a very rare wrong turn. One of the boys yelled out, "Mom! you made a wrong turn!"

Maria quickly caught herself and got back on track to drop off the boys. She still felt a bit dizzy when she dropped the boys off at their school. One of the parents waved and said something to her, but she was unable to focus. The vision of the dog and its deformed fangs started to sicken her. She pulled over to the side of the road and took deep breaths. She never liked dreaming of death, but that was a given considering the fact that she worked at a police station. Long ago she had abandoned her sensitivity to death and the dreams. It had no real effect on her life and overall the majority of the dreams were not gruesome, violent, or ugly. Even the dream she had last night was only ugly. Still, there was something different and there had been a dark feeling that no other dream had evoked. She tried to relax, but it took longer than she anticipated. She looked at her watch and now realized she had been sitting in her car for over five minutes and she had to get to work. She forced herself back on the road and drove. The dream faded away and being back at work snapped her mind back into reality. She quickly found some coffee and headed to her office.

## CHAPTER 3

The game had started at 5:30 PM and Tony lay on his couch with a pillow over his head. He was trying not to hear as the game blared from the televisions in every apartment in his building complex. He was getting very irritated though because he had a lot of money bet on the game and really couldn't bear to watch it. Finally, he decided he had no choice so he got up and turned on the television. Just as he turned the game on, he saw the Giants score a run in the top of the second inning to take a one to nothing lead. He knew he had to be the cause of the misfortune. "Oh my God. I just know I am going to lose this bet!" he yelled. He quickly turned off the television and nervously paced around his apartment. He didn't know what to do or where to go, but instinctively he grabbed his car keys and headed out of his apartment.

"I just know the Angels are going to lose," he said to himself as he started his car and pulled out. He put a "The Best of the Doors" tape into the tape player and cranked up the volume. He drove north down Sepulvada Boulevard heading toward Santa Monica. He didn't know exactly where he was going, but figured he might as well just drive until the game was over. When he reached Santa Monica, he turned onto the Coast Highway and drove into the Santa Monica Mountains. Driving had always made him feel better, but this time he didn't feel as good as he normally would because he was convinced he would lose his bet. When he got to Malibu, he turned right at Tuna Canyon. He knew the road well and figured he could stop at the top of the mountain for a while to kill time. Heading up the canyon, he started to think back on his last killing. He said out loud to himself, "I guess the person I really should have killed is that psycho-bitch from hell, my ex-wife."

Tony had raised his son Marco from the age of five pretty much on his own. His ex-wife was originally from Peru. He had met her at a club she had come to with some of her friends. They had dated for a few months and at the time he really liked her. She seemed very sweet and different from the American girls he had dated. She had that Latin spice and at the same time she had a domestic quality that most of the American girls didn't have, at least not in Los Angeles. She loved to cook and could cook Italian food very well. When she was at his place, she would clean up and wash his clothes. Her name was Adriana. She was tall for a Peruvian woman and she really looked more Italian than anything else. She had come to the United States to meet some other guy she had been corresponding with. She was 22 years old at the time and the relationship with the guy only lasted a year. She moved in with a girlfriend and that was when she met Tony. Tony let her stay at his place often and soon enough she moved in with him. They had a very passionate relationship. He found out that she was bisexual not long after she moved in with him. He wasn't sure if she would still want women now that she was living with him, but he wouldn't mind because he found the idea sort of exciting. He didn't mind if she did have another woman as long as he could at least watch and hopefully participate. They had been living together for only a month when one day he came home early from work and unexpectedly found her in bed with another woman. It happened to be someone that was a friend of someone whom lived in his building. Tony didn't realize that he would react the way he did...with anger. He caused a big scene. He was surprised and shocked, but didn't know why he was because he had told her it was fine for her to have another woman. He ended up grabbing the other woman by the hair and pulling her out of the bed. He made her leave and told her he never wanted to see her again. Adriana seemed hurt at first, but when Tony calmed down she laughed and told him she was happy he was jealous because it showed he really cared for her. She took Tony into bed and Tony couldn't help but fantasize about Adriana in bed with the other woman while they made love. Later that evening, he told Adriana that from now on if she wanted to be with another woman she would have to share. Adriana laughed again and said when the weekend came they could go out to the club and see if they could find someone together.

That Saturday night, they did exactly that and thereafter they went out almost every weekend with Adriana being the bait, trying to pick up a woman for them to bring home and share. It was wild and exciting. Of course there were times Adriana failed to be successful in meeting someone at one of the clubs when they went out, but just the attempt made them both excited. When they returned home they would make love into the early morning.

Tony didn't know until after they had been living together for more than a year that Adriana was in the country illegally. Tony had just started working at a job where there was little tolerance for any kind of illegal activities on his part. He was shocked and also pissed she hadn't told him sooner. Adriana said it wasn't her fault and that she didn't know how to go about changing her now expired tourist visa into a permanent visa. Tony looked into the details of her situation and realized the fastest and easiest thing to do was to marry her. He wasn't sure if he was ready to get married, but they had been living together for over a year and he really liked Adriana a lot. He proposed to her and she said yes immediately. He tried to act like it was not just so that she could become legal but also because he loved her and wanted her to be with him the rest of his life. Adriana loved Tony as well and wanted to start a family. They both were getting tired of going out to clubs and they both wanted to settle down and have a more stable life. They had a short engagement and then a simple wedding. Tony's family was very happy for him because they could see Adriana was quite domestic and they knew that would be good for Tony.

Tony and Adriana decided to go to Peru for their honeymoon so Tony could meet Adriana's family. Having grown up in southern California, Tony knew enough Spanish to get by pretty well, but when they arrived in Peru he realized his Spanish was pretty rusty. When he was in Lima where Adriana's family lived, it started to dawn on Tony that maybe he had made a mistake in marrying her, but what he didn't know at the time was that she was pregnant.

Adriana's brother kept talking to Tony and asking him how Adriana was doing in the United States. It had been over four years since Adriana's family had seen her. What bothered Tony was that he felt uncomfortable with Adriana's brother's tone of questioning. Tony began to feel uncomfortable and a bit suspicious. There was a dark side to his new wife, but he didn't know what it was and the brother was not providing enough information for him to find out. Tony's ability to speak Spanish was not good enough to ask the detailed questions that he wanted to ask.

The two of them had planned to be in Peru for a month. They had filed the papers at the embassy for Adriana's immigration visa and then headed out to Manchu Piccu to have their honeymoon away from Adriana's family. It was a wonderful and mystical place. One cool evening there, when they were sitting outside on the patio of their hotel room under the shadows of the Andes mountains and a night sky filled with billions of bright stars, Adriana told Tony that she was pregnant. Tony was surprised, excited, and scared all at once. He really did not plan on starting a family so soon, but he knew he would have to. Adriana was from a strict Catholic background and there was no way he would ever think of discussing an abortion with her. Yes, he loved Adriana and he wouldn't have married her if he didn't think she would make a great wife and mother, but he just had a feeling that there was a threatening grey storm on the horizon. He didn't like the feeling.

The following day they returned to Lima and went to the American Embassy to go to the interview for Adriana's immigration visa. They were supposed to go back to the United States in just three days. The storm had gathered and the skies burst with torrential rain, both literally and figuratively. Tony had never seen it rain so hard anywhere. He thought the old Volkswagen they had borrowed from his mother-in-law would start to float down the street as they made their way toward the embassy in downtown Lima. Strangely, just as quickly as the rain had started, it stopped as they reached the embassy. It was 8:45 AM so they waited outside in the long line until the embassy opened at 9 AM. Adriana commented that the line wasn't as long as usual; maybe it was due to the rain. At 9 AM they moved inside and took seats in the crowded waiting room with the other applicants. By 11 AM it started to get unbearably hot, as there was no air conditioning in the room. They both wished they could hurry up and get the interview over with. Finally their names were called, so they went to a small interview booth and sat down. On the other side of the barred window a man carrying papers came and sat down opposite them.

"My name is Justin Spencer. I am sorry to inform you of this, but after reviewing your case we can't grant Adriana an immigration visa at this time."

Tony couldn't believe what he was hearing. It seemed like some sort of surrealistic dream. "What do you mean? I am sure we filled out all the paperwork correctly. What is the problem? We have tickets to return to the United States in a few days. If there is some mistake with the paperwork I'm sure we can fix it immediately."

"No, there is not a problem with the application Mr. Salerno. Everything was filled out correctly and we have all of the supporting documents. You see...you applied for an I-130 Visa which is an immigration visa for an Alien Relative and since Adriana is already married to someone else it just is not possible for you to sponsor her. She can't be married to two people at the same time," said Mr. Spencer in a monotone voice as his eyes darted back and forth between Adriana and Tony. He was curious to see their reaction.

"What?" Tony's mind went numb. He looked first at the man across from him behind the window and bars, searching his eyes to see if he was playing some kind of cruel joke. He knew he wasn't. Not here; not at the U.S. Embassy. Then, Tony darted a look at his wife, his pregnant wife, but she was staring down with meek eyes at her hands crossed in her lap. There was a brief silence after his question and Tony could feel the pressure building in his head. Tony asked again. This time he was staring directly at Mr. Spencer and searching his eyes. "What are you talking about?"

Mr. Spencer smiled, knowing Tony had no clue. Having worked in the embassy for three years, he had seen a lot of cases and heard a lot of lies. He knew Tony was upset, but he also knew it was not his place to discuss anything further with him. "Well, Mr. Salerno. I really believe that is something you should discuss with Adriana. Not me!"

Tony looked again at Adriana and she remained silent still staring at her hands in her lap. Tony knew there was something wrong and something had been hidden from him, but at this point he didn't care what it was. He just wanted to get her papers and get back to the United States. Tony looked back at Mr. Spencer, who was now putting the papers back in their folder. "Wait, what are you saying? Adriana and I are married. You have a certified copy of the marriage certificate to prove that. What more do you want? Isn't that good enough for you?" Tony realized he was pushing the limit and stopped talking.

Mr. Spencer was now standing holding the folder under his arm. "Yes we do have your marriage certificate and you did fill out all the forms correctly. What you did not provide us with was a copy of Adriana's divorce certificate from her previous marriage. When you have that, then please come back and we can grant you another interview."

Tony was in shock and the dumbfounded expression on his face let Mr. Spencer know that Tony had no clue that Adriana was already married to someone else. Tony looked again at Adriana and this time she looked at him with a puzzled look on her face. She started to open her mouth to speak, but decided against it. Tony looked back at Mr. Spencer who was still standing and was obviously ready to just walk away. "Wait. Before you just leave us here, can I ask you what I am supposed to do? I have a pregnant wife and a job I only recently started back home. How am I supposed to get her back to the U.S with me?"

Mr. Spencer smiled. He was not feeling sorry for the young man in front of him. He had seen too many like him before. "I'm sorry Mr. Salerno. My job is not to give you advice, but I will say it is not advisable to marry someone who is already married!" Then he turned and walked away.

Tony was now livid and turning red. "Wait!" he yelled out to Mr. Spencer, "This is my embassy. I am an American. You are supposed to help me out here!"

Mr. Spencer turned back and looked at Tony with a glare before walking back to the window. He looked directly at Adriana and said something very brief and rapid to her in Spanish. Maria nodded to him and then he turned and walked away from the window. He closed the door on his side of the booth leaving Tony and Adriana alone. Tony grabbed Adriana by the hand and hurried her out of the booth and out of the embassy. It was raining again as hard as ever. He saw a small café across the street and pulled Adriana along with him to the café. He didn't say a word to her until they sat down at a booth.

"You're married! Adriana, what exactly is going on?" Tony was beside himself with anger as he sat down in the booth at the café. He felt like his head was enveloped in a thick fog. He could hear the rain as it pelted down on the canopy outside the café.

Adriana looked down again at her hands, which were in her lap as they had been in the embassy. She glanced up quickly at Tony and then started to tear up and cry, hoping to draw out some sympathy from him though the look on Tony's face remained stern. Finally she knew she had to start talking or he would yell at her in the café. "Well I told you I had a boyfriend here in Lima before I went to the U.S."

"A boyfriend, yes. But, you never said you were married to him! A husband is a little more serious than boyfriends. Are you out of your mind? What made you think the Immigration Department wouldn't know?"

Adriana had finally composed herself and decided she had no choice but to tell Tony the truth. At the very least she had to provide some of the truth so Tony would still love her and not be too mad. "Ok, yes, so we got married. I was only 17 at the time. I didn't think it mattered because I was less than eighteen years old. We only stayed together for six months and it is very difficult to get divorced down here. It is not like the states where you can get married and divorced whenever you want! Here you have to have the approval of the church and it takes a long time to go through the process and file all the papers. Most people here just stay married and then they just live with someone else if they meet the right person later. Oh Tony. I'm pregnant and I'm your wife. I want to be with you the rest of my life. I love you Tony. I promise I will the best wife in the world for you. The man in there said something to me in Spanish so don't worry. Everything is going to be fine. I am sure we can work things out so I can get the visa. It will just take a little time."

"Time? How much time are you talking about? We don't have a lot of time Adriana, nor do we have a lot of money. Adriana, how could you not tell me you were already married? Our marriage wasn't even legal. Why did you hide this from me? I have to get back to my job," Tony replied angrily.

"Oh, Tony. Everything would have been fine if we would have stayed in the states. You wanted to come here to see my family and go to Machu Piccu!" Adriana said. She wasn't sure why she said that when she saw the reaction on Tony's face.

"What did you say?" Tony was starting to raise his voice and people from the other tables were now looking at them. "Are you saying if we would have stayed in the states that you could have just gone on and hid this from me for as long as you wanted? I just can't believe this. What else are you hiding from me? Don't you understand I have a job back home that I just started and I need to be there? Do you want me to just leave you here and you can have the baby here!"

"Tony, the man there said all I need is divorce papers. It is not that hard here to get divorce papers." Adriana wanted to calm Tony down.

"You just told me how hard it was to get divorce papers and now you're saying it is not too hard. What are you talking about?" Tony shot back at her still in a loud voice.

"There is a way to get fake divorce papers here. It doesn't take too long and it doesn't cost too much either," Adriana said more softly with a smile.

Tony was even angrier now. He was confused and just wanted to be back in Redondo Beach in his apartment far away from where he actually was. He took a deep breath and tried to calm himself, but the idea of getting fake papers and turning them into the government was just too much for him to think about. "Do you know how much trouble we could get into if we got caught getting fake papers? It is a federal crime to do that!"

"Oh, Tony. It is not that hard here. People do it all the time. We just have to talk to my mother. She knows someone in the courts. All we have to do is get a divorce document for me and I'm sure I can get the visa. You have to just trust me on this Tony. Really, it is the only way. The papers will look real and be signed by a real judge," Adriana replied trying to make it sound easier than it was so Tony wouldn't be too worried.

It took over a month and cost Tony almost three thousand dollars. He took out money on all the credit cards he had and also drained his savings account. His mother-in-law knew someone who knew someone else, who knew a judge. There was a short fat man who constantly sweated acting as the go between in the transaction. He had two assistants, one sickly looking woman and some other man who seemed like an enforcer, but really was a wimp. They kept bleeding money out of Tony until one day Tony had reached the end of his rope and totally lost it. He grabbed the fat man by the neck and used a kitchen knife to hold off the other man right in the middle of his mother-in-law's dining room. He yelled at all of them at the top of his lungs and told them that he wanted the divorce papers by that evening or he would totally lose it and they all would pay. He told them he wasn't paying one more cent to anyone. He made threats that were totally untrue, but it did have an influence and the two assistants came back that evening with the phony divorce papers signed by the judge. Maybe it was the crazed look he had, but it worked.

Earlier Tony had called his work and explained that he would be stuck in Peru for another month. His boss was not happy, but told him he wouldn't fire him. Tony was happy he would still have his job when he returned to the U.S.

Tony and Adriana were not getting along well during the whole ordeal in Peru. The honeymoon was definitely over. They couldn't afford to stay anywhere else so they were stuck at his mother-in-law's house. Adriana's father had a job with the government as an accountant. He made a good salary, but it didn't help his mood. He was always cranky and Tony knew he wanted him out of his house as soon as possible. Tony was bored and unhappy during the wait, but he had no choice until the embassy called them with a date for another interview. As soon as they had the phony pre-dated divorce papers they took them to the embassy and requested an interview. Still they had to wait another two weeks until the embassy called granting them an interview.

When they arrived for the interview, both Tony and Adriana were scared. Tony knew if they questioned the divorce papers and found out they were forged then he would be in a lot of trouble. What made the whole situation worse was that during the drive to the embassy, Adriana decided for some sick reason to divulge to Tony that her ex-husband was involved with the mafia in Lima and that he was now in jail. He ran a stolen car ring. Adriana wanted Tony to know that the reason she had never asked for a divorce from him was because she was scared of him. Tony had been through too much and at that point he wished she wasn't pregnant. He just wanted to get rid of her and go back to his home in the U.S. He knew though that he had to get those thoughts out of his head because she was pregnant with his first child.

It was hotter than it had been the last time they had been to the embassy. Fortunately, they were called for the interview after only waiting an hour. They again sat inside the booth. This time there was a different man sitting across from them and Tony breathed a sigh of relief.

"Aren't you two the ones from Los Angeles that called me about a month ago asking about the procedure with divorce documents you were going to send in?" He was younger than the man that was there before.

Tony's heart stopped beating for a second. He knew he was in trouble. He had called the embassy more than once trying to find out what he could do to hurry the process along. He had asked for detailed information without revealing that he was in the process of getting phony divorce papers. He never thought anyone would remember and surely it wouldn't be the same man now giving the interview. Tony's mind raced with ideas. He knew he couldn't say yes to the man or the divorce papers could come into question and become the main focus of the interview. "No, we are from Redondo Beach. Not Los Angeles." Tony looked directly into his eyes when he said it and did not blink or take his eyes off the other man's eyes.

The man looked down at the file in front of him and then back up at Tony while Adriana sat casually not seeming to really care. "Oh, I see. I must be mistaken then," replied the interviewer. He then shuffled through the papers and pulled out the divorce certificate. He stared at it for what seemed like an eternity. He held it up to the light and touched the judge's signature and the seal. He then looked at Adriana and smiled as he set the certificate back down. Tension hung in the air and Tony didn't breath. He could feel the heat and started to perspire. They all passed glances at each other and the air seemed like soft butter just waiting to be cut. "We have to be careful here because we get a lot of forged documents. There are a lot of people that want to immigrate to the United States and they will do anything to get the visas you know!" Tony sweated even more and could feel his hands beginning to tremble, so he moved them off the counter and put them in his lap. Again, the man looked back and forth at Tony and Adriana trying to read their expressions. Finally, he picked up his pen and twirled it in his fingers like a toy. "Well, I guess all the papers seem to be in order so I am approving the visa application. Adriana can pick up the visa this afternoon at 3 PM." He then stood quickly and walked out of the interview booth and closed the door.

Tony finally breathed and Adriana turned to him and smiled, "See, I told you everything would work out fine!" Tony had nothing to say. He was in debt with his credit cards, had drained his bank account, and had almost lost his job. He just wanted to get on a plane back to Redondo Beach as soon as he could.

They made it back to the states just after the first of the year. They had stayed in Peru almost three months. Adriana was now five months pregnant and was really starting to feel the baby. Tony had gotten his job back and felt happier and more appreciative than ever to be living and working in the United States. He had seen more poverty and corruption in his brief time in Peru than he ever thought existed anywhere. His appreciation for life extended into his love for Adriana. He did everything he could to make her feel happy and comfortable, but she wasn't. She was pregnant and away from her family. She felt isolated and alone even though Tony was showing a lot of care and concern. Tony was thrilled at the idea of having his first child. He felt very good about himself and his new job. It might have been because of his high self-esteem, but he tended to ignore or pass off Adriana's tantrums and quirks. At times, he wondered what went through her mind.

Adriana was becoming insanely jealous as the pregnancy went on. She did bizarre things that were starting to add up and make Tony wonder even more what she was thinking. With the advice of family and friends, he wrote off her jealousy thinking it had to be due to the pregnancy. She took one of his credit cards without him knowing and rented a car for a whole week just to follow him to and from work. She went through his personal phone book and crossed out with a marker any female name and number. She went through all his drawers and paperwork and any bit of presumed evidence of a connection to a woman became the obsession of a nightly barrage of insults and inquisition. She would imagine and create scenarios that had Tony sleeping with just about any female he had ever had contact with at all. It was so bizarre that when Tony was in a good mood he laughed it off, but most of the time he felt uncomfortable and pressured almost to the point of snapping. Tony spent almost every evening after he came home from work explaining in detail his daily movements and conversations. If by chance he had spoken to any woman during the day, Adriana would extrapolate that into an affair and often begin to berate Tony late into the night. Tony was forcing himself to remain calm and composed no matter how crazy Adriana became because he knew it had to be due to her pregnancy and that the behavior would stop after the child was born.

It was a Monday, a day he would never forget, and a day that would influence him for the rest of his life. It was one of those clear, crisp, windless days. The air was thick with humidity, as it had rained during the night. Tony had come home early from work and found Adriana in bed. She was now six and a half months pregnant and having constant pains. Tony had tried his best to get her to follow the doctor's recommendations of not drinking or smoking during her pregnancy, but his warnings had little influence on her. He didn't keep any alcohol in the apartment, but that didn't stop her. Almost daily, she would walk down to the convenience store to get wine and cigarettes. Fortunately, she didn't drink every day and sometimes not for a week at a time, but it still concerned Tony.

Tony walked up to the bed and gave her a small kiss on the cheek. She seemed to be sleeping and he didn't smell wine, so he guessed she was just tired rather than passed out drunk. He started to go into the bathroom to take a shower when she woke up or at least half woke up. She moaned, gave him a fake smile, and then moaned again asking him if he would go to the store and buy some Tylenol. He nodded his head as he could see she was in pain, headed downstairs to the garage, and began to drive to the store. He drove for about a minute and then it hit him. He had bought a bottle of Tylenol just a few days before and it had been one of those big bottles. He turned the car around and speeded back home. He ran up the stairs to the apartment and hurried inside. Adriana was now almost completely passed out. He looked in the bathroom and sure enough the wastebasket contained the now empty bottle of pills. "Adriana, Adriana. What did you do?" he called out to her, knowing full well what she had done, but not wanting to believe it was true. He grabbed her by the shoulders and tried to shake her awake, but her eyes only half opened. He thought of calling 911, but knew he could get her to the emergency room faster on his own so he picked her up and headed back down the stairs to his car. As he put her in the car, she started to wake up somewhat, but he could see she was going to pass out again. He drove like a madman toward the hospital. Halfway there, Adriana grasped the door handle and opened the door screaming that she wanted to die. Tony held on to her other arm and drove the rest of the way to the hospital with one hand.

Tony sat with his head in his hands in the emergency room. He couldn't believe this was happening to him. How could she try to commit suicide while she was almost seven months pregnant? Did she hate herself or the unborn infant more? The doctor came out and said they had pumped her stomach. He said there were over fifty pills in her, the Tylenol and something else. The doctor told him that he had saved both her life and the life of the fetus. There was a definite possibility that the fetus could be damaged, but they would have to wait and see over the next few days. If he had brought her in any later the pills would have started to fully digest and most likely the fetus would have died and she possibly would have also. They would monitor both of them over the next few days and she would have to be in the intensive care unit for at least three days. A few minutes later one of the nurses came over to Tony, put her hand on his shoulder, and asked if was going to be okay. Tony tried to smile, but he didn't have a smile or an answer in him.

The next day he came back to the hospital to visit Adriana in the intensive care unit. Her face was drawn and there were dark spots under her eyes. She looked like she had aged over night. When he walked in, she had a plate of food in front of her and she immediately threw it at him when she saw him coming in the door. She screamed out in an eerie broken voice, "Why didn't you let me die? I wanted to die!" Tony turned around and went back home. He was very sad and very confused. He called the hospital and talked with the resident psychologist. They planned to meet the next day to go over the interview she had with Adriana.

"It appears what has happened to your wife, Mr. Sloan, is that she has experienced what we like to call an "anniversary reaction," said the overweight and most likely lesbian woman who sat in front of him. "Ms. Tanner" is what it read on her nametag. Tony looked at her quizzically, but let her continue. "Your wife explained to me that when she was pregnant before she had caught her ex-husband in bed with another woman. This caused her to go into hysteria and she subsequently had a stillbirth and lost her child."

It was another surprise for Tony. Adriana had become the woman of mystery and surprises. She had never told him that she was pregnant before. He found it hard to believe that she would tell all of this to a hospital physiologist that she had just met rather than him, but at this point nothing really surprised him that much. He had become sort of like a shell-shocked war veteran from the constant episodes of drama and trauma that his wife was putting him through.

Adriana stayed in the hospital for eight days. Tony came and visited her and she stopped being angry with him for not letting her commit suicide. She was obviously very depressed, but there was no medication that the doctors could put her on because she was so late in her pregnancy. She moped around the house and Tony made sure she wasn't alone. He paid an aunt of his to stay with her when he was at work. His aunt helped around the house and treated Adriana very well. It was working out well, but Tony still had reservations about the future so he mostly tried to not think about what it might hold.

Adriana ended up having the baby a month and a half premature. The doctors preformed a C-section and though the baby was very tiny, he was strong and made it through. Tony thanked his lucky stars and even went to the church and prayed for the first time in a long time because he felt so grateful that his son was born healthy. Adriana seemed a lot happier when she came home with their child. Not to say that she was normal, but the feeling of being a mother with her newborn made her somewhat happy again. Tony thought for sure that this was a good sign and things would look up. Maybe all the trauma of the past was behind him. After the first few weeks, he started to think that maybe everyone had been right and that she had only been acting irrationally because of the pregnancy. But, then something happened that changed Tony forever.

Tony had been helping Adriana with the breast-pump and had been storing the extra milk in the freezer. It actually turned out to be a good idea. It had only been 15 days since Adriana and their new son Marco had been home from the hospital. It was late at night and Marco started to cry because he wanted to feed. Tony gently woke up Adriana and passed the baby over to her so she could breast-feed him. The baby started to suckle and stopped crying, but then like a scene from some bizarre horror movie, Adriana pulled Marco off her breast and literally threw him at Tony. With a voice that sounded like she was possessed with some evil spirit, she hissed, "Here, he is your son, the son you always wanted, you take care of him. I'm not breast feeding him anymore!" She then turned her back on Tony and the now wailing baby and put the pillow over her head.

Tony was petrified. He wanted to confront her, but the baby was crying so he calmly went to the kitchen and took out one of the frozen bottles of breast milk to warm it up. He sat in the living room, fed the baby, and then put him to sleep. Tony then sat in the living room until dawn thinking about what he should do. The next day, Adrianna started drinking again and Tony realized he would have to take over the majority of the responsibility for taking care of his infant son. The reality that he had married a selfish and mentally unstable woman had finally sunk in. He had let her physical beauty and sexual wildness sway him to believing she was the woman for him. Now he would have to dedicate himself to raising his son. He decided he would be the best father any son could ever have. There was no other choice.

The ensuing seven years before Adriana and Tony officially became divorced were tumultuous to say the least. They had separated in the middle of the marriage for almost two years. Tony had Marco with him the majority of the time. While they were separated, one of the neighbors told him that the child cried for his daddy when he was with Adriana. The neighbor said that was the first time she had ever heard of a baby crying for his daddy rather than his mommy and thought it was a bit odd.

During the separation, Adriana went through numerous boyfriends, girlfriends, and jobs as well as Tony's money. She threatened to move back to Peru and take Marco with her unless Tony got back together with her. Tony felt trapped and decided he would make the effort so he could be with his son. It turned out to be a bad decision even though it seemed to go smoothly in the beginning. Adriana worked out of their apartment as a translator; this suited her well, as she could not keep a regular job due to personality conflicts with other employees and superiors.

Adriana was still insanely suspicious and jealous. She would often berate Tony for hours on end when he came home from work. She would accuse him of sleeping with any and every woman he had ever had a connection with. Tony became numb to her outbursts and lived for the happiness of his son. When he came home after work, he would take Marco to the park down the street to play. Tony held his anger and his temper inside. He wanted his son to have a "normal" life, so he maintained an image of stability to all his friends and family.

Once again, Tony fell into the trap of convincing himself that things were going more smoothly. He had learned to block out her rages and jealousy. He had lost most of his old friends because he didn't have time for them now that he had a son, but that was fine with him. He had become more of a sports fan due to the fact that they spent most of their time at home. Adriana seemed to be doing better with her translating business because she didn't ask him for money as much and she would actually buy things for the house now. The fact that she spent a lot of time on her computer didn't bother him because if she was busy she couldn't yell at him or think of things to criticize him about.

Once again though, it was only the calm before the storm and now that Tony had so many built up emotions and pent up anger it was a miracle that he didn't do something more drastic. It was a Saturday and he was watching football on the television in the bedroom when he heard the phone ring. He let Adriana answer because she was working on her computer in the adjacent room. Out of curiosity and instinct, he put the TV on mute. He could hear her talking and giggling while she talked. After her conversation ended, he got up and asked her who was on the phone. She replied that it was one of her clients that she was doing some translating work for. It was a private detective actually and Tony didn't know him. She told Tony that she had to go meet him because he had some papers to give her. It was early Saturday evening and Tony didn't understand why it couldn't wait until Monday, but he didn't question her. She left and didn't come home until 1 AM. They argued and Adriana slept on the couch. For the next few weeks the pattern continued with Adriana going out every few nights claiming she had to meet her client. Then she didn't come home for two days. She had gone to Las Vegas with her detective friend. When she came back after not saying she would be gone, she gave Tony some ridiculous story about a convention and that she didn't tell him because she knew he wouldn't let her go. Tony knew now that she was cheating on him and that was the last straw. He didn't blow up or even say anything to her. He simply packed his bags and went to a hotel. Tony had reached the end of his rope and he knew that there was no more "trying." The relationship was over forever.

The divorce dragged on for more than two years mainly because Adriana wanted more money as well as custody of Marco. She said she wanted to take Marco back to Peru, but she really just wanted Tony to offer her more money. Tony went into debt to pay for his attorney. Marco ended up being with Tony most of the time. They had agreed on a regular schedule of custody sharing Marco equally, but it never worked out that way because Adriana always had things to do and let Marco stay with Tony. Tony, at the request of his attorney, kept a log of how often Marco was with him. The attorney told him it would help because in California it was very rare for a father to be granted full custody unless the mother was either in jail or was incapacitated. The judicial system favored the woman in numerous ways. Finally, after two years, Tony paid Adriana $20,000 and settled for joint custody even though it was working out that Marco was with Tony almost 70% of the time. The good part was that Marco was a lot happier now. His father played sports with him and helped him with his schoolwork. Plus he didn't have to hear his parents argue.

Tony had been very patient just as his attorneys had advised him, yet it seemed like he had lost, at least financially because he was very much in debt. Most of his paychecks went to paying for his credit card debts, but he tried to keep them current. Less than a year after the divorce Adriana tried to commit suicide again, so the judge granted temporary full custody to Tony and a few weeks later the judge made it permanent. The journal Tony kept had paid off along with the fact that she was now unstable. Adriana was only upset that now her $800 per month child support was cut to nothing.

Tony was relieved and happy because now he could move on with his life and make sure his son had a great life.

Tony accepted the role of single father with care and commitment. He had always known that it would happen at some point and maybe he had waited too long to leave Adriana. Now it didn't matter because he had to raise his son virtually on his own. Marco saw his mother once a week or so, but he never spent the night. Marco and Tony became best friends, playing sports, and having a lot of fun together.

When Marco turned ten, Adriana moved back to Peru and stayed there for over a year. The whole time she was there she only called her son twice. Then, one day out of the blue, she knocked on Tony's door with a big smile and proclaimed she was back. At the time, Tony was dating a cute Asian woman who would be showing up in an hour or so, so he took Adriana to a hotel and paid for her room for a week. Before the week was up, Adriana had found a new boyfriend and moved in with him.

From the ages of 12 to 17, it was mostly Tony and Marco on their own. Marco spent time with his mother on occasions when he felt guilty for not seeing her for a long time or when he and his father had a disagreement.  It wasn't often though and usually not for any extended period of time. Neither Adriana nor Tony remarried or entered a long-term relationship. Adriana was still a very difficult person to get along with even though she had been able to curb her drinking by going to AA. Also, Tony really didn't have the time or feel the need to bring another woman into his son's life. Tony taught his son to play golf and they golfed together whenever they had a chance. Marco had talent, so Tony put out the money for a private instructor. It paid off because once in high school Marco not only won for his school, but also was offered several full scholarships to colleges. Tony was very proud of him when he accepted the full scholarship to the University of Phoenix because it was one of the best schools for golf. Tony knew his son had a good chance of becoming professional after he finished college. At Marco's high school graduation,

Adriana, in typical fashion, came up to Tony and said with total sincerity, "Wow Tony. Didn't we do a great job of raising our son!"

Fortunately for Tony, as he was driving into the Malibu hills and thinking that he should have killed his ex-wife and not the gang punk, his ex-wife was far away. She had moved to somewhere outside Phoenix, so she could be near her son and hopefully gain off his future success.

Tony was almost at the top of the mountain and it was dark now. He had been driving for well over two hours. He pulled his car off the road onto a dirt turnoff. It must be a spot where lovers come to see the view he thought to himself. He could see the city lights far below. It was almost 8:00 PM and he guessed the game should be close to being over. He just knew the Angels had lost. He said to himself that he would wait for 15 minutes before turning the car radio on so he could hear the outcome. He leaned back and crossed his hands behind his head. He could hear the crickets outside because there were no cars on the road and he felt very relaxed even though he knew he had lost his bet. He was enjoying the serenity of the Malibu hills. He almost fell asleep when the glare of headlights in his rearview mirror brought him out of his serenity. The car slowed down and pulled off, parking right next to him partially off the road and partially on the road. There were two Cholos staring at him. One had a red bandana tied around his head. The guy in the passenger side closest to him rolled down the window.

"Hey homie, what's up? What are you doing up here?" Tony could see the tattoos covering his arms as the window rolled down.

"Trying to be alone," Tony replied with sarcasm in his voice. He was very annoyed that these two idiots had broken his moment of serenity.

The Cholo scowled at Tony and laughed, "Oh sure, right. You want to be alone because you're up here flaming, aren't you? I bet you have some good smoke."

Now Tony was getting more than annoyed. He was getting angry. "Look. I am up here to be alone. I don't take drugs, so why don't you just move along now. Do you understand? Get lost!"

"What did you say to me? Listen Gabacho, I don't take any crap from any white man." He then lifted up his other arm and pointed a small handgun directly at Tony's head. "See this, you white piece of crap? I'll blow your brains out right here because you disrespected me. First throw your wallet over here right now!"

Tony knew he had made a mistake by being sarcastic, but that was his nature and he really didn't care. These two guys were obviously gang members and what the heck they were doing up in the Malibu hills was beyond him. He was supposed to be up here relaxing and keeping his mind off the game, but now it had turned into a bad situation. Very casually, Tony reached under his seat and found his 22-caliber handgun. It was the same one he had killed the black kid with so he knew he had five shots left if he needed them. "Ok, ok. Hey I'm sorry. I will give you my wallet." Tony acted the part of the scared victim because he had to make the guy let his guard down. At the same time, he had to calculate how he could take them both out or even if he should take them both out. This wasn't the first time someone had pointed a gun at him, but he knew he had to think fast. The guy in the driver's seat was looking at this friend with the gun, but not moving or talking. So after Tony had grabbed his gun from under the seat, he casually put it on the seat between his legs. He knew the guy holding the gun on him couldn't see it because it was below his vision, as it was blocked by the angle from his eyes to Tony's seat. Then Tony very slowly lifted his hands up in the air and said with fake fear, "I'm sorry if I said anything to offend you. Please don't take my wallet because I have a lot of credit cards in it." He knew this would make the Cholo want it even more.

"Shut up, you ugly white culero. Give me your wallet now or I will blow your brains out." The Cholo waved the gun up in the air trying to act like the gang member he was.

"Ok, ok. Here take it," said Tony as he slowly brought his gun up, waiting for the right second to make his move. The gang member gave Tony the opening as he briefly glanced back at his friend, who was in the driver's seat. Tony blasted him right between the eyes. He fired two quick shots and the Cholo fell back toward the driver giving Tony a chance to blast him. He let off two more shots. The first one hit him in the shoulder as he tried to duck, but Tony adjusted his aim on the next shot and hit him in the neck. The driver slammed his foot on the accelerator at the same time and the car lurched forward and careened off the road about fifty feet ahead of where Tony was parked. Tony started up his car and drove to where the other car had stopped and was now teetering at the edge of the cliff. Carefully, Tony walked over to the driver's side. He knew he only had one shot left and if the guy were still alive, he would need it to finish him off. Both the Cholos were sprawled out. Their bodies were limp so there would be no need for the last shot. But then, the driver sat up and moaned so Tony let off his last shot in his temple. Tony then leaned inside the car to make sure the other guy was dead too and he heard the radio announce, "The Angels have just won the World Series!" Tony smiled. He had just won his bet. Then he noticed the blood on the seat as it was starting to roll down to the floor of the car. "Angel red and Cholo blood he said out loud to himself." He grinned ear to ear and felt the same adrenaline rush he had felt a few days before. He was hyped to the max. He then turned and hurried back to his car, which he had left running. As he started to drive off, the euphoria of winning his bet and the adrenaline from this run-in made his thoughts flow like a fast running stream. He had to take care of this mess. It had been self-defense since he had been held up at gunpoint. The problem was he had used the same gun that he had killed the young black gang member with just a few nights before. That meant there was no way he could do anything but stay quiet. He went over the incident in his head reviewing every detail and knew the only evidence would be his tire marks and some possible footprints, but the ground was hard and dusty. He took some deep breaths and forced himself to relax. He then thought of winning his bet and grinned ear to ear.

As he was walking down the hall to his apartment, his fat neighbor opened his door as someone who had been there was leaving. Tony tried to sneak by, but the neighbor saw him. "Hey Tony, how did you like that game?" asked the neighbor.

"It was a good game. I'm happy the Angels won." Tony could see his neighbor had been drinking a little too much, so he hurried to get in his apartment before the fat neighbor started a longer conversation. Tony smiled at him and ducked into his apartment.

Tony immediately went to the TV and turned it on so he could see the highlights of the game. Now he was pissed at himself for not staying and watching it. It had been a great game plus he wouldn't have had the problem of running into the gang guys up in the Malibu hills. He turned off the TV after he had seen enough highlights and fixed himself a very stiff rum and coke. He could feel his heart still beating faster than usual and he knew he needed to relax. He had been through dangerous situations before, but now he knew he could possibly face some serious trouble. The best thing to do was to just go about his normal life and not worry about it. He thought back to when he had executed that black gang member. It felt like months ago, but it had been only a few days ago. He had planned that out and thought about it over and over for months. He had carried out his plan perfectly and when he had pulled the trigger there were no thoughts or remorse. This time though, it had been unplanned and he had been very angry. Heck, he would have found a way to beat the crap out of them even if he hadn't had his gun in his car. What bothered him the most was there would be evidence. There wouldn't be much, but there would be some. He wasn't too worried, but he knew he had to change his tires as soon as possible as well as get rid of the gun. He wasn't worried about them tracing the gun because it was illegal and he had lots of illegal guns. Still, he knew it had been stupid to use the same one. He had been too confident after the first killing by holding onto the gun. He should have disposed of it right away rather than keep it in his car. That was really careless. He decided he would throw the gun off the Redondo Beach pier in the morning before sunrise and get new tires. Now that he could collect on his bet he deserved new tires anyway. He smiled thinking about that as he fell asleep on his couch.

## Chapter 4

Maria woke at 5 AM. Her husband was asleep on the couch, as he had been asked. She felt sort of guilty because she had been so mean, but she also felt very relieved because he had not woken up and tried to come into the bedroom. She knew she didn't have to be at work until 9 AM, but she was determined now and wasn't going to put things off any longer. She was going to go to Home Depot before work and get a lock for her bedroom door. She lay back down and thought maybe she would sleep some more because she had plenty of time, but she knew she would just fall asleep again and start dreaming of Tim. She couldn't get him off her mind so she took off her night slip and decided to take a long shower.

She stood naked in front of the mirror in the bathroom. "God I look old in the morning." She rubbed her eyes and tried to smile at her image, but it was a smile without meaning.

The warm water felt very good as it cascaded over her. It was like Tim's hands caressing her. She started to smile for real now as his image came into her mind, the kissing and hugging. Then she got soap in her eyes and Tim's image left her. She washed the soap out with water and turned with her back to the showerhead. She smiled again as she took the soap and started to clean herself. The water reminded her of the softness of another woman. She thought to herself...no wonder so many women experiment with another woman. She had because it is like the water, soft warm, flowing, molding its wetness around you, sensing and probing all the most erotic parts. It touches your soul. Then she giggled at the thought of water touching her soul. Suddenly, Tim's image came back into her mind as she started to wash her sacred parts with the bar of soap. The kissing, the wanting, and the excitement of the game the night before...it all had been so masculine...baseball, the crowd, the noise, his smell, and his lips touching hers. She could feel again the passion in their kisses. She touched herself and it felt very good. She was strong and determined now that she would make the changes in her life that she needed to for her own happiness.

The morning for Tim was not as good. Last night when he had returned, he had been met with the cold shoulder from his wife and older daughter. His younger daughter April was a bit more sympathetic toward him. He left the house without, "Good morning, good bye, or have a good day." Instead, his wife was standing with her hands on her hips shaking her head and saying with anger, "I still can't believe you ran off on your own without telling us yesterday. That just wasn't right and you know it."

Maria was very determined. She dressed quickly after her shower and quietly left the apartment. She went to Home Depot and bought a lock. She felt sort of out of place with all the construction guys there early in the morning because she was dressed in her clothes for work. Several guys started to follow her around the store as she searched for the lock she needed. When she left the store she realized it was still way too early to go to work and she definitely didn't want to go back to the apartment and wait. She decided to stop and have breakfast. She didn't really eat much in the morning, but she needed to kill some time so she stopped at a Denny's on the way back to her apartment.

She picked up a newspaper from one of the newsstands in front and went inside. There was no one in the front so she walked over to an empty booth and sat down. The headlines had a full-page picture of the Angels winning the World Series; it made her smile as she thought of Tim.

"Hi, my name is Susi! Can I get you some coffee?" said the waitress. Maria, still smiling, looked up from the paper and saw a very attractive Asian woman holding a pencil and ordering pad. The woman was smiling maybe because Maria was still smiling from thinking about Tim.

"Yes, some coffee would be nice," replied Maria. Susi turned and walked away toward the kitchen to get the coffee. Maria watched her as she walked away and admired her body. She didn't know why...maybe because she was still aroused from last night and then her shower in the morning, or maybe this waitress just reminded her of someone she used to know. She wasn't sure, but she really enjoyed watching her walk. She was petite, but with a nice firm body. Instinctively, Maria looked around to see if anyone had noticed her staring, but there was only a couple in a booth and they were talking. Maria held the paper in front of her like she was reading, but really she was just daydreaming. She was thinking about the only time she had been with another woman. She was thinking about the softness and the details of their night together. Susi came back with the coffee and again they smiled at each other. Maria ordered some pancakes and then tried to read the paper in earnest.

Susi returned with the pancakes and noticed the big headline on the paper that Maria was holding, "Angels Win World Series!" She set down the pancakes in front of Maria and asked, "Did you see the game? I don't really know much about sports, but I watched with my roommate and boyfriend. It was pretty exciting."

Maria smiled. Now that she was close Maria could see that she had very smooth skin and pretty eyes. "I was at the game yesterday and it was very exciting," Maria replied. She was now noticing the soft colored lip-gloss on Susi's lips.

"Really, you were actually there?" Susi replied as she refilled Maria's coffee.

"Yes, I was really lucky. My boss gave me two tickets. I went with a friend from work," Maria replied. She was wondering how the word friend sounded as she said it to Susi because she wanted Tim to be more than a friend.

"Wow, you were lucky. I heard the tickets were selling for well over $1,000 a piece!" said Susi who was admiring the nice blue blouse and business suit that Maria was wearing. She wondered if this customer was an important businesswoman.

"I was thinking of selling them but I'm glad I went to the game instead. It was really a lot of fun," replied Maria.

Susi smiled at Maria again, wishing she were a businesswoman rather than a waitress at Denny's. "Well let me know if you need anything else." Susi turned and walked back again toward the kitchen with Maria watching her walk. Halfway to the kitchen Susi turned and they both flashed charming yet brief friendly smiles at each other.

Maria ate her pancakes and read some of the newspaper. Susi came over to give her the bill. They chatted again and afterward Maria gave Susi one of her business cards and asked her to call sometime. Maybe they could go shopping or something. Maria was happy time had passed and she could start her day. She stopped back at her apartment complex, gave the lock to the manager, and asked if he could install it on her bedroom door. She felt a bit embarrassed, but he was very polite and said he would take care of it. She then headed off to work.

Tim and Maria did not see each other at work on Monday until late in the afternoon. Tim again had received a call from the head of homicide. "I've got another report on two more gang related homicides. Mexican American gang members were shot this time. They were found late last night on La Tuna Canyon Road in Malibu. That's county land outside the city limit, so it's the jurisdiction of the Malibu Sheriff's Department, but I think it's something you might want to look into in case it's related to the other shooting. It says in the report they were most likely both shot with a 22-caliber bullet from a handgun. It could be just a coincidence, but with two shootings over the weekend with the same caliber handgun, it seems odd. I want you to look over the printout I have, call the Sheriff's Department in Malibu, and compare notes with them. I'll send down Maria with the report. Oh yeah, I hope you enjoyed the game last night. I am the one who gave her those tickets you know."

"Thanks boss. I really enjoyed the game. She told me that you had given them to her," replied Tim, who was now a little nervous that he had to see Maria. He had been hoping that the day would pass by and he wouldn't have to see her. He was feeling guilty and unsure if what he had done was right.

"Well, I am glad she took you. I know you are a big baseball fan," said MacIntosh.

"Thanks boss," said Tim as he wondered what else his boss knew about his trip to the game yesterday. He didn't think Maria would say anything else. As a matter of fact, he was sure she wouldn't, but she could have lied and said she took someone else.

This time Tim did not leave his desk and go to the vending machines so he could come back to see Maria standing at his desk with her backside to him. It wasn't something he thought of consciously; it was just that they had taken the flirting past innocent fun by going to the game and acting like young high school lovers. They were now on the border of entering territory that was both exciting and dangerous. Tim was trying to tell himself he would end it right here and right now. He was a bit nervous and scared about seeing Maria now and was also confused as to what he should to say to her. So he kept his eyes down on his desk and pretended like he was looking at some paperwork, but the papers were just blurry and his mind was the same. He tried silently rehearsing what to say to her, but the image of her body pressed up against his as they kissed kept coming into his mind.

As Tim was staring blankly at his desk, he could feel Maria coming so he looked up. She was smiling and holding out the file as she sauntered up close to the front of his desk. "Hi Mr. Sloan," she addressed him emphasizing the "Mr.," but at the same time raising her eyebrows in a sensually provocative way.

"Hi Maria," Tim answered back as his eyes went from hers and then down slowly to the papers in her hand, continuing on to take in a filling gaze at her breasts. Everything in his mind about ending what they had not even started yet disappeared in an instant of misty passion. Tim looked back up at her eyes and smiled. "Thanks for bringing the papers down. I had a great time with you last night at the game. How are you doing today?"

"I'm fine. Well, I'm a bit tired because I woke up very early this morning." Then Maria leaned over Tim's desk and Tim almost thought she would kiss him, but she stopped and smiled softly as her eyes darted to either side to be sure no one was watching them. "I've been thinking about you. I really enjoyed being with you at the game."

Tim whispered back, "Me too."

"When can we get together again?" Maria said, wanting to kiss him so badly that she could feel herself start to tremble.

"We have to be careful around here. Let me think of something and I will send you a note," Tim replied.

"Ok, that sounds good. I'll be waiting Tim." Maria smiled again, turned, and hurried back to her office. Knowing Tim was watching her walk, she turned and smiled at him one more time just as she rounded the corner into the hall.

It was the last smile that sealed their fate because even though Tim talked like he wanted to meet her again, he knew he wouldn't. Cheating on his wife would just be too much guilt on his mind and he didn't want that. Also, the ramifications of having an affair at work were too much to think about. So as Maria walked away, he tried not to watch, but he couldn't help it and he talked under his breath to himself saying, "Just leave her alone Tim." But then she turned and smiled and he smiled back and the thoughts and the guilt buried themselves under a soft pile of silken passions.

Tim told himself he had work to do so he could block the thought of kissing Maria out of his mind. His noticed his palms were sweating as he opened the file. He smiled to himself and thought of Maria in bed with him, but then quickly shook his head trying to take the images away so he could focus on the paperwork in front of him. But, he couldn't. He was staring blankly at the papers and trying to decide if he should go through with it. It would be worse he figured if she were single, but she was also married so maybe that made it less bad. He told himself that people had affairs all the time. He told himself that if he did that he would have to be very careful so no one at the office found out. For sure, Linda couldn't find out. He decided if he did get together with Maria again he had to plan it out very carefully. It couldn't be spur of the moment like going to the ballgame. He knew that was a mistake. Also, he told himself he would have to end it at some point. Exactly when he wasn't sure because Maria was very hot and sexy and his wife hadn't been that with him much in the past few years. He told himself the worst thing he could do for both himself and Maria would to be to fall in love with her; there was no way that could happen, at least not now.

Eventually, his thoughts of Maria faded and he focused on the report in front of him. It was a synopsis of a double homicide that had occurred the night before. It appeared there had been a car chase or a race and then a shooting. It all seemed like typical gang activity except that it had taken place in the Malibu hills. He called the given number for the Malibu Sheriff's Department so he could talk with the investigating officer.

"Hi, Tim Sloan here. I'm with the LAPD Gang Task Force Unit."

""Hi, I'm Steven Breeze. I work homicide here. What can I do for you?" replied Mr. Breeze.

Tim guessed from the tone of Steven's voice that this was not going to be very productive. Though they both were in law enforcement, the LAPD and the LA County Sheriff's Department had never been on the best terms. They cooperated when it was necessary, but there was always an underlying aura of animosity. The Sheriff's Department ran the LA County jail system and they did it their way. This had always caused tension from other law enforcement agencies. Tim had to do his job though so he continued, "We had a Crip shot near South Central last Friday night. He was shot with one bullet in the back of the head with a 22-caliber handgun. My boss gave me the summary of your shooting last night and said that a 22-caliber handgun was also used. He thinks we should compare notes just in case there is a connection. Do you have the full tests on the bullets back yet?"

"Sure we can compare notes. We should have the results on the bullets by tomorrow morning. We don't do things as fast as you guys! What I can tell you is that it was two Mexican gang members shot, not Crips. It appears they were either racing or being chased down when they were shot. One of them had a gun, but he never got a shot off. We are making castings of the other cars tire treads and we also have some pretty clean footprints so we know it was just one person involved. I will send over the results on the bullets as soon as I get them and you can send me the report on the other shooting," replied Mr. Breeze.

"Probably the soonest I can get the report over to you is by tomorrow afternoon. You know how entrenched in bureaucracy we are here," said Tim. Mr. Breeze laughed at the comment and they hung up.

Now that the immediacy of his work was done, Tim allowed his mind to wander back to Maria. He was trying to think of a way they could meet again. He would have to manipulate a few things around so it would work for both of them, but he was a detective and he knew he could do that. He had an idea now. He picked up the phone and called his boss. "Sir, I just talked with the Malibu Sheriff's Department. I spoke with Steven Breeze; he is handling the homicides. He wanted to know if we could meet in person and exchange files. I think it might be a good idea if I go up there tomorrow afternoon. You know how much they can delay things if they don't get their way, so if it's his suggestion...I think it might be the best way."

"That will fine Sloan. I'm glad you informed me you are going there tomorrow afternoon. Some of the idiots around here would just go and not tell me anything," replied MacIntosh.

Tim smiled. Things were working out pretty well. Now he just had to discreetly talk to Maria. Tim wrote a note for her asking if she could take off tomorrow afternoon at 2 PM. He explained about driving out to Malibu and told her they could have some time alone. He waited until 6 PM because he knew that was the time that she got off work. He then headed out to the parking structure and waited casually around her car. There were a lot of employees leaving at the time and Tim felt awkward until Maria showed up. She had a big smile and a big hug for him. She was very surprised to see him. Tim looked around and felt embarrassed at the idea that anyone might see them together. He handed her the note and told her he really wanted to see her and then hurried away hoping he had not been seen by anyone. Maria sat in her car and read the note. She giggled and knew she had her chance to be with Tim again. As she drove home, she imagined them at the ballgame. The kissing had been heavenly so she shivered at the thought of how the rest would be.

Maria stopped at the manager's apartment before she went upstairs to her apartment and picked up the keys to the new lock he had installed for her bedroom door. Fortunately, he didn't ask any questions, but rather just handed her the keys and gave her an odd smile. When she went inside, her two sons were eating chips and watching the television. "Where's your father?" she asked them.

Her younger son, Leo, came over to her and gave her a hug. "Dad left just before you got here."

"Did the two of you finish your homework?" she asked.

"Sort of," replied her older son.

"That means you didn't finish your homework," Maria said with her hands on her hips as she put her purse down. "I want that TV off and I want you two to go in your room and finish your homework before you watch TV."

Maria checked her phone messages and then went into the kitchen to cook dinner. She guessed Felix had gone off to be with his friends and get drunk. She knew if he left then she would have to find someone to help her out with the kids. She would need someone who could pick them up from school and watch them until she returned home from work. As she was cooking, she suddenly remembered she had to call into work so she could take the afternoon off and spend it with Tim! She called her boss's messenger service and said she had to go to her son's school for a meeting with the teacher tomorrow afternoon. She needed to leave work at 2 PM. When she hung up the phone, something bothered her. Then she realized that was the first time she had ever told a lie to her boss. Lying is not good she thought to herself. One lie always leads to the next. She promised herself that would be the one and last lie she would tell to her boss. She also promised herself that she would not fall in love with Tim. She would meet him tomorrow and maybe a few more times. She would enjoy him, but she would not get involved with him for long because he was married. Maybe she would meet someone in the future after Felix left. Hopefully he would get the message and move out soon. She knew it would be hard on the kids, but she couldn't accept being treated the way she was being treated. Maria stared to cry a little. Not a lot, but tears welled up. She wanted her own life, but she didn't want to become a person that lied all the time just to get the things she wanted.  She wished Felix would change, but she knew that was not going to happen. She wished that Tim was single, but he wasn't.

After dinner, Maria spent time playing and talking with her two boys. They laughed together and had fun. She put them to bed and then locked herself in her bedroom. She liked the feeling of being secure and she also enjoyed knowing that when and if Felix came home he couldn't come into the bed drunk and put his hands on her. She fell asleep quickly and slept very well for the first time in a long time. Felix came home late and very drunk; he slept in the living room on the couch.

When Tim returned home from work Monday at 6:35 PM he was expecting the worst. He was sure his wife would still be mad about him having gone to the game the day before. Instead, she was in the kitchen cooking dinner and wearing a very short tennis skirt. The girls were in their rooms doing their homework as usual. Tim entered the house through the back door as he always did because it was connected to the garage. The door led into the kitchen. "Hi honey, how was work today?" Linda asked as she turned and gave Tim a kiss on the cheek as well as a nice hug. She smiled at him in an inviting way. Tim smiled back, but he was confused because he was sure she would still be mad.

"Work was fine," he answered as he backed away a little from her embrace. "I thought you would still be upset at me for going to the game yesterday?"

Linda gave a little pout, "No, we all need to have a little fun once in a while. Really, I thought about it and understand. I know you really like baseball. Colleen is still upset though. She doesn't understand why you couldn't have taken her to the game. You know she loves sports just like you do. She gets that from you, honey."

"You're right; I'll have to do something to make it up to her. So what's with the tennis skirt Tim?" looked down at her as she turned back to the stove. The skirt was very short.

Linda turned halfway around to face him and made sure the skirt flew up a little so he could see she was wearing a thong underneath. "So do you like it? It's really short huh? I told you a few weeks ago I was thinking of taking tennis lessons. You said I needed to exercise more. So I took my first lesson today!" Linda was hoping he wouldn't ask too much more. The reality was she was still upset he had gone to the game, but didn't want to have any more conflicts with him. She didn't believe for a minute that he had gone to the game on his own, but she didn't really care if he did or he didn't. He had been too distant lately. He didn't cuddle with her that often, but instead would stay up late watching sports in the den. They rarely went out together. He didn't even take the girls places like he used to when they were younger. Life was becoming very routine and very boring. She had really enjoyed the time she had spent at her tennis lesson. Tim didn't need to know that the only reason she had decided to take any lessons at all was because three weeks earlier that tall, handsome, very fit and younger guy had given her his number in the market. He had told her he taught tennis, but really he was hitting on her and she knew it. Today was her second lesson and she didn't tell Tim she had taken a lesson the previous

Monday. Today the lesson had progressed a little further than the first one. She had bought the tennis skirt and she had worn thong bikini panties underneath. She could see the tennis instructor was getting turned on and she just loved the fact that she could turn him on. She knew she was in pretty good shape even though Tim thought she wasn't. She walked all the time and she was the only one that took the two dogs for walks. Sometimes she even jogged with them. Tim just didn't appreciate her. Maybe he was hitting on some woman at his job...she really didn't know. She just knew that the tennis instructor thought she was in great shape and that she turned him on. The lesson today had been very professional just like the first one. She figured he had to have a girlfriend because he was just too good looking. He said he didn't though when they talked afterward. Then she made a point to bend over while picking up the loose balls and she could tell he really got turned on. That was when he hinted at them meeting some time other than for tennis. It was all harmless flirting and really just a fun game for her until the very end of the lesson. They had stood face-to-face just talking about how her game was progressing and then when they said goodbye to meet again next Monday for the lesson, they kissed. It was a friendly kiss, but there was a hint of something more and Linda liked it.

Tim was standing near the doorway to the living room looking back at his wife as she leaned over the stove in her new tennis skirt. He liked her legs, but his mind drifted to Maria and the rendezvous they had planned for the following day. Before he headed upstairs to shower before dinner he turned and said to her, "Well I am glad you're taking up a sport honey. That is really good for you." Linda turned and gave him a curt sarcastic smile.

## Chapter 5

Tues October 29<sup>th</sup>

Tim and Maria met at 2 PM in front of the entrance to the large parking structure at their work. They hadn't seen each other all day at work and both were worried whether the other would show up as they had planned. When they both showed up almost at the same time though, they knew they would go through with it. They smiled at each other and the anticipation they each felt hung in the air like the scent of jasmine on a spring afternoon. "Hi, Maria!" said Tim, smiling ear to ear. Maria acted a bit shy and only half smiled trying to hold back for now. "Can you take your car and follow me? I have to meet with a detective at the Malibu Sheriff's Department and pick up a report from him. You can wait in the parking lot for me. It shouldn't take very long at all and then we can go somewhere together." Tim was trying to be confident. He knew all women liked confident men. The problem was he was trying to act confident and the reality was he didn't feel confident at all. Actually, he had been thinking most of the day about Linda in her tennis skirt. Normally he would have been very turned on and had a wonderful night with his wife, but last night he slept early thinking he needed the energy for his meeting with Maria today. Trying to cheat on his wife with Maria was just becoming way too crazy and stressful, but he felt the momentum taking control of him and he knew there was no way he could go back now.

Maria had no reservations whatsoever. When she left for work this morning Felix was passed out on the couch as usual. The alarm clock was set near his head so he could get up, take the boys to school, and go to work. She knew he had no desire to change at all. Hopefully at some point he would be sober enough so they could talk, but for now the fact that he slept on the couch and left her alone was good enough. Not only did Maria want to be with Tim, but also she felt like she deserved it. She felt like she deserved to enjoy life and start living again, even if she had a brief affair with a married man from work. She smiled at Tim again and leaned forward, giving him a soft kiss on his cheek. "Sure Tim. I can follow you."

It took about 25 minutes for them to drive to the Sheriff's Department in Malibu. Maria waited in her car in the parking lot while Tim went inside and met with Steven Breeze. The meeting went fast and was businesslike. Mr. Breeze was a large heavyset man, who seemed to have a constant scowl. He had a look that intimidated anyone, but really he was quite softhearted. He was older than Tim and obviously looked at Tim as an inferior officer. They exchanged reports and talked briefly about the homicides. They both agreed it was highly unlikely that the two homicides were linked, but they would know for sure when the results on the bullets were in the following day. The whole meeting took less than half an hour and every minute of it seemed to drag on for Tim because he knew Maria was waiting in her car in the parking lot. If she had to wait too long, she might get upset and that would not be good for him. When he headed back to her car, she was contently listening to music. She was leaning back in her seat with her eyes closed and had unbuttoned the first few buttons of her blouse.

"Well, I'm done Maria!" said Tim with a big grin. Maria turned her head and rolled down the window all the way. She reached down and turned off the radio.

"You know that wasn't too nice of you to make me wait in the car," Maria replied just to see where she stood with him.

"I'm sorry Maria," Tim said back apologetically.

Maria smiled now knowing he really was sorry. She was just anxious to be with him somewhere else than in the parking lot of a sheriff's station. The conversation was frozen and Tim had a quizzical look on his face as he was wondering now if either one of them really wanted to go through with it. This was when Maria leaned to the window, gently put her hand around Tim's neck pulling him into her, and kissed him passionately.  It sealed their fates. "Where are we going now, Tim?"

"There's a hotel a little ways down the coast highway. I saw it when we drove up," Tim said trying to sound as if he had not planned the whole escapade, but instead was acting spontaneously.

"Ok, I will follow you again," Maria replied as she started to button one of the buttons on her blouse. Tim smiled and knew inside he was caught up in something that he had no intent to control. He felt like a teenager again and could feel himself getting aroused during the 10-minute drive to the hotel. He constantly checked in his rear view mirror to make sure Maria was still following him.

The hotel was right along the Coast Highway. They pulled in and parked in the parking lot side by side. There was a series of small bungalows each with a romantic view of the ocean. Tim paid for the room with cash and said that Maria, who was by his side, was his wife. They walked down a little path to their room that was lined with birds of paradise.

Once inside, Maria walked over to the picture window and looked out at the ocean. Tim followed her and they stared out at the waves breaking on the rocks below. They both commented on the magnificent view and then they turned and faced each other. They looked into each other's eyes for only a brief instant and then their bodies crashed together just like the waves below were crashing into the rocks. They undressed each other while still kissing and fell onto the bed not caring to pull down the covers. There was no love or commitment...just pure lust and passion cascading from within each of them. Neither one of them wanted it to end so they would tease and caress each other until they almost reached a moment of exploding passion and then they would ease off and slow down almost to stillness each hearing the sound of the crashing waves below. Two hours later, they lay naked in each other's arms as the last rays of orange sunset reflected off the mirror over the dresser. The white walls of the room were fading to a burnt orange, as they lay entwined on top of the bed.

Tim was completely satisfied, but now the guilt started to seep into him. The room was almost dark now and Tim got out of the bed and went to the restroom. He turned the light on in the room afterward. Maria lay on her side and it reminded Tim of a painting he had once seen. Maria smiled at Tim wanting him to come back to bed and make love with her again, but she could feel Tim withdraw himself emotionally from her and she knew he was feeling remorse. She went to the restroom and dressed. They quietly left the hotel room. They kissed in the parking lot and then headed back to their respective homes.

## Chapter 6

Wednesday, Oct. 30

It was nearly 2 PM and fortunately or unfortunately, depending on whose point of view, Tim and Maria had not seen each other at work. Yesterday evening the drive from Malibu to Simi Valley took about the same time as it would have taken for him to go from the station to his home. Therefore, he arrived at his home about the same time he would on any normal workday. It was a mundane evening with his family. He helped his younger daughter with her homework and at last his older daughter stopped being mad at him over the Angels game. He bought some tickets to take her to a Lakers basketball game. When he handed her the tickets, she tried not to smile or act excited, but the smile cracked through and she was happy he thought of her. He admitted to her that it had been selfish for him to go to the Angels game and not think of taking her. She accepted his apology. No one in his family had any idea that he had gone with Maria to the game and that he was now involved with her. When Tim finally went upstairs, Linda was already asleep. He lay in bed next to her, watching her sleep and that was when the guilt broadsided him in full force. He thought about his wife and all they had been through together. He thought about his two daughters and how they were maturing so quickly and then he wept. He felt angry with himself. Maybe it was just the fact that he had been making love with his wife for so many years...the same body over and over again, and he had needed a change. He wanted to make love with Maria again, but there was no way he ever would and he knew it. He told himself that Maria had wanted him more than he had wanted her anyway. She always flirted with him and that was a sign she had wanted him. He knew she must have been having problems with her husband or she would never have flirted with him that much. The voices in his head went on and on trying to justify his actions, but in the end he knew the love for his wife and family outweighed his lust for Maria. Tim was the kind of person who made decisions quickly so as he lay next to his sleeping wife, he told himself he would tell Maria tomorrow that it was over. He put his arm around his wife and slept restlessly.

Tim had spent most of the day with these same thoughts dancing in his mind. He had not been able to concentrate on his work as he thought about what he would say to Maria if he saw her. He sat there staring blankly at the papers on his desk when his phone rang. For a second he didn't want to pick it up because it might be Maria, but he realized how stupid it would be to not pick up the phone so he picked it up on the second ring. "Detective Sloan speaking, what can I do for you?"

"This is Detective Breeze. I have the results on the analysis of the bullets and they match. They came from the same gun. We were both wrong. It looks like we may have the beginning of some kind of serial killings here or we just have someone that likes to shoot gang members."

Tim replied, "Well that definitely is very interesting. I would never have thought the homicides were connected. You know how many gang related killings we get here."

"Actually we don't get too many homicides at all up here in Malibu. We get some bodies dumped in the hills once in a while and an occasional domestic type of homicide, but we don't have too many gang shootings up here," replied Mr. Breeze.

"Yeah, I guess that is true," said Tim.

"The fact is Mr. Sloan, I have already cleared it with my boss here and we are turning over the case on the shootings to your department. We don't have the resources like you guys do to get too deep into this kind of thing. We will be sending over all the information we have on it to you as soon as possible."

"That's fine. I understand. Thanks for all your help in the matter," replied Tim.

"You're welcome and good luck. Let us know if you need anything else from us. To serve and protect, right?" said Mr.

Breeze, who was happy he wouldn't have to deal with the case.

Tim shook his head and smiled. He wondered why he had chosen to work for the LAPD rather than become a sheriff. Tim leaned back in his chair and crossed his hands behind his head. He always did this at his desk when he needed to gather his thoughts. He knew he had his work cut out for him and he also knew his boss was not going to be happy now. Whenever there was a possibility of a serial killer it woke up bad memories in the press and it was dramatized to an unbelievable level. There had been way too many movies about serial killers and now the public could be worked into frenzy by the press at even the hint of a serial killer. The markings on the bullets had matched so that meant the same gun had been used, but they would have them analyzed again to be certain. This obviously meant the same person had been involved in both homicides, but guns get thrown away and are then found again. Yet, that was highly unlikely. So now three known gang members were dead, murdered with a 22-caliber gun. It would not be too unusual to expect that the first one was from a black gang and the second one was from a Latino gang. Tim knew that his boss would bring in more people on the case, especially if another gang member were found dead soon with a 22-caliber bullet. The chances that the media would find out that the two recent shootings were linked were very high and that concerned Tim most. There were just too many leaks within the LAPD and someone would get the information out knowing the media would find it interesting that someone has been killing gang members from different gangs. Tim passed a lot of various scenarios and possibilities in his head. Was it another gang? Maybe one of the Chinese or Russian gangs were getting revenge or thinning their competition? He knew his boss would go all out on these two homicides before the press turned it into a circus.

At least Tim had stopped daydreaming about Maria. The problem was he would now have to see her face-to-face because he had to go to his boss's office to tell him in person that the bullets were a match. Maria, his boss's executive secretary, sat in the small office in front of his boss's office. When she looked up and saw Tim tapping on the glass door that led to her office, she couldn't help but smile. At the same time though she could see by the look on Tim's face that something serious was going on. Otherwise she knew he wouldn't come over without calling MacIntosh first. She motioned with her hand for him to come inside.

"Hi Tim. How are you?" Maria smiled as she looked into his eyes. They could both feel the heat between them once again now that they were near each other.

"Hi, Maria. I didn't come here to see you. Well I didn't mean it that way. I am happy to see you. What I mean is I need to talk to the boss." Tim felt awkward because he knew he needed to talk to Maria soon about stopping their affair. He couldn't keep getting away with it and he knew it. The problem was he still felt highly attracted to her and he could tell she felt the same. They hadn't talked or made any plans since they had gone to the hotel, but they both knew the other was married.

Maria could see Tim was a bit uncomfortable and she also knew that he almost always called when he needed to talk to MacIntosh unless it was very pressing. She smiled at him again and subconsciously played with the top buttons of her blouse almost as if she was going to unbutton them. "He will be back from lunch any minute now. Why don't you sit down and wait for him?"

Now it was worse than before for Tim. He couldn't say, "No" and not wait. That would be totally rude and he could only dally in small conversation for a while with Maria. He knew he would have to bring up what happened between them yesterday afternoon and that would be hard to talk about at work. He also knew he had to be the first to tell MacIntosh what had developed with the homicides so he sat down.

Maria shuffled some papers and then looked at Tim. "Tim, you know we need to talk about things, but not here and not now."

Tim was glad she had said it first. "I know Maria. We will for sure."

They both wanted to blurt out a bunch of things that were on their minds. They looked at each other trying not to smile, but they couldn't help it and they both laughed out loud at the same time. They both felt the passion and desire of the day before. The laugh was a way of feeling close to each other. The excitement and daring of what they had done the day before was still there and it lingered in the air. If it wasn't for the fact that Maria's office was composed mostly of glass walls open to the rest of the department, they might have embraced.

"Sloan, what are you doing here?" asked MacIntosh as he burst through the door. "Are you over here flirting with my secretary while I'm away?" He winked at Maria. Alex MacIntosh was a large man. Not too much overweight...just large. He had a way of being intimidating. He was in his late fifties and had dark hair, large bushy eyebrows that looked like they had never been trimmed because they almost grew together giving him the look of having a constant scowl. Tim's jaw dropped. He wondered if Maria had told MacIntosh, but he knew she would have never done that. "Sir, I need to discuss some information I just received from Detective Breeze at the Malibu Sheriff's Department. I just talked with him about half an hour ago."

"Ok Sloan, come in my office." MacIntosh sort of grumbled and barked at the same time as he spoke to Tim. Then he stopped dead in his tracks as he was heading through the door to his office and turned back to Maria. "Now Maria, you let me know if this detective or any of the others around here in this department bothers you in any way at all."

Maria turned and flashed her best smile at her boss. "Oh don't worry sir. Tim is always very polite and charming with me." She then turned back and winked at Tim making sure

MacIntosh wouldn't see and Tim followed MacIntosh into his office now more confused and nervous than ever.

"Sit down Sloan and tell me what's going on," MacIntosh said as he propped himself in his large leather chair behind his desk.

Tim relayed all the information he had on the cases while his boss sat there clicking his pen. The sound was annoying to Tim. When he was finished, MacIntosh stopped clicking the pen and put it down on his desk. "You know, Sloan, we have the beginnings of what we could call a, 'Situation.' You know what I'm talking about right? I am going to relay everything you have told me to the chief and see how he wants to proceed. He needs to be prepared for the media if this gets out that someone is executing gang members. Between you and me, my opinion is that this is most likely one of the Russian gangs taking out revenge or trying to take out some of the lesser gangs. They hate the blacks and the Latinos with a passion. They might actually be doing this city a service, but it is still murder so we have to solve it. The big problem here is that every liberal organization out there is going to make a fuss if word gets out what is going on. We need find out who is doing this and catch them as soon as we can or this is going to be a real mess for the department. I'm going to assign a few more detectives to your gang task force if the chief agrees. I'm gong to keep you as lead detective on these cases and I want to see some results and fast. Now get out of here and get to work. Oh yeah and one more thing. I see the way you flirt with my secretary and so do a lot of people around here so just remember you are married man and start acting like it."

"Yes sir," replied Tim as he stood up, feeling he should salute, but he didn't. He was thoroughly embarrassed and he now realized others knew how much he and Maria had been flirting. That was not good at this office and he knew it. He glanced with a frown at Maria as he hurried through her office almost as if to warn her not to say anything to him. Maria looked up from her desk and smiled at Tim, quickly saying, "Bye Tim!" Tim didn't respond or even look back.

When Tim arrived and sat back down at his desk, he felt very flustered and embarrassed. What his boss had said about people in the office knowing he flirted with Maria was not good at all. How could he have been so stupid as to think that no one noticed? If anyone ever found out that he and Maria had taken off work to go to a hotel, he would lose his job for sure. Even worse was the fact that so many of his co-workers knew his wife! If someone decided to tell Linda that he was flirting with some secretary at work that would be even worse. Tim tried to concentrate on his work. There was a meeting of the task force to go over the details and formulate a plan of action. He worked late with some of the other detectives and it was almost 8 PM when he finally went home.

Maria didn't think too much about the way Tim had left her office that afternoon because she had overheard the last part of the conversation. She knew Tim would be worried and upset, but he couldn't have been that naïve to think that their little flirting game would go unnoticed. It was a big office and people noticed people. Maria left work at 6 PM her usual time, but as she was driving on the freeway she suddenly got a bad stomachache and worse she shivered with a bad feeling about something. Was it Tim, her kids, her parents? She didn't really know but she felt something was wrong. She wanted to drive faster to get home, but she knew that would be stupid. She picked up her cell phone to call home, but the battery was too low.

When Maria turned around the corner to go down the street towards her apartment complex, she saw the ambulance parked directly in front of her building. As she got closer she saw her father standing there with his arms around her two boys. It seemed like she was in a dream. She sped the last fifty yards and saw the gurney, which had a body, being put into the ambulance. She double parked her car, flung open her door, and ran to where her father and sons were standing near the ambulance. The boys had tears in their eyes and flew into her arms when they saw her.

"What happened?" she asked her father, looking at the gurney with the body, which she noticed was covered as it was being put into the ambulance. Her boys were clinging to her and she started to shake already knowing her father's answer.

"Maria, I'm sorry," her father said softly.

"It's Felix isn't it?" she asked looking in her father's eyes.

"Yes, my child," replied her father trying to hold back his tears. The sound of their father's name made the two boys wail even more. Maria knew he was dead and she could only guess how. She looked at her boys and tried to comfort them, but she fainted. Maria's father, one of the neighbors, and her two sons carried Maria into her apartment and lay her down on her bed. She woke up a few minutes later and saw her two sons lying on the bed with her. They still had tears in their eyes, but were no longer wailing. Her father came in and took the boys out of the bedroom into the living room where Maria's mother was waiting.

Maria stared at her father as he walked back into the bedroom and closed the door. He pulled up a chair and sat next to the bed. "Are you going to be okay Maria?"

"I think I fainted," Maria replied.

"Yes, you did. We brought you in here. Do you need to see a doctor?" her father asked.

"No, I think I'll be fine," Maria said as she started at the ceiling wondering if this was really all just a bad dream. Then she started to feel the emotions come back again, but she steadied herself because she wanted to know what had happened and why. She looked back and her father sitting patiently next to her. "How did he die? What happened? I want to know everything."

"Are you sure you want to talk now? You can rest first if you want," her father replied.

"Yes, I want to talk now. I need to know what happened," Maria said trying to sound composed.

Her father looked straight in her eyes and leaned closer to her from his chair. "He committed suicide. He overdosed on pills."

"No, not Felix. He couldn't do something like that!" Maria put her hand over her mouth and her eyes fluttered. She fainted again.

She awoke about ten minutes later and this time her mother was sitting in the chair near her bed. "Mama, what are you doing here?" As Maria spoke everything came back to her. "Where are the boys?"

"They're sleeping now," her mother replied. Maria could hear voices from her living room. She knew there would be some relatives and friends over. The fact that people were near to support her made her feel secure. "I need to get up. What time is it?" Maria asked.

"Almost 10 PM" replied her mother as she leaned over and kissed Maria on the forehead. It made Maria feel like a child again.

"I should get up," Maria said in a distant voice.

"Why don't you take a shower and maybe you'll feel better and then we can talk a bit?" her mother suggested.

Maria could hear the concern in her mother's voice. She knew a lot of people would be concerned and she also wondered if God was punishing her for having an affair with a married man. Things were just happening too fast. She sat up and her mother gave her a hug.

When she closed the door to the bathroom and turned on the light, she stood looking at herself in the mirror. She put her hands on the counter to steady herself because she still felt weak. She shook her head and said to herself, "This can't be really happening to me!" She undressed and went in the shower hoping the water would wash away reality, but it didn't. The warm water made her feel more relaxed, but it also made her cry. When she came out of the bathroom, her mother was still sitting in the chair near her bed, but now she was holding an envelope. Maria walked toward her and she held out the envelope for Maria to take. "Felix left this for you. It says, 'To my Dearest wife, Maria.'"

Maria stared at the envelope in her mother's hand. She could see Felix's writing on it. She reached out slowly with her arm trembling and took it from her mother, who stood up, giving Maria the chair. The envelope felt hot in her hand. She didn't want to open it. Her mother stood in front of her and again reached out and put her hand on Maria's head, brushing Maria's wet hair out of her face. "Maria, you don't have to tell anyone what is in it if you don't want to. You know that is private between the two of you. Your father has gone to the hospital. Only he and I know that Felix left this for you and we don't know what it says. The boys are in their room sleeping now.  Your aunt and uncle are still here, but I am going to send them home now. Do you want your father and I to stay here tonight with you and the boys?"

Maria looked at the lines in her mother's face and wondered how long it would be before she got old too. "That would be good Mama; I am still sort of in a daze. I might need help with the boys for the next few days."

After her mother left the bedroom, Maria sat down on the edge of her bed, held the envelope in her hand, and stared at it. She thought to herself," God, I have the worst karma in the world.  He was so good to the boys. Then I cheat on him, and he kills himself. How could he have known? Why did he have to do this to me? Oh God! I stopped sleeping with him and put the lock on the door. That was probably the reason why. I have caused such a horrible mess all because I wanted another man." She started to cry again and watched as a tear fell onto the envelope. She wanted to bring Felix back. She wanted for him to be alive again and for them to be like they were when they first met. She held the envelope to her chest and hugged it. She remembered a time when they had gone to a resort in San Diego. It was the most romantic time they had spent together. San Diego then made her think of Felix's parents because they lived there and surely her mother had called them. They probably would be here in the morning or maybe even later tonight. What would she say to them? She held the envelope out and looked at it again. Then she remembered what her boss had said in the office today. "Everyone knew that Tim flirted with her!" Someone must

have seen her in Malibu with him and somehow Felix found
out! Her brain was running wild now and the suspense was
becoming too much so she tore the envelope open. The letter
read:

Dear Maria,
When you read this I will already be dead. I'm sitting
here with my gun and a handful of pills. Ok, here I go. I am
going to take the pills. Wait, I have to get another beer. Ok, I
took the pills. That was easy…a lot easier than shooting myself.
I thought of doing that, but it would really make a big mess
and I know the boys will be coming home before you.

I started this letter an hour ago and kept trying to think
what would be the best way for me to kill myself. I really didn't
know if I had the courage to go through with this but after all
that has happened lately I have decided that this is best for
everyone. Well since I have taken the pills now I am sure you
will find me here sleeping, but I won't be sleeping. I will be
dead.

(Actually it didn't happen that way as Julio kept trying to wake
up his father when he came home from school and when he
wouldn't wake up, he called 911 and his grandparents.)

I guess I could try to go in the bathroom and stick my finger
down my throat and throw up the pills! I am not going to do
that though because no matter what you think of me, I know I
have courage.

Oh Maria, you really don't know how much I love you.
You are the only woman I have ever loved. Why Maria have
you been so cold to me lately? Have you found someone new?
Really it doesn't matter now because I'm going to finally tell
you all the truth about me and why I am doing this. I guess I
should say why I have done this because I already took the
pills! God, I am crazy and I know it!

I have tried my best to be good to you and the boys. You
know I think of your son as mine also. I have tried to play the
role of a good father and good husband for all of you, for the
boys, my family and especially you. I do love you. Please take

care of our sons, Maria. I know you are a strong woman and that you will do a great job. Raise them to be men that are good to all people.

You have no idea how difficult this is for me to say or how hard it is for me to reveal to you because I know you may get the wrong idea and not see that I have not had control over my destiny. When I met you that day at the park you were the first woman that I had felt attracted too in so many ways. Your smile made me feel strong. Seeing you there with your son made me think about wanting to raise a family and I knew we could be great partners in doing that. I knew we would become friends, but I never thought we would marry. I really cared for you so there was just no way to tell you about myself at that time. It wouldn't have been fair to the happiness we shared. The truth is Maria I live a secret life. I have done what many would say are bad things. For me, I can't control myself and I don't want to control myself...not anymore at least. Maybe a few years ago I thought about trying to change and be different, but you started working and then I had more opportunity to do things and you ignored me more. It seemed you always had an excuse to go out with one of your friends or you took some class so you would be away from home. You were always the one who seemed tired. You were always thinking of yourself not me...well now I have become tired, tired of the life I have lived and tired of the lies I tell just to be whom I really am.

This is hard for me to say, but I can feel the pills starting to come on now so I might as well get on with it. God, I know I shouldn't kill myself, but really I think it is the best for everyone involved. I am starting to get tired and want to stop, to sleep...but I have to let you know why I am doing this. When I met you Maria, you were the first woman I ever made love with. It was very special, very nice, and I actually enjoyed it. You see before you I had only been with a man. Well actually more than one, but it was secret and no one knew. No, I'm not in love with anyone; I never have been except with you. I just like the thrill and the risk of meeting a man and having sex. I have done it a lot. I have met and slept with a lot of men, old ones, young ones, all races and I found out last month that I have AIDS. It is just too much for the boys to ever know or for anyone to ever know. I don't want to go through treatments and counseling and all that kind of stuff. I can't go on like this. I have become too crazy and I know it. I started going out to the racetrack after finding a guy and then I would gamble. I have lost a lot of our savings account and I know there would be no money for me to get treatments. I would rather you and the boys have what is left of the money. This is the best for me and I know it.  Please Maria, please never tell anyone this.

    I will always love you.

    Felix


    Maria's jaw dropped open in a state of ghastly shock. She blankly stared at the letter, put it down on the floor, and closed her eyes. When she opened her eyes a few seconds later, the letter was still there so she read it again. When she came to the part about AIDS she stared at the word. It seemed to get bigger and bigger. She scrunched the letter in her hands. She let out a muffled scream because she knew her mother was in the next room and she couldn't draw her attention. "That selfish bastard has given me AIDS. He was gay and he never told me. Oh my God! What am I going to do now?" She tore the letter into small pieces and then she pulled at her hair. She bit her lower lip to try and think without fainting. She picked up the pieces of the letter from the floor and when she stood up, she could fell herself getting sick to her stomach. She ran to her bathroom and heaved out her guts into the toilet and then she threw the pieces of the letter into the toilet and flushed it. Her blurry eyes were almost fading into blackness as two little pieces of the letter didn't get flushed, but rather floated back to the surface of the water and bounced around like two little boats. She quickly gripped the handle and flushed them down again. She pulled herself up in front of the sink and turned on the water. She washed her mouth out and tried to wash her face, but she felt too weak.

She looked up into the mirror and saw an old woman; it was an old, very old, grey haired and deeply wrinkled version of her. She closed her eyes, crawled to the edge of her bed, and began to pray like a child. She pleaded with God to take the bad dream away, but it didn't stop. Her mind raced and she begged for God to help her. Eventually she pulled herself into bed, curled up like a fetus, and rocked herself into a restless sleep.

Maria woke at 6 AM. She felt very weak and very thirsty. She was disoriented and wasn't sure if the night before was nothing but an incredibly horrible nightmare. She put on her robe and went to the kitchen to get some water, but as she passed through the living room, she noticed that Felix was not sleeping on the couch. With that, she knew it wasn't a bad nightmare, but reality and a new day. She drank two glasses of water and started some coffee. When the coffee was ready, she poured herself a large cup and sat down on the couch where Felix would be sleeping. She noticed the phone message machine had 22 calls on it. She dreaded playing them because she knew that some would be from Felix's friends and relatives. She listened to them anyway and took notes on who she should call back first. She had a message from her older sister who was living in San Francisco. She quickly called her and caught her before she left for work. She agreed to come down and stay with Maria for the weekend and maybe a few days longer. Maria wanted to just blurt out the whole story over the phone to her, but she held back and decided to wait until she saw her face-to-face. They were close and Maria knew she could confide in her sister.

Maria's father arrived at the apartment at 8 AM and waited around until the boys woke up before taking them for breakfast. Before they left, they asked Maria if they could still go trick or treating. Maria hadn't even realized that it was October 31st, Halloween. Her mother came a short while after and she had Felix's parents with her. Maria was surprised to see them. She thought they would be angry, but they weren't. They offered their comfort and support. The four of them made the arrangements for the funeral. As the day went on, other relatives and friends came by her apartment. Maria dressed in black and played the role of the mourning wife, but inside she was boiling with anger over the fact that Felix may have given her AIDS. She was scared and hurt more than grief stricken, but she knew she had to keep the contents of the suicide note to herself. She hoped her mother wouldn't tell Felix's parents about the note because they might feel they had a right to read it. She was also angry with herself because she had been blind to the fact that the man she married was gay. She kept searching the past to find clues of his behavior and came up with numerous incidents, but it was too late now and she knew it. She just wanted to get through the day and see her sister as soon as possible so she could talk with someone.

## Chapter 7

That same afternoon Tony Salerno sat on the couch in his apartment feeling pretty confident. His workweek had been boring as usual, but fortunately his boss had given him Thursday afternoon and all of Friday off. He would have to work on the weekend, but at least he had Halloween night free and he hadn't gone out on Halloween in years. He decided he would get a costume and have some fun at the local bars in the evening. He would drink, dance, and have fun.

When he clicked the remote and turned on the TV, it was right when the reporter came on and said, "We have new information from sources inside the LAPD that there is a link between the shooting of a young black male last Friday night and the shootings of two Mexican-American gang members last Sunday in the Malibu hills. Our sources have revealed that the police are now working on what they believe is the beginning of serial murders aimed at gang members." Tony laughed out loud. He sat up and leaned over so he could hear the rest, but nothing else was said so he turned the TV off. He knew what the "link" was between the murders. He knew they had matched the bullets. Fortunately, he had thrown the gun off the Redondo Beach pier Monday morning and had changed the tires on his old mustang so there wasn't a reason for him to be concerned. He had laughed at the reporter due to a nervous reaction more than anything else. He knew there wasn't any evidence that could allow him to ever be caught. What bothered him was that his plan to continue killing would have to go by the wayside because of the fact that those two Mexican-American gang members had tried to rob him. He knew he had shot them in self-defense, but it was impossible for him to ever reveal that to the authorities.

He thought out loud, "Reporters and detectives are just the same. They try and make guesses and then prove their guesses. Well, that theory will go down the drain because the gun is gone and I will never run into two Cholos again, at least not in the Malibu hills. God, how did that happen to me? I have such bad luck. I really have to be careful if I ever decide to kill anyone else like that. I really had no choice with those two guys. I don't know if they would have shot me or not, but I couldn't just hand over my money. I have to get out of here and have some fun. I have to get a good costume."

Tony knew of a costume rental store not too far from his place so he headed there. Most of the good costumes were already rented out and Tony almost decided that he would forget about wearing a costume. "Hey, don't you have any good costumes here?" he yelled at the balding clerk.

"I'm sorry sir. It is a bit late. Most of the better costumes have already been rented and we are closing in about ten minutes. If you like I can show you a few we have in the back that are a bit damaged. It isn't really that much to be noticeable and I could give you a discount on them also."

Tony was annoyed at this guy, but he realized he was looking at the last minute for a costume so he calmed himself and decided to see what the guy had in the back. When they arrived in the back storeroom and the clerk showed Tony the costume, Tony burst out laughing. He couldn't believe anyone could come up with an idea so bizarre.

"This is perfect! I can't believe anyone would wear something like this, but I will take it. How much do you want for it?" Tony asked the clerk.

"Well the truth is we usually don't sell costumes like this and it has been here in the back for a few years now. There is a stain on it that we couldn't get out so I can sell it to you for half price if you want," the clerk replied.

"Fantastic. I will take it," said Tony as he was already thinking about the reactions he would get when he hit the bars in the costume.

That evening Tony put on his costume and looked in the mirror. He started laughing. He decided to walk down to the Kings Head Bar as it was only about a mile from his apartment. He could always take a cab back home if he got too drunk and he planned on getting drunk for sure. He was out to have fun on Halloween night for the first time in years and he felt very good. When he opened his door to leave and walked into the hallway he, of course, ran right into his fat neighbor whose name he could never remember.

"Holy Jesus, is that you Tony?" asked the neighbor, who was standing with his mouth open in shock. He then burst out laughing. He had one of those big bellied laughs that made the whole hallway shake and Tony wondered if more of his neighbors would soon open their doors and see him. The fat neighbor laughed so hard he fell to his knees. But then, he plopped his big ass right in the middle of the hallway so there was no way Tony could squeeze through and get to the stairs.

"Yes, this is me," said Tony, who was hoping the guy would get up so he could get past him. Tony was happy that the first person to see him in the costume couldn't hold back the laughter, but he was not happy that it had to be his fat neighbor who was now blocking his progress to the stairs. For a second he just wanted to kick him, but he knew that would be really stupid so he just stood there and let him finish laughing. Finally, when he had stopped and started to stand back up, Tony realized he needed to work on some lines he was going to use at the bar so he tried one on the fat neighbor. "Meet my mother, Luciana."

The fat neighbor laughed again as Tony stood there smiling. He was dressed as a mother holding her infant baby and he was the baby! At last the neighbor got up from the hallway floor. "That is a great costume Tony. You will definitely win the best costume contest wherever you go."

"Well, my mother and I have to get going now," Tony replied back. He was happy that his line had worked and was even happier that he could finally get past his fat neighbor and head out of the apartment building before any of the other neighbors came out of their apartments.

When Tony began walking down the street to the bar, everyone stopped and stare at him. He wasn't sure if he liked all the attention and almost thought about going back home and calling a cab, but he didn't want to encounter his fat neighbor again. So he kept on walking down the street toward the bar and started to notice how cold his legs were in the dress. This made him wonder how women could ever walk around in a dress during the winter. He figured it would be great in the summer, but not in the winter.

Tony had changed and he knew it. Maybe it was because of the killings, but he wasn't sure. He knew that dressing up in a bizarre costume and going out on Halloween was not something he would normally think of doing, but he was starting to enjoy the new him. When he thought of the killings, he felt no remorse. He had put them in the past and they seemed very distant from him. Whenever he thought about the killings he had committed, he found himself smiling and sometimes even laughing out loud at the thought. It was not because he had derived any pleasure from them, but he felt satisfied that he had fulfilled a part of himself that had been dormant for so long. He always came back to blaming his ex-wife for the feelings of rage he felt and now that rage seemed to have dissipated into thin air and he liked that. The people he had killed were worthless humans in his mind and he felt as if he had merely squashed a cockroach. Even though the first murder had been planned, it had been executed on someone that he had seen over the past year, someone he knew was dealing drugs and was a gang member. The next two killings were totally in self-defense and he knew he could not have avoided them even if he had wanted to. What bothered him though was the fact that he didn't want to avoid anything anymore and if something like that happened again, he knew he would shoot even faster.

"Tony, is that you?" the Kings Head Bar bouncer asked.

"Yeah, this is me! Hey, meet my mother, Luciana," Tony replied with a smile.

"Oh, that's a good line. You know what Tony, I think I might have to charge you double!" replied the bouncer.

Tony started to laugh and everyone in line laughed also. It seemed like it was going to be a good night Tony thought to himself, as he scanned the line for how single women. The bouncer waved for Tony to come up to the front of the line.

"Hey, I think I am going to have to see some identification. We can't let a baby in the bar!" said the bouncer as Tony stood in front of him. He waved for Tony to go in and didn't charge him anything. Tony was feeling very good with all the attention he was getting.

Once inside, Tony looked around and again everyone either laughed at his costume or stared at him and mumbled some kind of remark. It was still early and the people inside were just milling about and talking. No one was dancing yet because it was still early. Tony headed for his favorite corner of the bar and smiled at the people he passed on his way especially the single girls, who were always in groups of three or four. He sat down at his favorite spot and when people would come up to him and comment on his costume, he would throw some quick line at them. His favorite was of course, "Hey, you had better show respect for my mama. You know she has twelve more kids at home!" When someone would introduce himself or herself, he would say, "Hi, I'm Tony and this is my mother, Luciana." Pretty soon people were buying him drinks so he had an unlimited supply of rum and cokes. By 10:30, the bar was really starting to fill up. Tony decided to stop drinking and he ordered an iced tea. He was having a lot of fun, but he knew he was getting way too drunk.

Tony suddenly noticed a very attractive blonde woman dressed up like some kind of fairy in a tight and very revealing white lace outfit. She was tall and had a great body. Her boyfriend was next to her, but he wasn't wearing a costume. He looked like an ex-football player. He was very tall and very muscular. The woman was dancing by herself and having a great time letting everyone watch her. The dance floor was starting to get packed with people in all kinds of costumes. There was an open stool next to Tony and the girl's boyfriend found it. He sat down keeping his eyes turned to the dance floor so he could watch his girlfriend. Tony struck up a conversation with the guy. His name was Josh. His girlfriend's name was Jessica. Josh commented on Tony's costume so Tony bought him a drink. When Jessica came back from the dance floor, Tony could see she was already pretty drunk. After Josh introduced them to each other, he bought her a drink anyway and offered for her to have his seat. She gladly accepted because she had been standing most of the night. Josh, a gentleman, offered Tony his seat, but Tony refused saying that he needed to stand for a while. As they continued to talk, Tony found out that Josh actually was an ex-football player and that he had injured his knee several times so now he refused to dance. He said that if he did dance he would just wake up the next day in too much pain. After Jessica had rested a bit she stood up and grabbed Tony by the hand to take him onto the dance floor. Tony looked over at Josh who nodded his approval and Tony and Jessica headed to the dance floor.

 The dance floor was packed and when they found a place to dance, they were chest-to-chest. Tony liked it except for the fact that this girl was someone else's girlfriend and he happened to be an ex-football player! Tony looked around and saw people in all kinds of costumes. As they continued to dance, Jessica would smile and every once in a while, one of her breasts would come out of the top of her low cut fairy costume because it was too small. She would casually smile at Tony and then stuff her breast back in the top that was obviously too small for her. As time went on, she just gave up and decided not to notice that her breast had came out of the top. Finally she was dancing very close to Tony and both her breasts were out of the top. She started to rub her body on Tony, but Tony would move away discreetly knowing that her ex-football player boyfriend was most likely watching from his seat at the bar. Tony was having a lot of fun and Jessica was definitely turning him on so he started to wonder how close she actually was to her boyfriend. Tony was definitely going to see how far she would take it and he wanted to get her phone number. As they continued to dance, Tony didn't really notice when two gay men started dancing next to him. The two gay men were dressed up as women and they figured that Tony must also be gay because of his costume. They danced close to him and tried to get his attention. In the heat of the moment, as the dance floor pulsated with movement and noise, one of the gay men reached out and groped Tony's rear end.

Tony turned and at first glance, mainly due to inebriation, he thought it was a woman. The gay guy was soft and not bad looking dressed up as a woman. Then he saw the eyes and the fat gay freak next to the guy who had groped him and Tony knew they were gay. Tony scowled and clenched his fists ready to pound the freak that had touched him, but he held back and yelled, "Hey you freak!" He then saw them smile and Tony couldn't stop himself. He reached out and grasped the guy who had touched him by the throat and pushed him back into the other gay man. They crashed to the floor and screamed like girls, but their screams were muffled by the noise of the dance floor. No one around even noticed as it just appeared the two of them had tripped over each other and fell to the floor. As they were falling, Tony realized that he should stop. He was drunk and in a public place. He knew that he had done enough so he gently leaned forward and pressed himself into the ex-football player's girlfriend and smiled. He kissed her and placed a hand on her exposed breast. Tony enjoyed the brief moment of pleasure and he wanted her, but knew it was too crazy. He slipped his hand into hers and took her off the dance floor as the two gay guys scurried in the opposite direction.

Fortunately Josh had only seen Tony push the two gay guys and had not seen him kiss and touch Jessica. "Hey, I thought you were going to pummel those two guys!" Josh said as Tony and Jessica sat down at the bar next to him. Josh handed both of them a drink.

"I didn't want to knock them down. I just wanted to scare them a little," Tony replied hoping Josh hadn't seen him touch Jessica on the dance floor. Just then though, since there was nowhere for her to sit, Jessica decided to sit on Tony's lap. She was getting a little too close especially in front of her boyfriend. Tony wondered to himself if maybe they were into threesomes or if maybe it wasn't just Josh's knee that didn't work so well. They talked for a little longer and Tony could feel himself starting to get aroused with Jessica on his lap. She was starting to go beyond the flirting stage and Tony noticed that Josh was looking at both of them too much now. He gently lifted Jessica off his lap and let her sit alone on the barstool. He shook Josh's hand, did the same with Jessica, and then told them he had to get going. Just at that moment though the music stopped and suddenly everyone was looking over his way. They had announced that he had won the costume contest. One of the hostesses came over to him and gave him the three hundred dollar prize. Tony smiled at Josh and Jessica and then headed outside.

Tony looked at his watch once he was outside the bar and it was 12:15 AM. There was still a small line to get in the bar. He couldn't stop thinking about Jessica. She had such a great body and he knew if he had pursued it he might have been able to take her home despite her boyfriend. Tony decided he needed one more drink before he went home. He went over to a nearby waiting cab and asked the driver to take him to the Gaslight Bar, which was only a few blocks from his home.

"That is some costume you have on," said the cab driver as Tony sat down in the back of the cab.

"Well I won the contest back there for best costume. I got three hundred bucks so I guess it paid off because I only paid forty for it. I had to get out of there though because otherwise I might have killed these two gay guys that were messing with me. Take me to the Gaslight," Tony replied back.

"Why would gay guys want to mess with a baby?" asked the cabby.

"I don't know but I would have killed them!" said Tony and they both had a laugh.

When Tony arrived at the Gaslight and saw how packed it was, he decided he might just as well walk home. He was drunk and he really didn't want to deal with more crazy costumed people the rest of the night. He talked to the bouncer for a few minutes because he knew him and then started walking down the street toward his home. It was past 1 AM now and the street wasn't too crowded. The Gaslight was at the end of a main street and Tony only had to go a few blocks before he turned down the street toward his apartment building. He walked for about a block and then decided to cross over to the other side of the street before heading down the street to his place. As he started to cross the street, he noticed a very attractive blonde woman on the other side of the street. At first he thought it was Jessica from the bar, but on second glance he could see it wasn't her. On a night like tonight Tony usually wouldn't stop and talk to her, but with the image of Jessica on the dance floor playing in his mind, his momentum drew him toward her and he said to himself, "Why not?" She was obviously a hooker.

When she noticed him coming close to her, she said, "Hi. Oh, you are a guy." She smiled at the crazy costume Tony had on and he smiled back. "At first I couldn't tell and I thought some old woman was coming over to talk to me. I almost ran off down the street!"

"Well I am a guy and I can see you are a woman," Tony said back as he looked her up and down. He liked what he saw. She was not bad looking at all and her body really did remind him of Jessica from the bar. Just to be safe though he needed to find out if she was with the police and working a sting because he had never seen her in his neighborhood before. Not that he knew all the prostitutes around, but it was just better to be safe and he knew it. "Are you a cop?" he asked her bluntly.

"No, are you?" she responded with a little shake of her head, as only women seem to know how to do.

"Of course I am not a cop. How many old women with babies are cops?" Tony said trying now to lighten up the conversation because he knew he wanted to take her back to his place and have sex with her and fantasize about Jessica from the bar.

"So, do you want to date or what?" she asked.

Tony's next question would usually be to ask how much it would be, but he couldn't stop thinking about Jessica from the dance floor. This girl was dressed in a short skirt and her legs looked like Jessica's. "Yeah, I want to date. My name is Tony. What is yours?"

"Hi Tony," she responded and reached out to shake his hand. "I'm Cici."

Tony liked her attitude. He could tell she had not been doing this for very long and probably wasn't enjoying it at all. She wouldn't be this far down on the main street if she had a pimp. She most likely was working on her own and just trying to make ends meet doing something she wasn't sure was a good idea. "I just live down the street. I'll tell you what...I'll give you $200 if you come and spend the rest of the night with me."

Cici had already made her money for the night. She hadn't slept with anyone. She had only performed oral sex on six men she had met at the club. She had taken them out to her car she had parked a block away from the club. She was actually heading back to the club now and thinking of doing one more guy. This guy seemed pretty nice and the offer of $200 was a lot more than the $50 she had been getting for the oral sex. She was a little hesitant about going to his place, but it was not like she hadn't done it before with others. She also could tell that Tony was pretty inebriated and she knew she wouldn't have to spend the night because he would fall asleep after they had sex. "Well, how far away do you live?" she asked.

They headed off toward Tony's apartment building, which was only a few blocks away. As they walked, Tony learned that she was from Long Beach, which was about twenty miles away. Like other women that Tony had met, Cici claimed this wasn't something she did on a regular basis. "Really, I am just doing this to save enough money so I can go to chiropractic school. It's really expensive and I need to have enough money to get through the school," Cici said.

Tony didn't believe a word she said and really couldn't care less. He was feeling a bit dizzy from so much drinking and wanted to get her back to his apartment as soon as possible. He couldn't stop thinking about the girl on the dance floor. When they got to the apartment building, Tony let her walk up the stairs in front of him and he liked what he saw.

When they were inside his apartment, Tony could tell by the look on Cici's face that she didn't like the apartment because it was so messy, but Tony didn't really care what she thought. He sat her down at his little two-seat bar in the corner and fixed her a strong rum and coke. He also fixed a drink for himself, but really just out of habit because he didn't want to drink more. He left her at the bar and went to his bedroom to take off the costume. When he came out of the bedroom, he could see that she was looking around and picking up things at the bar and he didn't like that. He had heard stories about hookers stealing from clients, but it had never happened to him and he would make sure it didn't. He went to the kitchen and found a half opened bag of potato chips and set them on the bar. On the way back from the kitchen, he locked the deadbolt and pulled off the handle, which was not screwed down. There was no way anyone could open the door from inside now unless they had the handle. This was his way of making sure he never had a hooker rip him off. He then went back to the bar, took her by the hand, and led her to the living room sofa. He threw off some old clothes that had been on the sofa and let her sit down. "You probably want to get paid first?" he asked as he took off his shirt.

"Yes, that would be good," Cici replied. She really wished she hadn't agreed to come with this guy to his apartment even though she wanted the money. The apartment was just too messy and Tony was very drunk. She felt a bit worried he wouldn't come up with the two hundred dollars and told herself the next time she should get the money before she went to the guy's apartment.

Tony smiled because he could tell she was worried and that meant she would feel relieved when he gave her the money. Then she would probably work even harder for him. He reached into the pocket of the bathrobe he had on, pulled out his wallet, and handed her two one hundred dollar bills. Cici smiled and took the money. Tony then walked over to the bar and picked up his drink. He took his wallet out and put it on the bar not really caring if she saw or not because there was no way she could rip him off. Of course Cici saw him put the wallet on the bar and she would think about that wallet until she had taken the rest of the money out. She could tell he was very drunk and he was drinking more now.

Tony went back to the couch and took his time with her. He wanted his moneys worth. He closed his eyes and thought about the ex-football player's girlfriend the whole time. Cici tried to get away with just giving him oral sex, but Tony stopped her at one point and bent her over the couch. He was taking longer than she wanted, but there was nothing she could do now because he had already paid her. After about half an hour Tony lay on the couch satisfied and half asleep. Cici went to the bathroom where she cleaned herself and redressed. When she came back into the living room, Tony was lying on the couch on his back and he was snoring. Cici looked at him laying there and snoring for a few minutes. Then she quickly went to the bar, opened his wallet, and took out the rest of the money in it. She put the money in her purse and took a quick look back at Tony on the couch. She then walked quickly to the front door and turned the handle, but then saw the door wouldn't open. She noticed he had locked the dead bolt and taken the handle with him. She tried to reach into it with her fingers and turn it, but it was hard to turn. She looked back at Tony asleep on the couch and tried to think what to do. The last thing she was going to do was give the bastard back the money she had taken out of his wallet.

She had no choice but to sneak quietly back over to the couch and look in the pocket of the robe he had draped over the sofa chair. He was still snoring so if she could find the handle in the robe, she could get out of the apartment without him waking up. The handle wasn't in the robe so she guessed he had put it in the bedroom. She quickly went into the bedroom and looked around. She found a watch and a gold ring on the stand next to the bed so she put those in her purse, but she didn't find the handle. She decided to go back to the door and try again to get it open without the handle. When she had gone to the bedroom, Tony woke up. He didn't know how long he had been asleep. He just knew he had heard her in his bedroom and that his head hurt. He wanted to drink some water and take some Advil. He watched her come out of the bedroom and he could tell by the way she was sneaking around that she was trying to rip him off. He watched as she went over to the door and again struggled trying to get it open. He sat up on the couch and when she turned and saw him sit up, he said with a smile, "Hey, you're not leaving yet are you? I paid you to spend the night with me." Tony then stood up and put his robe on.

 Cici was in hot water, but she had been in tighter situations before and had weaseled her way out of them. She knew she could do it again. "Well I did stay with you for the night and I need to get going now because it is really late. Do you think you could open the door because I can't seem to get it open?" she asked hoping he would just come over, open the door, and leave her alone. Tony put his hands in the pockets of his robe looking for his wallet, but then realized he had left it on the bar. He walked over to the bar, looked in his wallet, and saw that she had taken the rest of his money. His head hurt and he didn't want to have to make a big scene with the whore now. He reached under the magazine on the bar and took the handle to the door. He then walked over to where Cici was standing between the front door and the kitchen. He was holding the handle in one hand and his empty wallet in the other. "I have the handle right here and I am guessing you have the money from my wallet. I would like the money back and then I will let you go." Cici was now getting scared, but she still had confidence she could get away because Tony didn't look so good. His eyes were droopy and he obviously looked very drunk. Tony wasn't concerned about her getting away with his money because she couldn't get out of the apartment. He was concerned about his aching head though. He went to the kitchen and looked in the cupboard for some Advil. He found a bottle with a few left and took them with some water. Cici had come over to the kitchen and started to rub his back. She had her eyes on the handle that he had placed on the counter. "Don't touch me. Just give back my money and right now," Tony said turning and facing her. She smiled and knelt down on her knees. Tony leaned back against the cabinet and let her do what she did best. He didn't forget about his money, but he knew she couldn't leave anyway so she might as well take care of him. His head still hurt though and he wanted to lie down so he stopped her and took her by the hand into the bedroom and threw her on the bed. He held her down and smiled at her. He was aroused again and this time he was going to take out his aggression on her.

"Wait, I have to get the condoms. I left them in my purse," Cici said as she stopped him from taking her.

"Hurry up then," Tony said as Cici got off the bed and slowly walked out of the bedroom purposely leaving her blouse off. She knew the handle was sitting on the bar counter near the kitchen. She would get it, open the door, and leave. So what if she only had on her bra? It was Halloween and only a few blocks to her car. There was no way he would come after her if she went quickly. Tony felt dizzy and tired so his arousal disappeared as fast as it had come. She was up to something and he knew it. He struggled out of the bed and saw her fumbling with the handle at the door so he rushed over to her. Tony was angry now and he wanted to grab her by the neck. Just as he got to her, she opened the door so he pulled her down to the ground and slammed the door closed. He had planned on being nice to her, but now he wanted his money back and not just the money she had taken out of his wallet. He wanted whatever other money she had made working that night. He stood over her as she lay on the ground in her skirt and bra clutching her purse. "Get up off the ground you thieving whore!"

Cici stood up and backed away from Tony. She was now clutching her purse. "Oh please. I did a lot for you. I need the extra money for school. I didn't think you would miss it. Just let me go and I promise I'll come over whenever you want me for free," Cici pleaded still hoping he would let her go from a state of drunken mercy. She cowered back as he moved close to her. She closed her eyes and he leaned in and gave her a little kiss on the cheek. Tony wanted to play with her before he took all her money and sent her out into the cold night.

Cici opened her eyes and could smell the alcohol on his breath. He was close to her and smiling. She wondered if maybe he would let her go so she smiled back. Her smile was enough of a reward for Tony's sick mind and he then grabbed her on the forearm and scowled, "Listen whore. I am not someone you can steal from. That is why I took the handle off the door. So now you are going to let go of your purse and I'm going to rob you. I'm going to take all of the money you made tonight and then kick your sorry ass out of here. You had better pray that you never see me again or I will take all of your money again until you have learned your lesson."

Cici was really scared now for the first time. This guy was a freak and who knows what he could do to her. Still, she had to try to keep her money. She had worked all night for it and she needed the money. How could some guy she had just worked to satisfy take her money? Her mind became clouded with the thought of keeping her money and she instinctively tightened the grip on her purse. She had one last chance and she knew she had to try it now. Tony reached out for her purse. Cici clutched it, but did not pull it away from him too hard. "Ok, you have me. I know I shouldn't have taken your money. I'll give it back to you," she said as she stepped back from him, shielded her purse with her body, and reached into it. She was trapped halfway in the kitchen, but she could see the handle was still in the door. She had to get past Tony to the door so she pulled a small can of mace out quickly and sprayed it in Tony's face. The mace was old and it didn't really spray out well. Instead, it came out in a few short bursts and then stopped. There was enough though to hit Tony in one eye and the side of his face. Tony immediately jerked back from Cici because at first he wasn't sure what she had done. Cici tried to run past him, but Tony pushed her and tripped her at the same time. She lost her balance and her purse flew up in the air landing in the kitchen, with all of the purse's contents spilling out. Cici tried to grab the wall as she went down, but that only made her twist in an unnatural way as she fell. Her temple struck the corner of the bar as she went down. She only remembered seeing a lot of stars as the side of her head slammed into the tile floor.

Tony wanted to scream and kick her at the same time. His face was burning and he couldn't open his one eye. Then as the pain pulsed from his neurons to his brain, something flashed in his mind that eased the pain. He thought at that very instant that his life was just too screwed up and he had to change. He had studied Buddhism during his divorce and the concept was called "Honinmyo." It was interpreted as, "from this moment on." It was the essence and origin of causality. The situation for Tony had gone from simply getting his money to a situation where she had sprayed mace on him. Was it payback for killing the young black kid? He had fulfilled a fantasy, but it had only temporarily relieved him from his life of routine and boredom. Maybe if he had never killed the black kid he wouldn't have gone out on Halloween in that ridiculous costume and then later picked up the prostitute. Tony didn't know, but he did know he had to make some changes in his life or he could be the one lying on the floor. He promised to himself to make some changes in his life. He would clean his apartment, he would do something to volunteer for kids, he would call his own son who was in college more often, and he might even try meeting someone and having a relationship. Maybe he would fall in love with the right person. The thoughts came in a flash.

He looked at her lying on the floor with his one good eye, turned on the cold water in the kitchen sink, and stuck his head under it. After a few minutes, he could open his eye, but his face still burned from the mace. He looked over to where Cici was on the floor and saw a little pool of blood forming around her head. "Oh crap. The whore robs me and now she is probably dead!" he said in a moaning voice. He held a wet towel to his face, bent over to see where the blood was coming from, and saw it was coming out of her ear. He put his hand on her chest, didn't feel a pulse, and then bent close to see if she was breathing and she wasn't. The thought that she was now dead overwhelmed him. If he called 911 though, how would anyone know it was an accident? Tony stood up and looked back into the kitchen and saw her purse lying there. Next to it were with a bunch of things that had fallen out including his ring and watch. He bent down, picked them up, and then heard his doorbell ring. His eye and the side of his faced burned from the mace. He was angry that the crazy whore had tried to steal his money and now he was stunned at the sound of the doorbell because she was lying on the floor and blood was coming out of her ear. Tony held the towel to his face, quietly took the few steps to the door, and listened to see if he could figure out who might be there at this hour. He hoped no one had called the police, but the way his luck was going lately that was most likely what had happened.

"Hey, is everything alright in there?" said a voice. Then there was the sound of a knock. "Tony this is your neighbor, Al."

At first Tony froze, but then he recognized the voice as that of his fat neighbor. He then thought to himself that this was the first time he had ever heard the guy's name. He made a vow to remember it and to stop just thinking of him as the fat neighbor. He opened the door just a crack so it wouldn't seem like he had something to hide. He smiled as best he could with his eye still burning and his head aching from so much drinking. "Sorry, I had a girl over and she got a bit drunk, but she's sleeping now and everything is fine." The fat neighbor was in his bathrobe and Tony could see that it didn't close all the way around him because he was so fat.

The fat neighbor smiled back, "Ok. Ok well I was up watching a scary movie and heard a big thud. I thought something had happened, but I guess you are okay. Well let me know if you need anything." The fat neighbor then waddled off down the hall.

"Ok, thanks Al, for your concern." Tony closed the door and breathed a sigh of relief. The relief was temporary though because he saw the body still lying on the floor and his face and eye started to pulse again with the searing heat of the mace. Tony wanted to cry, but that is something he almost never did. Instead, he went to the shower and tried to think what he should do with a dead hooker in his apartment. After he showered, he lay down on his bed telling himself not to fall asleep, but he did fall asleep. It was a restless sleep filled with hazy dreams of fat people and blood.

Tony awoke at 9 AM with a huge headache and the side of his face felt like it was sunburned. He tried to remember what had happened, but all he could think about was that he had to go to work. He started to get out of his bed when it hit him that he had the day off. He sat on the edge of the bed and then recalled the previous night's activities. He wanted to believe it all had been a bad dream so he forced himself to walk out of the bedroom and peer over to where Cici lay sprawled on the floor near the kitchen. There was now a pool of blood around her head and the light coming through the window reflected off it making the blood seem to glow. He went to the kitchen and stared at the body on his way there. He grabbed a bottle of water out of the refrigerator and drank the whole bottle. He turned and looked at the body and saw how her left arm was curled under her and the wrist was pointing the wrong way. It must have been broken. The sight of it made him feel queasy. He started to walk around his apartment like a caged animal. Now he understood why people cut up their murder victims into a bunch of small pieces to dispose of them. It was almost impossible to get a full dead body out of your apartment without anyone noticing. It was an accident that she fell and he was not a murderer he kept telling himself. There was no way he was going to do something as morbid as cutting her up into small pieces. After he had looked at the body one time too many, he went to the closet, got a large sheet, and covered it up. Finally after the body was covered, he was able to go back into the kitchen. He made some coffee and some toast and sat down on his couch to seriously think about what he should do. He could see out the window that it was a beautiful day, clear and sunny, but it wasn't for him.

He kept wondering why this kind of thing would happen to him. It seemed his life was beyond his control and it felt very strange. He kept thinking that he had only wanted to kill a few people. He would not choose to have a prostitute fall down and die in his apartment. Again he started to think that he needed to change his life and get it together. He definitely would have to stop drinking, but a few minutes later he felt like he needed a drink. He knew he had to clean up the mess and get the body out of his apartment so he sat back down and tried to think.

After an hour or so of just lying on his couch and staring at the ceiling, he decided he had to take some action. He wrapped the body up in some blankets and cleaned up the blood. He gathered all the things that had fallen out of her purse and put the purse in with the blanket. He knew he was forgetting something and realized she didn't have her blouse. He went in the bedroom, found the blouse, and put it back on her. He had to be at work the next day at 7 AM and he didn't want to stay up all night worrying about what he should do with the body. He decided that when it got dark he would carry the body wrapped up in the blankets down to his car. He just hoped he would be lucky enough that no one would notice him. After he had everything cleaned up and ready to go, he made himself some lunch and watched TV for a while.

He decided to wait until at least 9 PM...otherwise it would just be too risky to carry the body down to his car. He got restless waiting though and at 8 PM he picked up the blanket with the body and headed out to his car. He was surprised at how light it felt. His adrenaline was pumping and he went as fast as he could down the stairs to the outside parking area where his car was. He saw a few kids playing nearby, but they didn't even look at him so he quickly stuffed the body into his trunk. He drove once again to the Malibu hills. He was not really aware that he was driving to the same area where he had encountered the gang member. He continued to drive and then realized the stupidity of getting rid of the body in the same area that he had been before. He decided to drive further north to find a more remote area. The air was colder than usual and the coastal fog started to creep into the hills. The whole scenario was weird and freaky to Tony. Death had overcome him and now it didn't matter what he did. It just seemed something bad was going to happen to him. He found a steep cliff where he threw the body down. As he was driving home, he felt a sense of relief that at last it was all over. Now he started making the promises to himself. He once again made a vow to stop drinking and to clean up his apartment. "I won't only clean the stinky blood this whore left, but I will clean my whole place. Maybe God's message to me is that I need to keep my place cleaner. I know it all has a message. When this much weird stuff happens it has to be a message from God." Tony wanted to make some changes in his life because he needed to change his fortune for the better. When he arrived back at his apartment, he started to clean the kitchen. He cleaned the floor really well, but then he felt tired and the exhaustion in his body overwhelmed him and he went to his bedroom. He stumbled onto the bed and fell asleep.

## Chapter 8

Maria's boss called when Maria didn't show up at work on Thursday morning. Maria's father answered the phone and said that Maria couldn't talk at the moment. He went ahead and explained what had happened. MacIntosh offered his condolences and said he would call back the next day. He said Maria could take off work as long as she needed due to the circumstances.

Funeral preparations were made for Sunday. Maria and Felix's relatives took up a collection to help pay for the funeral costs. People were coming and going most of the day offering their prayers and sympathy for Maria, her children, and Felix's parents. Maria stayed in her in her room most of the day mainly to avoid her in-laws. It seemed that no one really knew Felix had been bisexual or at least no one let on that they knew. Maria badly needed to talk with someone and she was waiting for her sister to arrive from her drive down from northern California. Maria talked with Victoria a few times on her cell phone as she drove down and Victoria could tell there was something she was waiting to tell her when she got there. When Victoria finally arrived at 3 PM, she went directly to Maria's room and the two of them cried and talked. Maria told her the whole story including the part about his letter, which she had flushed down the toilet.

"You know Mom is going to want to know what was in that letter because she is the one that gave it to you. How do you know she didn't read it before you did and then seal it back up?" asked Victoria.

"You know she wouldn't do that. You just say that because that is something you would do!" Maria now smiled for the first time since she had seen her sister. "I am glad you're here Victoria."

"Well you have to think of this also. Most likely Felix's parents are going to ask a lot of questions and if they find out he left a letter they are going to want to know what was in it. Everyone knows that people who commit suicide leave a letter or note. Most likely they will ask about it. If they find out he did leave a letter they will drill you with questions so they can find out every detail. I will talk to Mom and make sure she doesn't tell anyone there was a letter. I don't think she has told anyone yet. She would respect your feelings. I don't think she would want everyone talking. At some point maybe you will feel comfortable to tell her some of the details, but that is up to you," said Victoria.

Maria leaned over and put her head on her older sister's shoulder. Victoria stroked her hair and kissed her forehead. "I'm so scared to go to the doctor. What if I have AIDS? I don't know what I would do. I'm not happy Felix is gone, but I would be angrier if he was here. It is so horrible to feel this way about the father of my child, but I do. Do you know he blew most of our savings at the racetrack?" asked Maria.

Her sister replied still stroking her hair, "Well it is not for sure that you have AIDS. I don't know that much about it, but I do know that it is not really that easy to get it. I am almost positive they have a home test kit for it. Do you want me to go the pharmacy and see if they have one? You could try that before you go to the doctor, but you should go to the doctor also. Listen, just because he had it doesn't mean you have it. You have to have faith."

"I know you're saying all that because you are my sister and you love me, but the fact is we did have sex. We even had sex when I didn't want to." Maria started to cry and her sister knew that Maria had been very unhappy in the marriage even though this was the first time she had indicated that. "Do you know that he blew almost all of our savings betting on horses?" Maria repeated. The thoughts of how her life had changed in 24 hours had left her brain scrambled.

Victoria tried to console her sister. She really had no idea how bad things had been between Maria and Felix. "Maria, it will all work out. You're a strong person and we are all here to support you."

Maria was still weeping and her emotional state was on the edge of total despair. She didn't want to say what she was going to say, but it just burst out her. "I think God is punishing me for having an affair and cheating."

The conversation paused. Victoria was shocked because she never thought Maria would be the kind of person to ever cheat, but then she hadn't been around her sister for some time either. Obviously Maria's marriage had been a disaster and she had never told anyone. Victoria knew she had to lighten up the conversation and cheer up her little sister before she sunk into a deeper state of unhappiness and depression. "So you cheated on whom, God or Felix? Maria, stop with this kind of thinking right now. God is not punishing you. Felix cheated on you with men and he contracted AIDS. The truth is that he was selfish and he was a coward for not telling you that he preferred men."

Maria stared blankly at her sister trying to see hope in her face, but she only saw confusion. She was still unhappy and she still felt scared. "Yes, he was with a lot of men according to his letter and now I have AIDS!" Maria screamed in her sister's face, not wanting to be mean or sound angry. It came out that way though so she just broke down crying more.

Victoria had heard enough for now. What she really wanted to hear about was Maria's affair, but that would have to wait until later. She stood up and put her hands on her hips. "Ok, I am going right now to the pharmacy to get a test kit for AIDS. We need to know as soon as possible." Maria fell back on her bed and put the pillow over her head, waiting for her sister to return.

When Victoria came back, the two women locked themselves in Maria's bedroom and opened the test kit. "It says here that you should go to the doctor and have a second test no matter what the results are." Victoria put the swab under her sister's gum and put it in the solution to wait for the results. Maria reclined back on her bed and put the pillow over her head. Maria was very nervous. They waited what seemed like an eternity. Maria got up out of the bed and went to the foot of the bed on her knees. She clasped her hands together and began to pray.

Victoria went in the bathroom where they had put the swab in the solution and came out with a big smile. "Maria, it is negative. You don't have AIDS!" They hugged and kissed and Maria cried. She had been shaking with fear, but her fear had turned to joy. At last she had something to be thankful for and for the first time since Felix's suicide, she felt like she had some hope for her future.

Later that evening, Maria gathered Felix's parents, her own parents, and her sister together. She explained the contents of the letter that Felix had left her. Maybe it would have been best to hide it from them, but revealing the letter was the right thing to do. She wanted to have the freedom to live out her life and take care of her sons without ever feeling guilty or burdened about her past. She told them that she had taken the AIDS test, but that she was also going to the doctor to take another test. She also told them she would have her two sons tested. This statement brought a scowl and frown from Felix's parents, but she didn't care. She knew she had to do the right thing. Toward the end of the conversation they all agreed that they should keep Felix's past between them and not tell others. This also seemed like the right thing to do. Felix's mother broke down and began to cry and at one point she shook her head and refused to believe that Maria was telling the truth. Maria looked her square in the eyes though and persisted. Maria, of course, left out the affair she had with Tim. Her sister had convinced her that she should keep that private and Maria agreed. Maria knew though that she should tell Tim about Felix and that he should also get an AIDS test to be safe. She promised to get the courage to tell him on Monday.

The funeral took place on Sunday. It was a bright, clear, and warm day for the time of year. Maria wore a black dress and a black veil, but she did not shed any tears until she saw her sons start to cry. She cried for their loss, not for hers. She promised to care for her sons and to care for herself from now on. Her relatives and friends were loving and sympathetic, but they did not know the truth and most of them never would.

Many of her co-workers from the police department had come, but Tim was not there. She was happy he wasn't there because now was not the time she wanted to see him. It would distract her from the pain of going through the funeral. She was relieved and grateful when it was over because now she felt like her life was only beginning and she felt a sense of relief more than a sense of loss.

On Friday, Tim heard about Felix's suicide from the "grapevine" at work. He was shocked and at first was filled with thoughts that somehow Felix had found out about his affair with Maria. He wondered if Felix had followed them to the hotel in Malibu. He desperately wanted to talk with Maria, to console her, and to make love with her, but he was hesitant to call her at her home because he didn't want to draw suspicion from her family. Tim became very withdrawn and pensive at both his workplace and at his home for the rest of the week. By Saturday, he felt certain that Maria would at least have called him. He wondered if she was angry at him and if she thought maybe he had somehow caused the death of her husband. Linda kept asking him what was on his mind, but Tim would always reply that he was just worried about the case he was working on and that seemed to satisfy her. He told her that they were getting pressure from the media and his boss was on him to come up with some suspects soon. As the week progressed, he became obsessed with the idea that his affair had caused Felix to commit suicide. The guilt and potential ramifications for his relationship with his wife and daughters was almost becoming too much to bear. He had no choice but to try and call Maria and talk with her at home. By Sunday evening he had reached the end of his emotional rope. His wife and daughters were out shopping at the grocery market, so he had the chance and he called Maria.

"Hello," Victoria answered from the living room. Maria's apartment was filled with friends and relatives who had come over after the funeral.

"Hi, this is Tim Sloan. I work with Maria. May I speak with her?" Tim could hear the people in the background and realized that he had called at a bad time. He had completely forgotten that the funeral was today even though some people he knew from work had gone to it.

"I'm Victoria, her sister. Hold on a second and let me see if she is taking calls now." Victoria put down the phone and went to Maria's bedroom where Maria had just finishing taking a shower. She was standing in the bathroom in front of a mirror with a towel around her. She turned when she heard the bedroom door open, but she knew it was her sister because she was the only person who didn't knock. Victoria was smiling at her.

"I wish I had your body!" Victoria said as she came toward the bathroom.

"I've been working out you know," Maria replied.

"Your friend from work is on the phone," Victoria said and gave her sister a little wink. Maria knew she meant Tim, but decided to ask anyway.

"You mean Tim?" she asked and Victoria nodded, smiling.

"Well, do you want to talk to him or not?" Victoria asked.

"Sure, you go in the other room and hang up the phone and I'll take the call in here. Don't you dare try to listen in on the other phone!" Maria said.

Maria wrapped a towel around her and went to sit on the edge of her bed to pick up the phone. She hesitated for a second and tried to recall Tim's face, but she couldn't. It seemed like ages since she had talked with him and she hadn't thought about him since Felix had died. She finally picked up the phone. "Hello Tim." Maria heard the other line click so she knew her sister had hung up the phone in the other room.

"Hi Maria. I'm so sorry about what happened. How are you doing?" Tim asked.

"I'm much better now, but it has been a real ordeal. I guess I have gone through a lot of stress," Maria replied.

Tim was dying to know if Felix had found out about them, but he didn't know if he should ask now or wait until he saw her at some later time. He loved the sound of her voice though and he really did miss her. He wanted to be there and hold her and kiss her. "Oh, Maria. Really, I'm so sorry. I really miss you. I guess I have to ask if Felix knew about us." Even though it hadn't been his intention, he had just blurted the question out. Tim winced after he asked the question.

Maria felt uncomfortable now. She had lost the image of Tim in her mind and he sounded very distant. He was like everyone else that she seemed to meet...worried or self-interested. His sympathy was phony and she could feel it. "No, Tim. That is not the reason Felix committed suicide." She could hear his sigh of relief on the other end of the line and it disgusted her. She wanted to hang up the phone, but she knew she had to say a few more things. She knew she had to end whatever relationship it was that she had with him. The hotel, the sunset, the ball game, they all seemed like vague memories. It seemed like it had all happened years ago, not days ago. The intimacy and feelings of lust that had been so predominate for months had all faded into a surrealistic landscape of blood and drifting clouds in her mind. The dream of the dog with the deformed teeth welled up inside her and the dog's face morphed into that of Tim's face. She saw Tim for the first time and it was a different man than the one she had made love with in the hotel only a few days ago. He was male and represented the evil in the world. She started to piece together scenarios of all the men she had ever known as lovers or boyfriends and each one had the face of the dog with the deformed teeth. She tried to open her mouth and continue talking on the phone with Tim, but it was like her own words were part of a distant conversation and that conversation was not even worth listening to. She felt like time was passing and Tim was wasting her time.

"Well, that's good. Really Maria, I miss you very much."

He sounded deceptive now and Maria knew he only wanted to try and get on her good side because he wanted to have sex with her again. She had never felt like he had used her. Actually, she had felt just the opposite because it had been her that had done most of the flirting. Now though she felt used. "I have a lot of things I need to do Tim. Maybe you could call me on Tuesday. We do have to meet and have a serious talk." Maria knew she had to tell him about the AIDS so he could get himself tested. Also, she had to tell him that she didn't want to continue the affair. It was better they met face-to-face so he really got the point.

"Ok, I will call you on Tuesday and if there is anything I can do for you at all just let me know," Tim replied. He felt very relieved that he had not been involved in the death of her husband. The guy must have just been depressed or something he thought to himself. Tim was holding the phone to his ear when he heard the click. Maria had hung up without even saying goodbye. He reached for a tooth pick on the desk in front of him and picked at his teeth.

## Chapter 9

When Tim arrived at work on Monday morning, he met with the detectives in his unit to go over the details of the two homicides. Because the victims were gang members, the department was keeping the work on the cases within the Gang Task Force. Fortunately there had not been any more killings in the past ten days so the media had buried the story. It appeared at least for the present that they were not dealing with a serial killer. Tim and his partners in the unit had talked with many gang members over the past ten days and it seemed that hostilities were no greater than usual even though there had been two shootings. The detectives were still pursuing the theory that it was one of the Asian or Russian gangs that had committed the murders and that they were trying to stir up animosities between the Latino and black gangs. They didn't have much evidence other than the fact that the same gun had been used in both shootings. The motives seemed sketchy to say the least. Most of the detectives were just hoping that time would drag on and the case would be closed because past experience showed that these cases usually went unsolved.

At noon, Tim bought a few snacks out of the vending machines and went to his car to be alone. He had been thinking about Maria and he wanted to continue his thoughts alone during his lunch hour. He wanted to see her, to touch her, and to make love with her again. He knew he had said he would call her tomorrow, but he almost wanted to call her now. He kept thinking about how sad she must feel knowing she would have to raise her sons on her own. He wanted to be the person to give her sympathy and affection. He kept having a fantasy of the sympathy and comfort turning into an afternoon of lovemaking.

After lunch, Tim started to get a bad headache so he took aspirin hoping that it would go away, but it didn't. He called his boss and told him he didn't feel well and that he wanted to go home early. Tim rarely came home from work early, but today he just didn't feel that well. Once on the freeway his headache started to go away and he felt better. He started thinking about Maria again, but then he felt guilty knowing that he was going home to his wife so he pulled off the freeway and bought his wife some flowers. He knew Monday was one of her days off so he figured she would be home. He then remembered that she had her tennis lesson today and that made him think about her in the short tennis skirt. They would have a few hours alone before the girls came home from school. He was going to call her and tell her he was on his way home, but decided it would be more exciting to surprise her. He smiled to himself knowing the reaction he would get from his wife when he gave her the flowers. They had been together many years and she always loved to get unexpected flowers. Tim rarely gave the "make-up" flowers because he had learned long ago that those flowers didn't mean much. Now he gave flowers on random occasions and the gesture had almost turned into one of foreplay and they both loved that aspect of the flower giving. He knew that he needed to show her more attention, especially now because he had been ignoring her and dreaming about Maria so much. He loved his wife and he knew that someone would find out if he carried on with Maria for much longer. If that someone were his wife then he would be in a deep mess. As he drove, he made a vow to himself to only make love with Maria a few more times and then he would end it.

When Tim pulled into his driveway he saw that the garage door was still open and Linda's car was there. She must have just returned from her tennis lesson. He parked his car in the driveway and went through the garage to go into the house where the garage and kitchen were adjoined. He held the flowers behind his back hoping to surprise her. When he went in the kitchen he didn't see her so he sort of half whispered, "Linda, I am home from work early today. Are you here?" He continued on from the kitchen to the living room and he saw her tennis skirt and blouse on the floor near the couch. At first that seemed a little odd because Linda never left her clothes lying around, but then he thought she must have went upstairs to take a shower. That would be even more perfect as he could surprise her with the flowers as she came out of the shower. He headed up the stairs toward his bedroom with the flowers held behind his back. When he got to the top of the stairs and turned to go down the hall to his bedroom he thought he heard noises from the bedroom and as he got closer he knew he heard noises. He thought maybe she was watching TV. He approached the bedroom door, which was closed and then flung the door open holding the flowers out in front of him in a dramatic gesture. Tim was smiling, hoping his wife would be there so he could surprise her with the flowers. What he saw made his jaw drop and the flowers fell to the floor.

Linda was on top riding her twenty-year-old tennis instructor, Derrick, like there was no tomorrow. Her back was to the door and she didn't even notice that it had been opened. Tim just stood there in shock with his mouth open and his eyes not believing what he was seeing. It seemed like a long time that he watched her. He noticed how her long hair bounced around, but really he only watched for a few seconds. Derrick saw Tim before Linda did and when he saw Tim, he grabbed Linda by the hips and flung her off to the side of the bed. Linda was mad at him and wondered why he had that look on his face. She thought maybe she had been too rough or something, but then Tim finally yelled out, "Linda, what are you doing? Who is this?" The blood started to pound in Tim's head and he wanted to kill both his wife and whomever she was screwing in his bedroom.

Derrick had hurriedly rolled off the side of the bed and started pulling on his shorts. He was scared to death because Linda had told him that her husband was a detective. He thought about jumping out the bedroom window as it might be better to jump two stories than to get shot. Before anyone said anything else Tim rushed at Derrick and immediately had him in a choke hold. "Who are you? What are you doing here?" Tim yelled out. Tim was ready to choke the guy to death and would have if Linda didn't help. Linda first pulled the sheet around her naked body and then jumped off the bed screaming at Tim to let Derrick go. Tim held on and Derrick was getting close to fainting. "Stop it! Stop it! It is not his fault," yelled Linda and this time she pounded on Tim's shoulder with her fist to get him to stop. Tim let go of Derrick and turned back to his half-naked wife.

"Oh, so it's not his fault, then whose is it?" he yelled at her as she sulked back to the corner of the bed trying to wrap the sheet around her again. Derrick fell to the floor, but saw his opening and he scurried as fast as he could for the open bedroom door. He ran down the stairs and out of the house completely naked. Linda curled up in the bed and pulled the covers over herself. Tim started to head after Derrick, but then thought better of it and stopped at the doorway. He looked down and saw the flowers at his feet.

"Why did you have to try and choke him?" Linda yelled at him.

Tim was burning with anger and now the anger was directed at his wife. He rushed toward the bed where she was lying under the covers. Linda held her hand up in the air as if that would stop him. "Don't you dare come near me. If you lay a hand on me I guarantee you will go to jail," she said sternly.

Tim stopped at the foot of the bed. He wanted to cry and beat her at the same time. He backed away from the bed and grabbed the flowers that were on the floor and hurled them at the bed. "Here, I got these for you," Tim yelled back at her angrily. He tried to take some deep breaths, but he could feel his pulse pounding in his head. "How could you do this to me? Haven't I been good to you?" Now he was starting to plead and he knew he sounded like a fool.

"Good to me?" replied Linda still trying to hide under the covers and wishing she had never been caught because the sex had been really good. "Good to me? No, I have been the one who has been good to you. I have been the perfect wife taking care of your house and family. I cook, I clean, and you almost never take me out. You have been the one who has been cold and distant toward me! So why have you been so cold and distant lately, tell me Tim?" Linda felt confident and unafraid that her husband would hurt her. Now she wanted to confront him and turn her infidelity around to make it look like she deserved to have an affair.

Tim couldn't take it anymore. He had caught his wife cheating on him and he felt like his life was out of control and crumbling. He started to see himself and Maria in bed at the hotel, the light coming in from the window, and the sounds of the ocean. He turned and stormed out of the bedroom. He ran down the stairs, jumped in his car, and drove off quickly so the tires screeched out the driveway.

Tim drove fast at first not even knowing where he was going. He burned inside with anger and guilt. He wondered if somehow Linda had known that he had slept with Maria. He decided it just wasn't possible for her to have known unless Maria had told her and that was out of the question. He wondered how long Linda had been having sex with her tennis instructor. He thought about trying to find the tennis instructor and having it out with him, but decided that wouldn't solve anything. He kept driving and thinking to himself about what he should do now. He thought about calling Maria and asking her if she would see him, but he was afraid at what might happen if she said yes and he got himself further into an affair with her. He wanted to go back home and confront his wife again, but he knew he was still too angry and might lose control of himself. He saw a bar that he had been to a few times and stopped in front of it. He sat in his car for over half an hour just thinking with his head in his hands. Then he went into the bar. After four stiff drinks his anger flattened out, but now the problem was that he didn't want to face himself anymore. He looked at his watch and it was already 6 PM. He wondered what had happened to the time. The afternoon had started out so well with his idea of surprising his wife with flowers, but now here he was feeling sad and lonely in a bar. He knew he was too drunk and he shouldn't drive, but he didn't really care anymore so he got in his car and headed home. He had no idea what he was going to do or say when he got home, but he did know that his life was now a complete mess.

When he pulled into his garage it was dark and he could see the lights on in the house. He sat in his car again with his head slumped over the steering wheel. He tried to think about what he would say when he went inside. Things started to spin and he knew he was drunk. It felt good to be drunk so he smiled to himself hoping that would make him feel better, but it really didn't. He finally staggered out of the car and went into the house. His wife and two daughters were sitting in the living room on the couch watching some show on television. They didn't even look up when he came in. He started to head for the staircase to go upstairs to his bedroom when his younger daughter said, "Hello Daddy!" His wife kept her eyes on the television. "You don't look so good." April was staring at him because he was holding onto the railing near the stairs.

"I'm just really tired," Tim said back, trying to smile. He didn't want her to know he had been drinking. "I'm going upstairs to take a shower." He went up the stairs and into his bedroom. The bed was made and the flowers that had been strewn about were cleaned up. There was no remnant of what had gone on that afternoon. He went to the bathroom and took a long hot shower. The water sobered him up a bit, but he still didn't know what he should do so he just climbed in the bed with the images of his wife on top of the young tennis instructor stuck in his head. He closed his eyes and willed himself to sleep. After the girls went to sleep, Linda crept up the stairs and peered into the bedroom where she saw her husband was asleep. She quietly went back downstairs to the kitchen and called Derrick.

Derrick didn't want to answer his phone because Linda had called early and left a message, but he picked up the phone anyway. "Hello," he said tentatively.

"Derrick, oh God. I'm so sorry what happened. He came home and he is upstairs passed out drunk in the bed. I really don't know why he came home early. He never does that," Linda said.

"Linda, really, I just can't keep doing this. You're married and what is worse is he is a detective. He was going to kill me if you hadn't stopped him," Derrick replied.

Linda was hurt that he didn't want her anymore, but she knew he was right and that he was scared. "No, don't worry Derrick. He won't do anything stupid. I agree we can't have more tennis lessons, but I really miss you. I want to see you again."

Derrick liked being with her, but there was no way he ever wanted to see her again. "God, I hope he doesn't come after me. Really Linda, I don't know if we should meet anymore."

Linda could hear the fear in his voice and she could feel his coldness now. So they had fun and great sex for a while. That was it; she knew it was over. "I know Derrick. I guess you are right. I just wanted to call to let you know that you don't need to be scared. He is not going to come after you or do anything. I will make sure he doesn't. Maybe after a few months or so we could be friends or something. Just make sure of one thing for my sake. If he does ever talk to you, be sure to tell him that we only were together that one time. I am going to tell him that and I just want to be sure that you tell him the same if he ever does contact you."

"I understand, Linda. I can do that, but I hope he doesn't ever contact me," said Derrick

"I don't think he will, but just in case we both need to have the same story," Linda said.

"Ok, so we will say that it was only that one time. I wish it didn't have to end Linda. You were really great and I will miss you a lot," Derrick said.

"I will miss you too. I think I was falling in love with you." Linda smiled not really knowing why she said that, but it felt good to her.

"I guess I was starting to fall in love with you too," replied Derrick because he held out hope that maybe some day he would meet with her again though he knew it was not very likely.

"Goodbye Derrick." Linda was starting to cry.

"Goodbye, Linda. Call me again in a month or so," said Derrick.

"I will," Linda replied now fully crying as she hung up the phone. She went to the bar, fixed herself a very strong drink, and then sat on the couch. She turned on the television, but she wasn't really watching because it looked blurry through her tears. She thought about how she was going to get up the courage to make her way upstairs to her bedroom where her husband was asleep. After two more drinks, she was feeling drunk and the tears had dried up. Who really cared about some young tennis instructor? She knew she was fooling herself and she knew why she was fooling herself. She stayed on the couch until well after midnight pretending to watch some movie she had seen one too many times, but really thinking about her life. She decided she really did love Tim. After all, they had two children together and they had been together a long time. Sometimes couples just go through these things she told herself. He was still her first love and that should count for something. She made her way upstairs finally and curled up in bed next to Tim, making sure she did not wake him. Tim was sleeping restlessly and he felt her when she came into the bed, but he was still half asleep. He wasn't remembering the afternoon fiasco so he snuggled her close to him and went back into a deep sleep.

Tim woke up like he had been hit by lighting at 5 AM. Linda was next to him asleep. Tim instantly recalled the day before and his anger came back like a flash of hot wind. He quickly got out of the bed and dressed. He didn't want to be near his wife when she woke up. He wondered how she could think of coming into the bed with him last night after what she had done. He went to the kitchen after he dressed and left her a note, "Linda, we will talk when I come home from work." He then drove to a nearby restaurant and ate a prolonged breakfast while reading the morning newspaper. He was trying to kill time before he went to work.

Usually Tim arrived at work promptly at 9 AM, but today he arrived at 7 AM more than wide-awake after about four cups of coffee at the restaurant. He went over some reports on his desk and picked up a printout of the activities from the night before. He saw that yesterday afternoon a young woman's body had been discovered in Malibu hills. He usually wouldn't have thought about it twice except that it was in the same general area where the two gang members had been shot in their car. He called the Malibu Sheriff's Department because it was their jurisdiction. The detective in charge told him that there wasn't any identification on the body and that there had been no missing person report that fit the description of the victim. The woman had apparently been hit over the head with a blunt object. They calculated the time of death as being sometime late on Halloween night or the following morning. Tim asked them to call him when they were able to get identification. He was told it might be a few days because they would have to rely on dental records if they couldn't match the prints. The coroner was taking the prints now and they would get back to him later in the day. The body had been wrapped in a blanket so they might get some evidence from that if they were lucky. After the call, Tim started to think again about what had happened yesterday afternoon. He wondered if his wife was going to see the tennis instructor again and he started to get worried. He decided he needed to find out more about the guy.

By 10 AM the coffee had worn off completely and the effect of drinking the night before kicked in. Tim felt very tired and lethargic. He made it to lunch and at noon he went to his car and took a nap. When he woke up, it was well past 1 PM so he hurried back to his desk. He didn't have too much to do so he started looking for information about the tennis instructor even though he didn't know his last name. He had his methods and called the local recreation club near his home. He was able to get enough information to start his search. He dreaded going home and seeing his wife. He felt like he could never be close to her again.

During his drive home from work, Tim kept trying to rehearse what he was going to say to his wife. He wanted to tell her how angry, repulsed, and hurt he was, but somehow the guilt he felt from being with Maria made it all seem less severe now that he thought about it. He wanted to tell her that he no longer loved her and that he could never love her again, but he knew that was just a lie. What he really wanted was his "old Linda," the woman he had known years ago in college. He knew that was not very realistic though because they had both matured and changed. What he realized was that what he really wanted was to feel the romance and passion that he had felt with Maria. He had felt like that with Linda, but that was years ago and now they had grown apart from each other in so many ways. He knew there was a big part of it that was his fault. Before he knew it, he was pulling into his garage and still mulling over his options.

Sitting in the car in his garage, he felt the dread of having to face his wife. He really wanted to just go somewhere and start drinking again, but he knew he had to face her. He walked through the garage door into the kitchen and his wife was there cooking dinner with his two daughters.

"Hi Daddy. How was work? Are you feeling better today?" asked his daughter April, as she came over and gave him a hug. He saw his wife smile while his daughter hugged him and he knew there was no way he could ever divorce his wife and break up the family. His daughters thrived on the love and concern they received from both of them.

"Work was fine and yes, I am feeling better," Tim announced with one eye on his wife, who refused to meet his glance. "Girls, your mother and I need to go out after dinner so we can talk about some things. I trust the two of you can be left alone for a few hours."

"So you and Mom are having trouble with your relationship?" asked Colleen, the oldest, as she picked up a pot and handed it to her mom. Colleen was at the age where she sort of knew what was going on. Her woman's sixth sense was developing quickly.

"Colleen, you shouldn't say those kinds of things!" said Linda, as she put her hands on her hips and stared at her daughter.

"She is just saying that because she doesn't have a relationship!" said April feeling more than happy to stir things up with her sister. She knew her father would take her side like he usually did.

"So what if I don't have a relationship. If I did it would be none of your business anyway!" replied Colleen as she turned toward her sister, put her hands on her hips, and made that little side to side head movement that only women can make when they need to emphasize a point.

"Well that's because you are a lesbian!" April snapped back knowing she would now get everyone's attention.

"What did you say?" responded Colleen, as she now started toward her sister ready to slap her as hard as she could. Linda grabbed April by the arm to restrain her from going after her sister.

"April, don't call your sister a lesbian. That's a mean thing to say," Tim interjected with a raised voice. Tim then sat down at the kitchen table and put his hands over his ears wishing he were somewhere else. He was tired. His life flashed before him and the scene in front of him seemed surreal. He was tired of being a father and husband. He hated his work and now his wife had cheated on him. He saw through his so-called "American Dream" and saw the reality of his life. He feared his future. He didn't know if he could continue to live the life he was living. Colleen pulled her arm away from her mother's grasp and came over and sat on Tim's lap.

"Well, she is a lesbian. I saw her kiss her friend Sara in her room the other day," said April still standing by the entry between the kitchen and the den.

"You little witch. You were spying on me," Colleen shouted as she tried to jump off her father's lap. Tim restrained her from going after her sister. Then she realized she had better say something because she was in front of her parents and they might be wondering what April was talking about.

Linda now turned away from the stove and looked at both her daughters. "Girls, stop it now." Then Linda looked at Colleen wondering if there was an explanation.

Colleen could feel her mother's inquisitive eyes. "So, we kissed. You guys know Sara is from France and she is very affectionate. We just kissed on the cheeks and once on the lips, but we didn't make out. I am not a lesbian." Colleen emphasized the last sentence.

"This conversation is over. Are you two sure we can trust you to be alone if you father and I go out after dinner?" Linda was looking at Tim and could see he was distraught. She was amazed that he actually came home after work and that he was calm enough to ask her to go out and talk with him.

"You never know Mom; you might come back and find April missing," said Colleen.

"Well, most girls that play softball are lesbians and everyone knows that," replied April, trying to make a statement that would ease her way out of the trouble she was getting herself into. Tim couldn't help it and he laughed at the comment. His wife smiled, but Colleen just glared at her sister.

Tim stood up. "April, that is enough. Drop the subject now." Tim knew life with three females was never going to be easy. "I'm going upstairs to take a shower before dinner." Tim stared April down and she knew she had to stop.

During dinner, Linda remained shy and quiet. She only looked up at Tim once and smiled sheepishly when he made some joke with the girls. The tension between the two of them was obvious to the girls though they tried to hide it. Linda excused herself first from the table by saying she was going upstairs to change. Before she left, she turned to Tim and asked, "Where are we going? Should I wear anything fancy?"

"I don't know yet. You don't have to dress up," Tim replied. The girls left the table shortly after and Tim sat alone trying to decide what to say when he talked with his wife.

Twenty minutes later they entered the car and could both feel the silent tension begin to mount. They didn't look at each other as Tim started the car and began to drive. Neither wanted to start the conversation and both feared where it would lead. Tim pulled out of the driveway and the feeling of driving made him feel in control. He wanted to control the situation, but his emotions were too strong. "So how long have you been banging this guy?" he blurted out turning quickly. Right at that instant, a neighbor's kid darted out on his bike and swerved in front of him. Fortunately, Tim saw him and slammed on the brakes. The kid rode on unharmed, but the moment let the tension hang even more. Tim pulled the car over, parked only half a block from the house, put his head on the steering wheel, and closed his eyes.

Linda let out a deep sigh, turned, and placed her hand on Tim's shoulder. "It is not what you think, Tim."

Tim jerked himself up, pulling away from her comfort. "What do you mean by that? I saw what I saw. Answer my question. How long have you been with this man?"

"Tim, really, it was the first time. I don't love him," Linda said. She knew she had to lie to save her marriage.

Tim didn't know whether to believe her or not. What he did know was that if he couldn't find the power within him to forgive her, then things would only get worse. Knowing he had also cheated made him want to forgive her more, but the reality of what he saw wouldn't let him forgive her. He thought it must have only been an uncontrollable sexual attraction like his affair had been, but what if it wasn't? What if his wife was in love with this guy?

Linda continued, "Tim, I am so sorry. I never wanted to hurt you. It is just that things haven't been so good for us lately. You haven't been paying a lot of attention to me for some time now. We never go out anymore."

Tim had heard enough. He started the car and headed back down the street. He needed a drink and figured he would stop at a bar not too far from his house. He was angry and he was frustrated. "Linda, what you did was wrong and you know it...even if it was only one time with your tennis instructor. Is he really your tennis instructor? Is that how you met him?" Now Tim wanted to know the details. At least they were talking and not screaming at each other. He wanted to know as much as possible.

They stopped at a hotel bar a few blocks away. They found a corner booth and when they sat down, Linda tried to give Tim a little smile. Tim remained stoic and ordered some drinks. After the drinks came, Tim once again started with the questions. He wanted to know everything and he wanted to decide here and now if he should try to stay with his wife. Maria only existed in the far corner of his mind and he didn't even think of that as cheating.

Linda wanted to just get through the conversation without crying or having Tim make a scene in the bar. After she had her drink in her hand, she decided she had no choice but to answer as many of his questions as possible. She didn't want to break up her marriage, but at the same time she didn't want end the relationship with Derrick because it had only started and it was getting to be very fun. She looked up from her hands and tried to focus on Tim's face. She wanted to see him like she had seen him when they were lovers in college, but the vision wouldn't come. She could only see the sadness in his eyes now. "Look Tim. I don't want to end our marriage either. This is just a stupid mistake I made. Yes, Derrick is a tennis instructor. He came on to me and it just sort of happened that way. He only came over that one time to the house." Linda was lying and she didn't even care now. It was the second time Derrick had been over and she didn't want to end it. She did love Derrick. At least she told herself that because she would never make love with someone that she didn't love.

"So you enjoyed having sex with him?" Tim couldn't get the picture out of his mind and he was feeling sick and disgusted. "Linda, this guy is like half your age." Now the feeling of inadequacy was creeping into Tim like a thick fog. Tim looked at Linda and then at his drink. He watched the ice move around as he stirred his drink and tried to remember how he and Linda had made love two or three times a day back in college. Now it was more like once a week and he knew it was not because he physically couldn't do it, but because he had lost his passion while his mind strayed to Maria. He didn't know what to say and then he just blurted out, "So are you still in love with me?" He regretted asking it as soon as he did.

"Tim, of course I am still in love with you." Linda was sincere and she started to tear up. She tried to hold back her tears, but she knew that she still loved her husband. At that same instant, she drifted to that afternoon and to the passion and lust in Derrick's eyes. She began to cry in earnest for what she had felt years ago with Tim and for what she may never experience again with Derrick. Tim tried to comfort her and at first she accepted his touch from across the table, but then he could feel the distant emotion coming from within his wife. He leaned back in his chair and she cried for a minute before composing herself. Tim waited until she looked at him.

"Honey, I'm sorry too. I'm sorry I haven't been taking better care of you." Tim said the words softly and with meaning. For an instant they both saw the glimmer in each other's eyes that they had once cherished with awe and tenderness. Tim was waiting for his wife to say she was sorry also, but Linda looked down and stared at her drink. "So are you in love with this guy?"

Linda replied quickly because she didn't want to have a major blow up in the bar. "No, I'm not in love with him, but I'm not going to say I am sorry either."

Tim felt hurt. Here was his wife sitting in front of him and she had been in bed with some tennis instructor and she didn't regret it. "So you cheat on me and you're not even sorry about what you have done?" He was hoping he would hear her apologize though he knew he had probably cheated on her for the same reasons.

"No, I am not sorry for what happened. I don't want to go there, Tim. It just happened. I think we should be talking about what we can do to save our marriage and not go into what happened." Linda wanted to keep her experience with Derrick untainted in her mind. She did love Derrick or at least she felt passion for him and that wasn't something that would just disappear because she had been caught by her husband.

At this, the macho stud detective broke down and tears welled up. He realized the depths of the mess that his marriage was in. He wanted to say something, but he couldn't think of words to say. "So was he better than me?" Tim's feelings of inadequacy deepened.

"I said I don't want to go there. The truth is 'We' haven't been passionate and caring like we used to." Linda wanted her old Tim back, but really felt the chances of that happening were remote.

Tim was able to stop his tears and now his jealousy reared its ugly head. "So did you see him today?"

"No, I did not see him today and I don't know if I will ever see him again. If I did want to see him I would because I am a free person and I haven't felt that you really love me for some time now. I am here with you in this bar talking to you and seeing if you want to save our marriage. Now you tell me...have you ever been with another woman since we have been married?" Linda had turned the tables and she could see Tim cringe at the mention of him cheating.

Tim looked her dead in the eye and knew that she really had no idea; there was no way she could know anything of his life outside of home. He was a detective, not his wife. He also knew that if he wanted to stay with his wife that he would have to admit to something. Partial truth seemed to be the best option. "Ok, I did cheat. It was over seven years ago at the convention in Dallas. I never did that again. "

"Oh, really, just the one time? Yeah right, how many conventions have you gone to without me? At least ten!" Linda had suspected as much and now the footing was equal and for the first time they shined a brief smile at each other. "Well, I don't believe it was only once, but right now it doesn't matter. Really Tim, we have drifted apart and we both know it. Do you want to try and makes things work? Do you think we can make the changes we need to make?"

Tim didn't know what to say. He wanted to forgive her, but the picture in his mind of the two of them in his bed was way too fresh. He really wanted to find this guy and kick him in the teeth. "I do want to save our marriage, but what am I supposed to do? Just forgive you and forget about everything? I mean you brought this guy into our house and into our bed!"

"Look Tim, I didn't say you had to forgive me and I didn't say I wasn't sorry for what happened. I am just not going to say that I am sorry to you. At least not right now. I think we should be here to talk about what it is we can do to make things better between us or we need to think about getting separated." Linda was now thinking that there really was not going to be much of a chance that her husband was going to forgive her or more importantly that he would admit there was anything he needed to change.

Tim saw the gravity of the situation and took a second to choose his words. He didn't want to break up his family and he didn't want to separate because he knew that would only be the first step in getting a divorce. "Linda, I do love you. I have always loved you from the very first time we met. I will admit that our marriage has not been so great lately and I will admit that a lot of the blame is on me. I have not been giving you the attention you deserve and I have not been thinking about the two of us doing things together that much. I have become complacent and I have taken it for granted that you would always be there for me. I have been concentrating too much on my work and not enough on you and the girls. I still don't see how that makes it right for you to cheat on me, but I think over a period of time I can get over that. I do want our relationship to improve and I know a lot of it has to do with me improving the way I treat you."

Now Tim was starting to feel impatient. He looked at Linda who was breathing in deep sighs and was obviously pondering the thought of leaving him and going to the young stud. "So what is this guy's name?" Tim asked, only slightly raising his voice.

Linda knew he would calm down so she purred at him and said softly, "You know I love you honey. Yes, I was caught, but it was just a one time thing and I don't want to be with him." She knew her husband was a detective and could do anything he wanted to the tennis instructor. They both knew they could pull at each other's strings if they wanted.

Tim did calm down. He knew he loved his wife and even though he had his escapes, he knew he didn't want to be married to anyone else. So they made up in their own ways. One was with deceit and selfishness and the other was with an even worst deceit, the deceit of love. That night their feelings remained edgy and intense. At first, Tim didn't want to touch his wife, but then he did though she didn't want him. Then it almost blew up late in the night. But because they both knew the best life they could have would be with each other, they stopped and made up. They made love with cautious passion and their sleep was restless and filled with fears.

In the morning it dawned on Tim that he had promised to call Maria last night and understandably he had completely forgotten. He sat at his desk and did some paperwork deciding that he would call her in an hour or so at around 10 AM. He had a hard time concentrating. He kept thinking about his wife on top of the tennis instructor. He wanted to call his home and check on her, but he knew that would just make him seem paranoid. He wanted to believe his wife, but at the same time he wanted to make sure this guy never came back. He decided to run a background check on the this Derrick guy to find out as much as he could about him in case he ever wanted to do anything against him. It didn't take long and there wasn't much on the guy. He had a few traffic tickets and he had only been in Los Angeles for a little over a year. He was originally from Maryland and he had played tennis in college. By now it was almost 10 AM and Tim picked up the phone to call Maria.

"Hello, this is Maria speaking."

Tim felt a calm come over him as he heard her voice. He smiled and recalled the intimacy they had shared, but it now seemed like only a fading distant memory. He couldn't feel the passion inside of him after what he had seen at his home with his wife and Derrick. "Hi, Maria. This is Tim. I am sorry I didn't call you last night. I was very busy and some unexpected things came up."

"That's okay," Maria replied, though in her heart it wasn't. She had waited for his call last night until after midnight. She had even thought about calling him. She had wanted to talk and hear his voice. She was going to tell him everything and maybe even see him again. She wanted to be close to someone and wanted someone who would listen to her. She had thought of calling him, but she knew that would be crazy because he would be there with his wife and family. As the evening progressed, she told herself to end the affair with him and to forget about him. Her feelings of hatred toward men had been pushed to the past and she wanted Tim to at least be a friend. She ended up falling asleep with the television on while watching some stupid movie.

"So, how are you doing, Maria?" Tim asked with genuine concern.

"I am a lot better now. Thanks for asking. Actually, I guess the worst of the shock is over." Maria was now realizing she didn't want to talk with Tim, not now and maybe not ever again. Yes, he was attractive, but just because they had been intimate didn't mean he was her type. Worse was the feeling that she had wanted him to call last night and he didn't and that made her angry. She started to drift back to the memory of her dreams and the teeth.

"When do you think you will be coming back to work?" Tim asked.

"I talked with Mr. MacIntosh today and told him I would be coming back on Monday," Maria replied.

"Well some people might think that is a little soon, but I think it is a good idea. Work always has taken my mind off of my problems." Tim didn't know if he had said the right thing and he was starting to feel quiet awkward.

Maria felt the same way, but she knew she needed to talk to him. "Tim, listen. I really think we should get together in person and talk."

Tim immediately wondered if it was anything serious or if she wanted to be with him again. He felt confused, but he knew they needed to see other soon. "I think that would be a good idea, but I am not sure when we can meet. I have been really busy at work."

Maria didn't want to wait. She had been through way too much in the past few days and the thought of not clarifying things with Tim right away made her feel very anxious. "Tim, I really need to talk to you. Could we meet at lunch today?"

Now Tim was a bit scared because he could hear the urgency in her voice. He hoped it was just that she wanted to call off their affair because that was what he needed to do if he wanted to keep his wife. He liked Maria way too much and the fact that they worked together made the risk of his wife finding out way too high. "I guess that would be fine. Where do you want to meet?"

Maria thought quickly because she did not want to meet him somewhere that other people from work might also go. "Tim, can we meet at the Yogananda Gardens? Do you know where I am talking about?"

"Yes, I was there once years ago. It is off Sunset Boulevard, isn't it?" Tim was trying to remember how long ago he had been there.

"Yes, it is just a little off of the Pacific Coast Highway on Sunset. I will be there around noon. If you can come and meet me there then we can talk for a while," Maria said.

"Ok Maria. I will be there around noon." Tim hung up not sure exactly what Maria felt she needed to say to him. He knew what he needed to say to her though. He wanted her again, but he had to resist or he could further jeopardize his marriage. He needed to tell Maria that he cared for her, but that he couldn't have a relationship with her.

## Chapter 10

The Yogananda Gardens and Shrine is a 10-acre garden with a small lake in the center. It is just off the Coast Highway in a small box canyon. For the people that could actually find the place, it was a special place of beauty. Well-maintained pathways and gardens surrounded it and it was open to the public during the day. It was not a place that was in any phone book or tourist brochure so it was rarely crowded. It was a very peaceful place and people would go there to meditate, relax, or to just enjoy the beauty.

Maria had been through a lot of stress and she needed to go somewhere and think about her life. She had been planning to go there and spend part of the day by herself anyway. So it made sense to have Tim come meet her there. Last night, as she had been waiting for him to call, she thought about maybe going to a hotel again with him, but since he never called, she had changed her mind. She realized she needed to tell Tim that Felix had AIDS and that she didn't want to carry on their romance. She had gone to the doctor yesterday and he had confirmed that she was not infected with the virus, but it was still only right to tell Tim and let him get his own test. Really, the things she had to think about were very depressing and she didn't like feeling depressed. She needed time to think and to plan out her future. Worse was the fact that her sister had gone back home and Maria didn't have anyone to share her thoughts with. There were so many emotions to deal with that she sometimes just wanted to escape, but she knew she couldn't do that because she had the responsibility of taking care of her two sons. Her parents and relatives had been very supportive, but she realized that from now on she would be alone and she would have to raise her sons by herself. The worst part was trying to hide the anger she felt toward Felix from both her family and his family. Even when Felix's parents had been told the truth they refused to believe it and looked at Maria like she had somehow been the cause of the problems. Deep down, she realized that Felix's death had made her feel very lost. Yes, she had grown tired of Felix's ego and macho behavior and she had planned to make changes in her life even before he committed suicide, but she had never expected him to be gay and to commit suicide. The shock of the past few days made Maria wonder about her views on life and on the world around her. She realized she was not a good judge of people's real character and that made her sad.

It was rare that the Santana winds came up in November, but they did. It was more than just warm. It was hot and the sun was very bright. Maria brought a few snacks and a large bottle of water with her. She thought for sure that there would be quite a few people at the gardens, but to her surprise there were only a handful. She wandered to the far part of the lake and found a small concrete bench against a flowery hillside that was partially hidden by fragrant jasmine bushes from the path below. She sat down on her bench, took a few deep breaths, and tried to fully relax for the first time in a few days. The beauty of the flowers and the shimmering lake in front of her let her escape from her problems for the time being. It was almost 11:30 and she actually hoped Tim wouldn't show up, but she knew he would. It wasn't going to be easy to tell the guy that she had been infatuated with and then finally had sex with that her ex-husband had been infected with the AIDS virus. She wanted to rehearse exactly how she was going to say it, but thought it'd be better to just let it come out. She knew from the distance in Tim's voice when she had talked to him that he was planning to end the affair and that was fine with her except that she now was starting to imagine kissing him in such a romantic place. She laughed out loud at her quandary. It felt good to laugh with no one around, but the laugh turned to tears when she noticed a couple walking in the distance. Her own dream of having a happy family with Felix was gone and even worse she now realized that her whole life with him had been a complete facade. Through her tears she saw Tim at the entrance of the garden. For a second, she felt like hiding as she watched him trying to find her. He was almost a hundred yards away on the other side of the lake and she knew it would be easy to just sneak off and hide, but she didn't. She stood up and waved to him as she wiped her tears away with a napkin.

Tim noticed her waving and casually sauntered over to where Maria was sitting alone. As he approached he wanted to smile because physically he remembered the joy of their sexual encounter. The smile faded quickly though when he saw her confusion and sadness. She had lost her husband and he knew he needed to be sympathetic to that. He thought to himself as he greeted her with a neutral handshake and then gentle hug that maybe he shouldn't tell her he couldn't see her anymore. Maybe he shouldn't hurt her feelings if she really liked him. The brief hug excited Tim and for a second he noticed the beauty around him and realized he saw Maria only as a sexual creature and that his sexual fantasy had come true.

"Maria, I am so sorry for your loss," Tim said with an even and calm voice. Maria smiled at him. She had a way of always smiling when she needed to. Maria sat down and Tim sat next to her. Tim continued, "I am really sorry about what happened to Felix. I am sure it is a big loss for you."

There was a pause and Tim turned to look at Maria and once again tears welled up, but this time they turned to anger as she thought about the situation Felix had caused her to be in now. Then Maria shook her head and let out a long sigh. "Look Tim, this life is crazy. I mean really crazy. Here I am with someone that I really like, maybe even someone that is my soulmate and he is married. Basically my life with Felix was a disaster, but you and your wife have been together a long time. You are a lovely couple and I don't want to interfere with your relationship. Maybe I wouldn't have been able to say that to you before Felix died and maybe you feel you want to be with me or maybe you feel you don't. The truth is I know now that I have to stick by the choices I make and I have to make them quickly. We can be friends and I will be back at work soon so we can talk, but we will not be romantic while you are with your wife."

Tim nodded slowly as if that was not what he wanted. He turned and put his arm on Maria's shoulder and said, "Ok, friends." It sounded stupid and awkward as soon as he said it. Maria felt awkward with his hand on her shoulder. The tension built quickly and Tim removed his hand from Maria's shoulder.

"The truth is, Maria...Linda and I have been having our differences. We had a long talk last night and that is why I didn't call. We decided to try harder in our marriage. Hey, I like you a lot Maria. I am very attracted to you. It just wasn't the right time."

"It is never the right time. Tim, there is something else I have to tell you and I want to trust that you will keep this completely between us. Felix had AIDS. I have been tested and I am negative, but I think I need to tell you because you are the only other man I have slept with," Maria said.

Tim wasn't sure at first what he had heard, but then it sunk in. The "AIDS" highlighted the sentence and suddenly Tim's mind went blank. He didn't know what to say or what to think.

Maria looked at Tim and could see his shock so she continued and tried to ease his mind. "Felix committed suicide because he had AIDS."

At this point, Tim didn't want to hear anymore. He knew he had used a condom and his chance of being infected if Maria wasn't was highly unlikely. Still, it was a shock to him. He looked down at his watch out of habit and stood up. "Maria thanks for being honest with me. Like you said, we can be friends. I will get tested, but you know it is unlikely that I have the virus. You don't have to worry. I will never tell anyone."

Maria stood up and they hugged. The hug was brief, as they both knew they were parting ways. They smiled and then kissed. It was almost like their first passionate kiss, but this time with a forced retreat. They both thought about what could have been and they both recalled their perfect afternoon in the Malibu hotel. They stopped their kiss and Tim began to walk away. He wanted to turn and look back, but he acted like he needed to hurry by looking at his watch.

Maria realized the moment had ended and that sometimes moments can be more than moments. An affair, a marriage, choices, and suddenly, two beautiful bluish-purple butterflies flew in front of her almost like one of those three dimensional movies. They danced not more than five yards in front of her. The butterflies moved off and played in some pink flowers. They were so free and beautiful she thought. When she looked back toward the entrance, Tim was out of sight. She noticed another man walking around the path. He was tall and elegant. He melted into her view just as Tim had melted away. The man was looking around as he approached slowly with his hands clasped behind his back. When he reached the area where Maria was off to his right above the path, he stopped and paused. Maria stared at him and wondered if he would move on or turn and say something to her. Then the man turned and gently smiled. Maria smiled back. She liked the way he looked. He had similar features to Tom Petty from Tom Petty and the Heartbreakers.

"How are you?" he asked softly, but with an earnest tone.

"I'm fine," Maria replied. But, she instantly realized she had just said that out of pure habit because she was speaking to a stranger. He looked nice, but she wanted to be left alone.

He smiled at her and she smiled back. He was ready to move on, but Maria realized that she didn't know if she wanted to be alone. He stood still and Maria sat back down on the bench. "I saw you from across the lake with your friend. I just wanted to tell you that you are very lovely." Maria sighed and took a breath like she wanted to say something, but the man continued speaking. "I didn't say that because I want to hit on you." Maria smiled again. She liked the sound of his voice. It was mellow and soothing. His eyes were dark blue, bright, and ageless. She was trying to guess his age, but it was hard. He could be anywhere from 35 to 50. He was tall, lean, and very fit. He had the typical California tan and skin that was clear and smooth. He was dressed in a casual golf shirt and Bermuda shorts. She noticed that the hair on his legs looked like fine threads of gold as they glittered in the sunlight. He continued, "The truth is I came here to see if you would like to have a conversation for a while?"

Maria was startled at his words. It was rare if ever that someone had asked her to have a conversation. People asked if they could talk, but she had never heard anyone use the phrase, "have a conversation." Maria wondered if the man was one of those really crazy intelligent types. She thought it might be best to just refuse him and let him go his way, but his eyes were so kind and soft.

"I might, but I am not in a talkative mood. I think it is best I be alone for a while." Maria looked off to where Tim had walked away into the parking lot and her mind wandered to her problems. The butterflies flew away. She looked up and the soft blue eyes were still looking at her.

"Well if you would like to talk after you have been alone a while, I will be sitting over there," the man said as he slowly walked away and pointed to an empty bench about fifty feet down the path. Maria watched him walk away and saw the butterflies hovering halfway between them. Maria sat alone and tried to force herself to not look over to the bench where the man was sitting. He was sort of like a magnet for her eyes though and she had to look. He was reading something and didn't appear to look over at her. She didn't want to just dwell on her problems so she stood up and said, "Ok, why not?" She walked slowly over to where he was sitting and when she was within a few yards of him, he looked up from his paperback book and smiled at her. Maria smiled back, "Well I guess it wouldn't hurt to have a conversation with you. My name is Maria." She reached out and they shook hands. He then motioned for her to sit down and she sat next to him on the concrete bench.

"Nice to meet you Maria. My name is, "The Writer.""

"What? I don't understand" What he had said sounded odd, not threatening, but just a bit too offbeat for her. She tensed up a bit and thought maybe she should leave.

"Well for today anyway. I just want to think of myself as, "The Writer." My real name is Brent, but today I am pretending I am the writer of the rest of my life. It is just sort of a way for me to try and think of things in a different way for a while. I come here sometimes to be alone, but when I saw you I thought it might be nice to be alone with someone else. Do you know what I mean?"

Maria wasn't sure that she did know what he meant, but she felt comfortable because he talked softly and seemed kind. "Well that seems like something different to do, but I think I am going to call you Brent if that is alright." She didn't want to flirt with him, but Maria knew she was flirting and she didn't mind it.

"Who was your friend that left?" Brent asked.

"He was just someone from work," Maria said. Then a silence set in. No words were spoken. The pause was brief, but in that few seconds Maria felt something shift around her. She felt the sun on her skin and it made her feel happy; it was the happiest she had felt in days.

"Hmm." Brent spoke softly and clasped his hands in his lap. "Well, because I am the writer today, let me take a guess. The two of you had an affair. You are both married and he came here to tell you that the affair had to end."

Maria turned and stared at him with her mouth opened, wondering if he was just taking a wild guess or if he had some way of reading her mind. "How did you know that?"

Brent smiled back at her. He wanted to tell her that he had the power to read her mind, but that would be a lie and he didn't want to lie to her. "Really, it was just sort of a guess. I saw the two of you together and he left pretty quickly without looking back at you. I just guessed that whatever he had to say was something serious and not romantic."

Maria felt comfortable with his answer, but she really didn't want to have the conversation go in that direction. "It is a really nice day, don't you think?"

Brent understood her hint. "Absolutely. It is a wonderful day. May I ask you some questions? I promise I won't pursue the past."

"That would fine," Maria replied knowing that he had understood her hint.

"What is your God?" Brent asked bluntly.

"What do you mean? Do you mean who is my God?" Maria replied.

"I mean exactly that; what is your God?" Brent said.

"Well, I am still a bit confused. I will say that I do believe in God. I believe in God now more than I ever have before," Maria said.

"Why do you believe in God now more than before?" Brent asked.

"Because God has recently protected me more than ever," said Maria.

"Well being protected is definitely a reason to believe in God, but I asked what your God is," Brent persisted.

Now Maria paused and tried to think exactly what Brent was asking. The past few weeks of turmoil weighed on her shoulders. For the first time, she thought neither on a level of rote answers from memorization nor on a level of emotions, but on a level that was uniquely hers. The two butterflies came back into her view. "God is the texture of love," she said with confidence.

"Wow that is a very beautiful and poetic answer!" Brent replied as he smiled at her.

"Thank you, but now it is your turn to answer the question," Maria said.

"Well, I am not very religious in the normal sense of the word so I will have to answer in terms of physics. There are four known forces in the universe: gravity, electro-magnetism, the strong nuclear force, and the weak nuclear force," Brent said.

"Well that sounds very interesting, but the only thing I know anything about is gravity," Maria replied hoping the conversation wouldn't turn into one that was too technical for her.

"Well let's just say I support the concept of God, but not as a creator. You see if we go by the idea that the universe is infinite then the concept of creation is moot. Most of the scientific community today believes in what is called a closed universe. In other words, the universe expands and then contracts in an infinite cycle," Brent continued.

"I haven't given much thought to it myself, but that sort of makes sense to me," Maria said.

"Do you believe in aliens?" Brent asked.

"Sort of. My aunt said that she saw a flying saucer once in Mexico. She said that a lot of people in the town saw it." Maria was feeling very comfortable sitting and talking with Brent. She had just met him, but she liked the way he talked softly and the way he showed interest in her. For the first time in days she wasn't thinking about her problems and that was good. The warm sun on her shoulders felt nice and she felt calm inside.

There was a pause in the conversation as they looked out over the lake and just enjoyed each other's company.

Brent broke the silence. "This is a place that honors all religions and in that way it has to be quite unique because most religions spend a lot of time trying to prove that their religion is the best. The truth is that men created all religions, rules, laws, mores, and social structures in order to control other men. It is our way of trying to survive as a species. I think it was Socrates that deemed us "Man the Thinker." Today though the sad fact is that a lot of intelligent people would change that to, "Man the Destroyer." Global warming is no longer a theory, but part of our present and future reality. I don't think we can say that life is either rare or common in the universe because the universe is just too vast. Based on mathematical formulas it is predicted that there are multitudes of planets with life and even more bizarre, there are most likely multitudes of planets that have exactly the same circumstances we have. In other words, there are other planets where a Maria and a Brent are sitting and talking exactly as we are. The universe is just so vast that the odds allow for those circumstances. There is a Japanese physicist who classified intelligent life into three types of civilizations. The first is a Type I in which the life on a planet has evolved to a point of complete balance and harmony. This would mean that they would utilize the energy source, their sun, in a way that their planet was assured a clean and safe future. The ecosystem of the planet would be balanced. They would realize that some day their sun would die out and they would have to migrate to another planet or planets."

"Well we definitely haven't reached that level yet!" Maria interjected. She was enjoying listen to this intelligent man because she didn't have to think about her problems for the time being.

"I hope someday we will, but for now it doesn't look very good. Actually just reaching a level of a balanced and harmonious planet may be the hardest thing for any intelligent life form to do. There is a program called SETI, the Search for Extraterrestrial Intelligence, which has been going on for over 30 years. We have hundred of thousands of computers, including personal computers that analyze any radio waves that may come from beyond our planet, and to date we have yet to find any intelligent life. We have been sending out radio signals into outer space ever since we invented the radio, which is almost 60 years ago. That means that our radio waves that travel at the speed of light have gone out 60 light years in all directions. Within that distance of 60 light years there should be numerous stars with planets and at least one should have intelligent life. So far, we seem to be alone in our universe. What that most likely means is that it must be very difficult for a planet to evolve a Type I civilization and have a balanced planet. In other words, most forms of life constantly compete with and destroy each other. It seems that our planet is headed in that direction also. We haven't even reached a point where humans don't have wars with other humans. Worse is the fact that we are on the verge of causing serious changes to our biosphere, which may lead to future climatic catastrophes. We haven't even reached the point where we utilize clean energy sources and that is mainly because of human greed." Brent took a breath.

"Wow, I never really thought of those things, but what you're saying makes a lot of sense. What are the other two types of civilizations?" Maria asked.

"A Type II civilization is one that uses their energy source against their sun to begin to explore and migrate to other planets within their galaxy. A Type III civilization is one that utilizes not only their own sun, but also other suns as energy sources to travel to different galaxies. Both Type II and Type III civilizations must be very rare indeed and most likely would also have evolved levels of longevity we can only imagine. So basically there must be three different reasons that we have not yet encountered intelligent life outside of our planet. First would be the fact that it must be incredible difficult to just reach a point of having a balanced and harmonious planet. Second, it is possible that when a life form develops harmony on their planet that they may never have the need to develop advanced technologies such as radios. Third, there may actually be other intelligent life that is watching us. If so, they must have decided that we are just too primitive to be worth communicating with," Brent said.

"It seems very interesting to think about, but I guess if you thought about it too much you would feel sort of depressed because there doesn't seem to be much hope for mankind," Maria said.

"Yes, I agree. I really think that most of us want to have peace. I am hoping it will just be a matter of time and then the leaders of the world will realize that there is a lot of benefit and value in us all getting along," Brent replied.

"Well, one thing is for sure. It makes me realize it is very nice just to be alive!" Maria didn't know why she said that, but she did. Immediately, she thought about Felix, but now it wasn't with anger, but with gratitude for the fact that he had allowed her to move on with her life.

"Do you believe in life after death?" Brent asked softly searching Maria's eyes.

Maria smiled at him and at the same time tears began to well up in her eyes, but she held them back. It was like this man had followed her thoughts about Felix and then asked the question to make her analyze her thoughts. "Honestly, I don't know if I really even care about that," Maria said very casually. She was feeling satisfied to just stay in the moment with her new friend and she didn't want to get out of it and think anymore about her past.

"You are the first person that has ever said anything like that to me. Usually everyone seems to care. For me, I find it very unlikely that there is any life after death. Of course our atoms are recycled; we all have atoms of the past, but the religions have created a concept in order to control people. The religions want us to believe that what we do in this life will have an effect on us in the next. It is a survival tool so that we can live in defined and controlled social orders. The reality is that what we do in this life has an effect on how we live in this life and how others around us live," Brent said.

"I definitely agree with that and I say that from personal experience," Maria replied. "Do you think they will come up with a cure for AIDS?" She had stopped thinking about her past, but somehow the past just jumped into her conversation with this very polite and interesting man.

"I am sure they will. It won't be too long." He smiled at her again almost as if he knew she really didn't want to ask that question. "Actually I believe in the future we will be able to cure almost any disease. There is field of study called nanotechnology that works with manipulating atoms, the building blocks of cells and matter. We have already used them to basically cure breast cancer and a number of other diseases. We will also be able to live extraordinarily long lives in the future. Maybe we can live almost an unlimited amount of years as they find new methods to prevent aging. What's said is that even though science is advancing at an incredible rate, we still cannot come up for a cure for our own selfishness and greed," Brent replied. He could feel a sadness in Maria and he wanted to comfort her, but he knew now was not the time. She had to go through whatever it was she was going through before he could attempt to get any closer to her.

"That is so true. It just seems like everyone wants to be satisfied in their own way and it doesn't seem to bother anyone if they take away from some other person's happiness to get their own. I have definitely experienced that enough in my short life!" Maria replied laughing. It was the first time she had actually let out a laugh in a few days. She felt relieved. She wanted to reach over and pull this man close to her and hug him, but she had just met him and she couldn't do that.

"That is why today I am the "Writer." Brent smiled and only slight moved closer to her. He could feel the electricity between them, but he could also sense her pain because her laugh had been tainted with sorrow. He wanted to ask her for her phone number, but that just seemed too inappropriate at the moment. "Well really, Maria. I need to get going to pick up my son." He wanted to prolong the conversation, but end it at the same time so he could get the courage to see her again.

"Oh, you have a son!" Maria smiled again. This time it was more with a feeling of passion and love for the man who had met her out of the blue. "Now I finally get some information about you and you have to leave!" Maria teasingly said.

"Yes, yes. I have a 15 year old boy; I share custody with my ex- wife," Brent replied.

Maria smiled again and thought of her two boys, but then the darkness of them being left without their father hit her. The emotions were forcing tears, but she fought back and did not want to cry in front of her new friend. She had barely met him and now she could feel herself starting to break down. She wanted to tell him everything because she could feel his compassion. There was no lust or desire, just pure concern. He was a complete stranger and she had just met him here on some random afternoon. The sun felt warmer now against her face and almost too warm like it was going to burn her. She continued to fight back the tears the best that she could. She wanted to be calm and yet she wanted to cry and have this stranger hold her in his arms. She forced a smile and again tried to look into his penetrating eyes. She could see a light in his eyes. It was a soft greenish light and then she realized it was the reflection from the lake water glimmering off his eyes. They held each other's eyes for what seemed like a very long time, but really it was only a few seconds. "I have two sons. They are really good boys too."

Brent took a deep sigh. He saw this lovely creature in front of him had been suffering tremendously. "Tell you what Maria. I can tell you are going through a difficult time with something. Why don't we do this? First, let me tell you upfront that I like you and I would like to hear about your life and your desires. Why don't we meet here again in one month? We can sit and talk and get to know each other better. I promise next time I will tell you more about myself."

"That would be nice. We can meet on Dec 1$^{st}$. I like that idea." Maria felt her whole spirit calm. She saw her past and her present and felt the joy of what might actually be a bright future. She closed her eyes for a brief second and "The Writer" kissed her gently on the cheek. He then turned and walked away slowly. He stopped a few yards away from her and said, "It is a date right!" Maria opened her eyes and nodded with a soft smile. Her eyes glistened in the sun from holding back the tears.

## Chapter 11

Thursday, Nov. 7

It was 8 PM and Tony had decided he had gone long enough without drinking so he went out and bought a six-pack of Zima. When he returned home, he sat down on the couch and turned on the television. He had known from reading the morning newspaper that the body of the prostitute had been found. The situation had made him feel anxious. He kept telling himself that he should have found a better way to dispose of her body, but he knew there was nothing he could do about it now. He had been careless and he knew it, but he kept telling himself not to worry because he didn't have a criminal record. He was sure it would end up as just another of the thousands of unsolved crimes and besides...who really cared that much? She was a prostitute. Also, it really had just been an accident! The news came on television and they mentioned the body being found. Now he started to feel uncomfortable all over again so he downed his Zima, popped open a fresh one, and changed the channel.

Tony's work had been a grind all week so he sipped his Zima and tried to think ahead to the weekend. He went to his bedroom to get his phone book to see whom he could call for a date. He wanted to go out and have some fun. He needed to stop thinking about what had happened recently and get back to a normal life. A "normal life!" When had his life been normal! Well, it didn't matter now. Life went on. He looked through the phone numbers and eliminated the ones he didn't want to call. He knew that if he called enough numbers that he would find someone who wanted to go out. He picked up the phone, but just as he was going to try the first number, the phone rang!!

"Hello," he said with a slight hesitation because the past few weeks jumped back into the forefront of his mind and he wondered if he had been caught.

"Hi Tony. This is Susi. Do you remember me?"

Tony recognized her voice right away, but he hadn't thought she would really call him. "Yes, you are the waitress from Denny's. How are you?" He was smiling now because he knew if a girl called him after he had given her his phone number that could only mean he had a great chance of going to bed with her! He knew she either had to be lonely or that she had a fight with her boyfriend. Yes, that must have been it because he recalled their conversation and she had said she had a boyfriend.

"I just wanted to call and say hello." Now Susi had some hesitation in her voice. She had never really called a guy on her own like this and she was getting a little nervous. It wasn't the norm for her to call a guy. They called her.

"Well I'm glad you did!" Tony could sense her hesitation. "I have been thinking about you."

Susi warmed up immediately. "You have, really?" she replied with a smile from her end. She thought maybe this guy really was a nice guy.

"Yes, really. I couldn't stop thinking about you. You had such a pretty smile." Tony knew it was time to compliment her and make her feel at ease.

"So how is everything going with you?" Susi asked.

"Everything is going well. I guess maybe I have just been a little bored lately." Tony felt stupid saying the word "bored," as it was just an outright lie, but it was his way of trying to hide the recent past and make a new beginning. "How would you like to go out tomorrow night just as friends of course?" Tony asked. He wanted to see right away if she would go for his offer or if he would have to convince her. He really didn't want to stay on the phone and listen to a sob story about her boyfriend.

"Yeah, I think I would like that. It would be nice," said Susi, who was glad she didn't have to ask him. She was actually steaming with anger because just a short time ago she found out from one of her girlfriends that her fiancé was visiting another woman on his supposed business trip to San Francisco. Her friend also told her that the only reason he had wanted to marry her was so he could get a green card. That was the last straw. She had called him and ended the whole engagement even though she knew her family would be very upset. She knew she had to marry another Korean or her family would disown her, but there was no reason she should lie around and mope. She could have some fun before she got involved with another Korean man. To hell with the Korean traditions she thought to herself. She wanted to see what an American guy was like, at least for now!

They chatted for a while longer on the phone and then Tony agreed to pick her up at 7:30 PM the next day. When they hung up, Tony was very happy and he felt like his luck was starting to change for the better. He knew Susi was a very attractive woman and at least 15 years younger than him. Maybe he would even take it slow and get to know her he thought to himself. Maybe she would be a keeper. He knew he could change his ways now. No more drinking he told himself. He immediately got back to the unending task of cleaning his place.

Thursday - earlier.

Maria stopped at Denny's to eat breakfast. Susi was working and came to the table to wait on her. "Hi, I remember you," said Susi with a smile. "You were here a few weeks ago, but you're not dressed up like you were last time!"

Maria remembered her also. "No, I'm off work until Monday."

"Well, you still look very nice," said Susi again flashing her magnetic smile and thinking how she wished she could be a businesswoman. She wanted to wear nice clothes and go to a good job. She wished she could make friends with this lady. Most all of her friends were other Koreans. Now that she was single again she wanted to make some American friends.

"Thank you," replied Maria. She could tell Susi was sincere in her compliment and not someone that just complimented her because she wanted something. It felt refreshing and she needed that now. Maria now recalled the feelings she had the last time she came to the restaurant and it made her feel warm inside, but it felt like ages ago because so much had happened since then.

Susi took Maria's order and then went back to wait on the other tables. Maria ate quickly and tried to read the newspaper, but found she was just staring blankly at the paper and thinking. When Maria got up to leave she sought out Susi and handed her a business card with her phone number. "Here is my phone number. Call me and maybe we can hang out sometime if you like." Susi was very happy. She smiled and told Maria that she had given her card to her the last time she came in. She quickly wrote her own number on the back of Maria's card and handed it back to her. Maria felt a bit embarrassed, but Susi thought nothing of it.

Friday

Tony picked up Susi as planned, but he intentionally arrived a little bit late because he knew the anticipation would make her more excited. When he went to the door and met her she was dressed nicely, but did not look as sexy as he was hoping. She sort of looked like a businesswoman with a conservative black skirt and white blouse. She still looked very nice with her straight jet-black hair that went past her shoulders and her black Asian eyes. Tony smiled too much and he knew it, but he was excited at the prospect of getting to know her intimately.

They went to an Italian restaurant. It was cozy, dimly lit, and romantic. There was a candle on the table in one of those round red vases. It burnt out and Tony asked the waiter to bring a new one. Susi liked the way he paid attention to detail and the way he was paying attention to her. Her fiancé always looked around at other women when they went to dinner.

Once they had ordered and had completed all the small talk, Tony decided to try and find out what her motives were. "Susi, I have to ask you. Is this the first time you have gone out with an American guy?" Tony knew a little about Korean culture and he wanted to know if he was the first. If he were then he would have to go a little more slowly even if she was on the rebound.

Susi wanted to lie and say no, but it wasn't in her nature to lie and she really liked the way Tony was treating her. "Yes, it is the first time." She felt a bit shy now and looked down after answering.

Tony felt that maybe he shouldn't have asked because she seemed a bit uncomfortable. "Well, I am really glad you called me back and I am glad we could meet each other. I just asked because I was wondering if the guy you had told me about was an American guy."

"I don't have a fiancé anymore," Susi said bluntly, not looking in Tony's eyes.

Tony had figured that much, but now he knew it was really something she didn't want to talk about. He was curious, but knew to leave the subject alone.

"What kind of work do you do?" asked Susi quickly changing the subject.

"I work for the government, really just a boring regular job," replied Tony.

Susi felt more comfortable now and she liked the fact he had a government job because that meant he was stable financially. She smiled at him.

Tony went on hoping he could get away from the topic of his work because it was not something he really liked talking about. "Actually I have saved quite a bit of money and in the future I hope to start a business of my own. What are your goals?"

"Wait, first I have to ask. You aren't married, are you?" Susi had it on her mind all day and she finally blurted it out.

Tony laughed. "No, I'm not married. I have been divorced now for quite a long time," Tony replied.

"Do you have children?" asked Susi wondering if she was getting herself into something she really didn't want to. All she needed was to get to know a divorced guy that had to pay his ex-wife and kids all the time.

"I have a son who is in college," said Tony as he wondered to himself if maybe this woman was just too young and immature for him.

"I want to go to UCLA someday," said Susi with a smile and gleam in her eye knowing that she now did not have to fear him paying his ex-wife. "Tell me Tony. Have you ever dated a Korean woman?" Susi wondered if he knew that she might even want to get very serious with him in the future.

"Nope, you are the first one my dear!" Tony smiled at her and Susi smiled back. For the first time during the date they both felt the attraction deepen.

"Well maybe I can teach you some things about my culture," Susi replied. "I am a really good cook! I could cook you some Korean dishes for you some time, but they are pretty spicy!" Susi was starting to have ideas about Tony. She liked the idea of being with a man who was older and more stable. The fact that he had money in the bank was really great. Maybe he would help her and support her dream of going to college!

"Wow, really? I would love that," said Tony knowing that now they were getting comfortable with each other and that his chances of going to bed with her were very good. The idea of her cooking for him brought visions of her in a kitchen wearing something enticing.

The food arrived and they continued to smile at each other and talk. Tony asked her if she wanted to go out dancing after dinner but Susi politely refused because she knew she had to get up early for work. When Tony drove her home and walked her up to her apartment they held hands. Tony tried to kiss her, but it was an awkward moment because another tenant opened their door at the same time so Susi turned away. They said their goodbyes and Susi went inside. Just as Tony was turning to walk down the hall feeling like maybe he had blown it with her, she opened the door and poked her head out. "Tony, can we go dancing tomorrow night?" Susi asked with a cute probing smile.

Tony turned around and smiled back at her. "Yes, I will call, ok?"

Tony drove home thinking to himself that maybe things were changing for the better. When he entered his apartment he noticed how it looked like a complete mess and he started to clean up again.

The next evening they went out dancing and this time Susi wore a short turquoise blue skirt and a halter-top. She was hot and Tony loved it. She danced very well and she stayed close to him the whole time. They kissed in the booth when they were alone. She wanted him and he wanted her.

Tony invited her back to his apartment, but Susi preferred that they go back to her apartment. Susi had a roommate who slept on the couch and Susi knew her roommate would hear them. Later she would spread the rumor that Susi had a handsome American boyfriend. Susi wanted the rumor to be spread and she hoped after a few months Tony would want to marry her. To hell with marrying a Korean man and to hell with my family she thought. If Tony decided to marry her, she would have a stable life and be able to go to college! They made love more than once and Susi made sure her roommate would hear. When morning came Susi acted like she had to have Tony sneak out. Tony tried to leave without being noticed, but he saw the roommate peeking at him from under her covers on the couch. Tony went home and slept most of the day.

Susi's roommate smiled at her in the morning, but didn't ask any questions and Susi went back to bed. When she woke up, she called her ex-fiancé in San Francisco and told him to never call her or contact her ever again. Susi knew this would upset her family and her other relatives, but she didn't care. She knew if she played her cards right it would make no difference if they were mad at her. She wanted to move in with Tony as soon as possible if she could start a new life.

When Tony finally got around in the afternoon he felt happier than he had felt in years. Susi was very cute and great in bed. She was obviously never going to be a brain surgeon, but that was better for him anyway. He didn't like being around women who acted too intelligent. They annoyed him. Susi lived 30 minutes away via the freeway and that was good also because he knew she wouldn't be one of those girls that just showed up unexpectedly at his door. Most of all he just liked the fact that she acted like a woman. She liked cooking and fashion and didn't talk about social issues at all. She never used a swear word in any conversation they had unlike most of the American women he had dated. He smiled to himself and recalled that one nutty woman he had dated that liked to smoke cigars! Tony felt fortunate and decided he would make the effort to be serious about Susi and not play games with her like he had done with almost every other woman he had dated.

They talked on the phone that night and made plans to see each other again the next weekend. Tony didn't want to hurry things and Susi knew she had to act coy if she wanted to be with him. She was sure a man like him had a lot of options.

## Chapter 12

**MONDAY NOVEMEBER 11**

Maria went back to work with a feeling of dread. She thought to herself that it was one thing to be married to a police officer and have him get killed in the line of duty and another to have been married to an auto mechanic who committed suicide because he had AIDS. She really was not too sure that she wanted to keep her job, but she really had no choice with two sons to raise on her own. When she arrived at work, her boss surprised her with a kind hug and a plain manila envelope. There was a card inside that was handmade and signed by probably over two hundred of the people she worked with, many of whom she had never even met. There was also a cashier's check in her name for $50,000. She was shocked to say the least. She sat down at her desk and began crying because she was so overwhelmed.

"We took up a collection Maria," said her boss very softly. "There are a lot of people here that like you very much and also appreciate the dedication you have shown to your job. We really hope this helps you out. I know it is going to be hard raising those two boys on your own."

Maria looked up with tears in her eyes and wiped them with a tissue. "Thank you so much. I have to thank everyone that did this for me," said Maria. It was at that instant that the burden and anger that Felix had left her with evaporated into thin air. For the first time, she was able to feel that there was a world of security around her. She wiped the tears away again and smiled and looked at the signatures on the card. Tim's name was at the top, but she also realized that she only knew a handful of the people who had signed the card. It was her fault and she knew it. She rarely attended any of the office social functions or special events and yet these people had still contributed to help her out. She suddenly felt very determined to raise her two sons to be caring and productive young men. All during the day at work people kept coming over to her and for hugs or words of encouragement. The day went by very quickly and Maria was the happiest she had remembered being in a very long time.

That evening she called her family and told them what had happened. They were all very happy for her. After tucking the boys in bed she sat in the kitchen. She felt alone again, but knew the feeling would pass. She noticed her business card with Susi's phone number was in her purse and she smiled to herself recalling Susi's bright smile. She needed some new friends so she picked up the phone and called her.

"Hello," answered Susi.

"Hi, this is Maria. I met you at the restaurant," said Maria.

"Oh, hi. Yes, I remember you...the pretty lady in the nice business suit! How are you? I am happy you called me!" said Susi.

"I am fairly well all things considered." Maria wanted to talk and share some of the things that had happened, but not over the phone. She thought that could scare her new friend away. "I called to see if you would like to get together and go shopping or something?"

"Yeah, that would be great. When?" asked Susi.

"Well, my two sons are going over to their grandparents for dinner tomorrow evening. How about you come by around 6:30 PM?" asked Maria.

"Ok, that sounds like a plan," said Susi. She was smiling to herself. She really felt like things were changing for the better. She had her new boyfriend and now she would get to have her first American female friend. She liked her new life already. Yes she was Korean, but she was going to be American also!

The next day at 6:30 on the nose Susi was knocking on the door. They decided to go to a mall nearby where they went to a little café and sat down to eat. They both felt like it would be a nice friendship even though Maria was a few years older and they were from different cultures.

"So tell me where do you work?" asked Susi.

"I'm a secretary at the police department," said Maria.

"Wow, that sounds really exciting!" replied Susi with enthusiasm. She wanted to do something exciting. She hated working as a waitress at Denny's.

"Well really, it's not that exciting. It actually can get pretty boring and there is a lot of paperwork. It can be sort of stressful at times, but I like my job," replied Maria sipping on her Diet Coke and thinking that she had better not go into any details about what had happened with her husband committing suicide. That would just be too much too fast to share with anyone right now even though she wanted to.

"So you have two sons and you're married? How is married life?" asked Susi wanting to know because she wanted to get married as soon as possible if she could get Tony to ask her!

Maria felt uneasy and unsure of how to avoid the subject. "Actually, I'm a single mom. My husband died a while ago." Maria said the minimum and hoped it would end there. She looked down and stared into her drink.

Susi felt her sadness. She wanted to give Maria a hug. "Oh, I am really sorry," she replied very softly.

"Thanks, but actually I am much better now and it really wasn't that great of a marriage. What about you? Do you have a boyfriend?" Maria asked hoping to avoid any further questions about the past.

'Well actually, I recently broke up with my fiancé! I found out he was cheating on me. I met this other guy though last weekend and I really like him. We are going to see each other again this weekend!" Susi said smiling.

"Well it seems like it is just the nature of guys. They all cheat!" said Maria as she let out a little sarcastic laugh.

"Yeah, sometimes I just hate men. What is wrong with them!" said Susi and they laughed together.

"In my case my ex-fiancé was my first real boyfriend. He came from a fairly prominent family in Korea. My family really wanted me to marry him. Some people told me though that he really just wanted to marry me because he was here illegally and wanted to get a green card. Actually, I never liked him that much so when I found out he had gone to San Francisco to meet some other girl...well, I just ended it. I am American now right?" said Susi.

Maria smiled and realized how immature and inexperienced this girl was compared to her. "So how long have you been here from Korea?" asked Maria.

"I came here when I was eight years old. My father was a doctor. We had been here only a year when my parents split up. They never divorced. They just stopped living together. I went back to Korea with my mother for 10 years and then I came back here to live with my father. He had started another family so I have two half brothers. When I was 18, my father told me I had to get married, but I didn't want to right away. He was mad at me because I didn't have the best grades out of high school and couldn't get a full scholarship. He didn't want to pay for me to go to college. I heard from other people that he lost a lot of money on some kind of bad business deal, but I don't really know for sure what happened. He told me I had to move out. I had some money saved so I bought a car and found an apartment I share with another Korean girl. It worked out fine and my father even gave me some money every month. I went to junior college part-time and finished my first year, but then my father got arrested for some kind of medical billing fraud. He left the country and went back to Korea. He sends money still to help his sons out, but he never talks to me. So now I work and try to save money so I can go back to college. I'm really hoping now that things will work out well with this guy I met, Tony. He is almost twice my age, but in a way that is very good because he has a stable job. I know he really likes me!"

Maria had a gentle smile on her face. She was thinking back to when she was struggling on her own after her first husband had deserted her. This girl was in a similar situation only she didn't have a child to take care of. "I'm sure you will be able to go back to school soon. You seem like a determined person. The important thing is that you know what you want for your future. So should we shop now? Is there anything you want to look for in particular?"

Susi felt very relaxed and happy that Maria had just sat and listened to her. "Let's go to Victoria's Secret! I just want to see if there is something I can get for this weekend!"

As they walked through the mall toward the store, Maria remembered the man she had met at the Lake Shrine. She remembered their promise to meet there again. She wondered if she would ever see him again or if he would even remember.

They browsed around the store and Susi found a few things that she wanted to try on. Maria let her indulge herself even though she didn't feel in any mood to buy lingerie. Actually, she had always felt that it was sort of silly. The one time in the past when she had bought some sexy lingerie and worn it for Felix, he had told her that she looked fat. She was totally humiliated, but had held the feeling in. The sex was disgusting though and afterward she promised herself she would never buy lingerie again.

"Come on Maria! Come in the dressing room with me and tell me how this looks!" Susi said enthusiastically dragging Maria by the hand and holding up a few very sexy pieces.

Maria smiled and let herself get caught up in her new friend's enthusiasm as they went into the dressing room together. Susi's excitement and smile made Maria realize that she had to stop going over the past and start living more in the moment.

They stood in the dressing room together with Maria holding the lingerie that Susi had picked out. Susi undressed casually in front of her. Maria stared and admired how beautiful and tight Susi's body was. She thought back to a time when her body was like that, when she didn't have any stretch marks from having children. Susi put on a very sexy little blue satin Teddy and turned around modeling for Maria. "What do you think?" Susi asked with a big grin.

"I think you look great! I mean the Teddy looks great on you!" Maria caught herself, but it made them both laugh again.

"Really?" Susi put her hands over her breasts. "I wish my breasts were larger," she said with a little pout. "Now yours are really perfect. I wish mine were like yours! Here you try this one." Susi said handed Maria a different style red Teddy.

"No, I'm too fat. I can't fit in that," replied Maria smiling back at her.

"Yes you can. Come on," said Susi now reaching over and starting to unbutton Maria's blouse. Maria was used to having her sister or friends dress her. This seemed the same and even though she had just met this new friend she could tell that she liked girly things and enjoyed life. Right now Maria felt she needed to enjoy life and to enjoy the world around her in a secure environment. Risks had led to trauma and she didn't want any more trauma. The fact that Susi was a young woman and was less mature than her made her feel like the older sister for the first time in her life. She had always been the younger sister and had always seemed to know other women that way as the younger sister. Most of her friends were older than her and she was close to her mother and aunts but she was never close to her younger female cousins. They were cute as far as Maria was concerned, but they were immature and the secrets she knew as a woman were hers alone. They were not to be shared by anyone younger.

Maria let her unbutton the blouse. "Ok, I'll try it on," she said smiling and wondering if this was a cultural thing with Korean women to feel so open and comfortable with someone they had only recently met. It really didn't matter, but in a way it did for Maria because she liked the feeling of another woman. She liked the closeness that evolved from a brief interlude of intimacy with another woman. It was wholesome, healing, and energizing in Maria's mind and from Maria's past experiences. But now was not really the time. Too much had happened too fast. She didn't want to dream of teeth for a long time.

They were smiling and giggling and feeling very comfortable with each other. There was a soft sexual tension building inside both of them and they liked the feeling. Maria was shy, but she undressed anyway and tried on the Teddy.

"God, you look really nice. I would love to have breasts like yours. I think I should get a boob job for sure when I have the money!" said Susi as Maria stood there in the red Teddy.

Maria felt like her older sister. "Really, Susi, you look just fine the way you are," Maria replied.

They stood there for a few minutes turning and posing in the mirror for each other. They were starting to feel the sexual tension mount between them. They both wanted to kiss the other, but it was just too scary. It was frightening and exciting at the same time so they took off the Teddies and got dressed. After they had dressed Maria leaned forward and softly kissed Susi on the cheek. "Thanks Susi. That was a lot fun. I'm really glad we did this." Maria spoke softly almost in a whisper into Susi's ear.

Susi turned her head as they pulled away and looked Maria directly in the eyes. She had never felt like this for another woman. She was aroused and it frightened her, but she liked it also. She was making a new life for herself and she wanted to be free.

"Maria, I've never kissed another woman. I mean I am not a lesbian or anything. But, well, I want to kiss you." Susi leaned forward and closed her eyes. She didn't really know what she was doing, but knew other girls who had been with women and now her newfound feeling of freedom made her spontaneously decide it was something she wanted to try. Maria stared at this lovely Korean girl standing innocently in front of her with her lips puckered out and her eyes closed. Maria grinned ear to ear and then shook her head left to right as if to let out a sigh of both disbelief and amazement. There was no feeling of love and no feeling of anyone wanting to use anyone except for one kiss. Maria's smile broadened and she slowly leaned forward to meet the statuesque and lovely young female in front of her.

When their lips met, Maria was smiling. It was a gentle probing kiss and they both liked it. It was very short and very simple without expectations, but it held a passion that fueled desires inside both of them. They left the dressing room and each paid for their piece of lingerie. They window-shopped on the way back to the car, talking, and feeling close to each other. On the way back, Maria stopped by her parents' house, picked up her two boys, and introduced them to her friend. Before Susi left they promised to call each other and to meet again soon. The kiss in the store lingered on their minds, but they both resisted the temptation of making anything out of it other than just a fun time shopping together.

## Chapter 13

During the following week, Tony and Susi talked on the phone almost every evening. Susi could tell sometimes that Tony had been drinking and in the back of her mind, she wondered if he drank too often. Tony had to work on Saturday so they decided to get together on Saturday evening. Susi insisted on meeting him at his place this time using the excuse that her roommate would be having friends over. The actual reason was that she wanted to see what his place looked like because she was thinking of moving in with him if things worked out well. Tony hesitantly agreed to have her come to his place because he knew that would force him to clean things up. Tony was starting to have second thoughts about getting too close with her so fast mainly because she seemed like the clingy type. He liked that, but at the same time he wasn't sure if he wanted to be tied down. Granted, she was young, sexy, and definitely the domestic type, but he had been single for a long time and he wasn't sure he wanted to commit to anything. He knew he had started the relationship because he had wanted her sexually. All men did. Women on the other hand always had sex to start a relationship and he knew that too. So the fact that they had become intimate so quickly led him to think that she really wanted to have a relationship and he was starting to wonder what was inside her head. He kept telling himself that everything was fine for now; he was getting older and the nights were getting boring so he needed someone around. The other thing was that when he thought of Susi, he easily was able to block out the crazy things he had done recently. "God, I have to take it easy and relax," he kept thinking to himself. He knew tons of murders went unsolved and he was sure his would be unsolved also, but he had to force himself to not worry about it. The other killing was out of self-defense and he didn't worry much about that anyway. Still, it was the incident with the prostitute that bothered him from a technical point of view. Even though that was an accident, what if someone had seen him bring her to his place?

It bothered him and weighed on his mind. He just hoped luck would stay on his side. Heck, he had met Susi and he had won his bet on the Angels! Luck would stay with him now; he just had to relax. He really wanted a drink, but he had been sober a few days and decided he could resist.

Susi showed up at 7 PM. She came prepared with a little overnight bag, which made Tony smile because they had never talked about her spending the night.

"Wow, you have a really nice place!" Susi said as she went inside. She was drawn to the view from the patio and walked there immediately looking out at the beach. She turned back to Tony and gave him a long hug and kiss. Tony was getting aroused just from the sight of her and by the way she was dressed. Susi had on a silky blue dress that clung to her every move. Tony wanted to take her to the bedroom immediately, but he controlled himself because he didn't want her to think she was just some piece of ass he had to have.

"Would you like to have a drink before we go out to dinner" he asked as he gently pushed her off.

"Ok. That would be nice!" Susi replied. She walked over to peer into the bedroom as Tony went to fix the drink. She was thinking that she would love to live with him.

Tony went to his little bar and fixed two apple martinis. It wasn't that he really liked drinking them, but that was what she had ordered the last time they went out and he wanted to make her happy. Susi was now sitting on the couch feeling very comfortable. Tony brought the drinks and sat down next to her. "Here's to us!" he said as they clinked glasses together. It had been a full week since he had been with her and he was excited about the night ahead.

They went out to a very nice Italian restaurant. They talked and ate late into the night. The conversation was light and enjoyable. They avoided talking about their jobs or about their pasts. Susi talked a lot about her desire to go to college.

It was almost midnight when they returned to his apartment. They made more martinis and ended up making love on the couch. They went to bed very late and Susi cuddled close to Tony all night. When they woke up, they made love again and then fell back asleep. When Tony finally woke up again it was almost noon. He could hear Susi in the kitchen and he could smell the breakfast she was cooking. He lay in bed with his hands behind his head trying to think how long it had been since anyone had cooked breakfast for him. He felt like his luck was really changing and that maybe this woman would be good for him.

Susi had woken up more than an hour ago. She had washed up and then gone to the living room to look out at the view in the morning light. She loved the view of the ocean. She knew she wanted to live with Tony. His apartment was so much bigger than hers. He was a good lover and he seemed very gentle. He had remembered that she liked apple martinis and he was always opening doors for her. Cooking breakfast would be a good way to show her love and impress him.

She took everything she needed out of the refrigerator and placed it on the counter. As she looked around she could tell the kitchen was not cleaned very well, but he had tried and that counted. Anyway once she moved in she would change everything and make it much nicer for both of them. She had found eggs, tomatoes, onions, and some potatoes, but no bread. She decided she would cook him an omelet. She found some utensils in one of the top drawers and there was a frying pan under the stove. She just needed a grate for the potatoes. When she opened one of the bottom drawers, she found a dark blue business card sitting on top of some tools that Tony had in the drawer. Out of curiosity, she picked up the card and looked at it. "Cici" it said in bold metallic letters and underneath, "Outcalls Only." It had a phone number at the bottom. She turned the card over and saw it was plain except for a small dark stain near one corner. She knew that "Outcalls Only" meant that this woman, Cici, was a prostitute. "So he sleeps with hookers!" she thought to herself. It hurt, but what single guy didn't at some point in time? It was not good, but it wasn't that bad as long as he never did it when he was with her. She was going to tear up the card and put it in the trash, but instead she decided to put it in her purse. Maybe she would call this girl and try to find out if this was something Tony did on a regular basis. She felt distant from him, but she knew she should not say anything to him and create an argument. Now wouldn't be good; she needed for him to like her. She needed for him to ask her to move in. She went ahead and cooked a nice breakfast with all kinds of thoughts swirling in her head.

Tony lazily got up out of bed and put on his bathrobe. He could smell the breakfast and that brought a smile to his face. He came out of the bedroom just as Susi was putting the food on the table. "Good morning sweetie!" he said with a smile. He came over and put his arms around her.

"I got up early and made you some breakfast," Susi replied. The card she had found had changed her romantic mood. She pulled away from Tony after only a few seconds of hugging. "Why don't you sit down and eat?" she said. Tony complied and sat down at the table. The food looked good, better that what he normally ate for breakfast. Susi sat down and toyed with her coffee. She didn't feel like eating now. She wondered if maybe she was jumping into this too fast. She still didn't even know what his job was other than the fact that he worked for the government. Maybe he was lying about that also she thought to herself.

As they sat there at the table, Susi wanted to start asking him more questions. He was happy now though and she liked the fact that she could make him happy. She held back her questions and let him eat. Tony on the other hand was still in a world of rapture after last night and with breakfast in front of him. He wondered if she really liked to cook. He didn't notice that she had become a bit more distant. After they finished eating, Tony wanted to take her back to the bedroom. It was Sunday and he had absolutely nothing to do so the thought of her in bed with him again seemed perfect. Susi resisted and said that she had to get back home because she had promised to help her roommate with a school project that she was working on. That was a lie of course, but she didn't care that she was lying. She needed to be alone to think.

After Susi returned to her apartment she pulled the card from her purse and blankly stared at it trying to decide if she should call the number or just throw the thing away and forget about it. She liked Tony and she could tell that he liked her also. She felt that it wouldn't be much longer before she could talk to him about moving in with him. The curiosity was getting the best of her though so she grabbed the phone and decided to call the number on the card. After she dialed the number and started to hear the phone ring, she changed her mind and hung up before anyone could answer. She thought maybe it would be better if she just asked Tony about the girl. Then again, if she asked him maybe he would think that she is getting too possessive. She was really hoping that she could move in with him in less than a month or so. The whole situation was confusing so she started to bend the card in half with the intent of throwing it away, but just at that moment her roommate called out to her from the living room so she just put the card back in her purse.

## Chapter 14

Monday, November 18th

It had been a very busy day for Maria at work and she was glad it was almost time to go home. Just a few minutes before she was to leave though, her boss called her to his office.

"Maria, can you take these files down to Detective Sloan before you leave?"

Maria did not want to do anything but go home and she especially did not want to see Detective Sloan, but she knew she had to. "Sure Mr. MacIntosh," she replied. She took the files from his hand, picked up her purse, and headed down the corridor hoping Detective Sloan would not be at his desk. That way she could just drop them on the desk and leave.

Tim Sloan had his head buried in paperwork spread out over his desk and didn't notice Maria as she approached.

"Hi Tim," Maria said with a tired tone. "Here are some more files for you."

Tim looked up from the papers and took off his reading glasses. He had been in deep thought and when he saw Maria standing in front of him he thought she looked as lovely as ever. But, he could also see her lack of expression and her tired eyes. He felt sorry for her and wanted to give her a hug, but he knew that would never happen. "Hi Maria. How is everything going?" he asked as sincerely as he could without trying to probe.

"It has been a long day," Maria replied.

"How are your boys?" Tim asked.

Maria could tell he cared and she could also tell the attraction they had in the past had vanished like an early morning mist and only a whitewashed friendship remained.

"They are doing as well as expected I guess," replied Maria now starting to feel a bit uncomfortable. "They miss their dad of course and find it hard to understand why he did what he did." That was too much information and Maria regretted saying it so she looked away from Tim. "Really, I guess we are all just angry." She didn't know why she blurted that out and now she was feeling tears start to well up.

"Hang in there, Maria. It will take some time," Tim replied. Now he wanted to get up and give her hug, but he knew he couldn't do that in the office.

Maria bit her lip to hold back the tears. "What about you and Linda?" she asked out of curiosity though she was also trying to change the subject.

"We are both making an effort, but it is not easy," Tim replied.

The conversation ended cordially with some small talk as both had come to the realization that their brief affair was completely over and a friendship was unlikely to endure. Time moved on and the circumstances for both of them had changed. They knew what they had experienced was only a result of lust and selfishness.

Tony and Susi talked on the phone early in the week and made plans to go to Las Vegas over the weekend. Tony had suggested the idea and Susi was thrilled because she had never been to Las Vegas. They planned to go on Friday morning because Thursday was Thanksgiving. Tony said he had to work on Thanksgiving Day. Susi kept thinking that a weekend together in Las Vegas would be the perfect prelude to bringing up the idea of moving in with him. She really hoped he would invite her to move in so she wouldn't have to ask. She had decided that she loved Tony and that she wanted to marry him someday. She would show him over the weekend how much he meant to her. She felt that he loved her also and that he would adore having her live with him. She looked forward to the weekend and started to plan what she would take with her besides the new Teddy she had bought with Maria.

On Wednesday, Maria called Susi and invited her to come over for Thanksgiving dinner. She told Susi that if she didn't have anywhere to go that it would be nice to have her over. Susi accepted the offer. Maria almost told her parents she didn't want to go to Thanksgiving this year, but she knew she couldn't refuse because it was always a happy time for her boys. Maria had been feeling a little concerned about seeing her family on Thanksgiving and thought it would be nice to have someone else there besides just her family. Susi would help keep the atmosphere a bit lighter.

Susi came by Maria's house around 4 PM on Thanksgiving Day and went with Maria's sons over to the parents' house. It was a nice sunny day for November and warmer than normal. Once they arrived, the boys went immediately outside to play with some of their friends. Maria took Susi into the kitchen and introduced her to her mother and aunts who were all busy preparing the feast. Maria received a lot of hugs and condolences. Susi was amazed how much hugging and kissing went on between the women; this was not typical for Koreans, especially the strict family that she had come from. She thought about how little actual physical closeness there was between her and her own mother.

Susi enjoyed herself tremendously and everyone went out of their way to make her feel at home. The dinner was lavish with all of the traditional Thanksgiving foods plus tamales and a few other Mexican dishes. After the desserts, which consisted of homemade pies and flan, they all sat around while the men watched sports. Around 9 PM, Maria and Susi headed back to Maria's apartment. Maria's two sons had decided to spend the night with their grandparents.

"Wow, I am so stuffed," Susi laughed as they drove back. "That was really nice. I really appreciate you inviting me."

"Well, I am glad you could come. It was fun for me also," replied Maria.

Once inside the apartment, Susi sat down on the couch. Maria went to the kitchen and came out with a bottle of champagne in her hand smiling. Susi smiled back and nodded her approval. They sat next to each other and had a little toast to each other.

"So how did you like my family?" asked Maria.

"They were all very nice. Everyone is so warm and friendly. My culture is very different. What I mean is that your family is very affectionate. It was really nice to see that. All your relatives hugged you and in Korean culture that just would not happen," said Susi.

"Really, I didn't know that. Actually, I don't know too much about other cultures. I'm Mexican–American so my culture is sort of a blend of the two. We still have a lot of Mexican traditions, but we adopted them to our American identity. There was always a lot of affection in my family, but it just seemed normal and I never thought about it that much. I am that way with my children also. Felix was that way also. They miss him a lot and I think that is why they want to spend so much time with their grandparents now. It is fine though because at least I get a little time to myself," Maria replied.

"My new boyfriend is like that too, affectionate, I mean. He is from an Italian background, but he was born here. He told me all Italian families have two things in common; they are all loud and affectionate!" said Susi.

They both giggled and then sipped their champagne.

"I may have to spend the night here if that is okay. I think I have had too much to drink with the wine and now this champagne, but it is so good!" Susi said smiling at Maria.

Suddenly, Susi went back to thinking about the kiss in the dressing room the last time they had been together. She wanted to kiss her again, but she wasn't sure she should. Maybe it was just the fact she was drinking too much. It felt good though. She was free really for the first time in her life and she liked it.

Maria smiled back at her reading her mind. "Sure you can spend the night. Actually, I would like that because I don't like being alone."

They both reached for their glasses at the same time and Susi stopped Maria from sipping hers by gently putting her hand on her wrist. "Wait, lets have another toast!"

Maria smiled and they could both feel the anticipation of their desires for each other. "So what should we toast to?" Maria asked.

Susi held her glass up, looked at Maria in the eyes, and then quickly looked away. She was nervous. "Lets see, how about we toast to...um, well, how about my second kiss with you!" She blurted it out quickly and then giggled.

They clinked glasses again and then gently set them down. They turned to each other; Maria leaned toward Susi and delicately kissed her. The kiss lingered and they kissed more passionately with willing hearts and bodies.

"Maria, I've never done this before. I have never been with a woman." Susi was still scared, but now she was willing to explore further.

"Actually, I have only been with one other woman and that was quite a long time ago!" Maria replied. "I am not a lesbian. I just feel good with you."

They both giggled and then continued to kiss. Susi pulled away first. "I really like you and I want to do this, but you know I have a boyfriend right?" Susi asked. It was more for her own sense of morals than Maria's.

"I know. You told me about him. I would never do anything to interfere with that," Maria replied. She felt very drunk from all the alcohol and was not really sure what she was doing though she was more than willing to go ahead with it.

Susi picked up her glass of champagne and drained it in one gulp before setting down the glass. "Yes, we are here now and this just feels so natural." She then turned toward Maria and for the first time, she initiated the kiss. It was long and deep and they both felt the growing heat well up inside of them. "Lets dance." She grabbed Maria by the hand and they went to the stereo to turn up the volume. Susi was feeling wild and crazy. She loved the way she felt. This is how life should be she thought to herself.

Maria laughed as they danced. She felt happy and completely at ease with her new friend. Susi was younger than her and she enjoyed that she was feeling young again. After the song ended, Maria put on some salsa music and tried to teach Susi to salsa dance. They were both very drunk. The dancing turned erotic and they started to undress each other. They were both almost completely naked and they danced holding each other. Both were perspiring and feeling their bodies slide sensuously together in a rhythmic dance of prolonged foreplay.

They made their way to the bedroom where Maria took the role of aggressor. She kissed and teased Susi in ways that took her to orgasmic heights that she had never experienced. Then Susi took the role of aggressor and tried to do to Maria the things Maria had done to her. Maria loved it and they made love late into the night only falling asleep when they were both completely satisfied.

Susi awoke in the morning before Maria. She wanted to go back to sleep, but she had a headache and felt guilty. She couldn't believe she had done all the things she had done last night, but it was so good! She tried to smile, but her head hurt. Maria rolled over and put her arms around her. They smiled at each other and then went back to sleep. When they finally woke up again, it was almost noon.

They showered together and again the passion arose. They kissed in the shower and played with each other for over an hour. Then, they dressed and went to the kitchen to fix something to eat. They sat at the kitchen table both feeling tired, but both smiled in the afterglow of their lovemaking. They sipped coffee.

"Maria, I feel sort of guilty, but that was so incredible. I mean it was so different than being with my boyfriend. I don't know how I'm going to feel when I make love with him again. Oh my God. He and I are going to Las Vegas this afternoon! I almost completely forgot!" Susi said.

"Oh don't say that. Not about going to Vega...I mean about making love with him. Look. This is just something that happened. It was great and we both enjoyed it, but I don't think it means you have to give up your boyfriend," Maria said thinking that it would be nice to see her again whether she kept her boyfriend or not. "Look, first and foremost we are friends. That is how it has to be."

"I know. I feel the same. Plus, I think we both drank way too much. I mean I just don't want to think of myself as a lesbian. This was my first time and the truth is I really liked it!" said Susi.

"Like I said before, let's just say we are friends and go from there. I don't think this is something I would normally do either, but I have had a lot of emotions going on lately and you made me forget about a lot of things," Maria replied.

"Maria, I care about you a lot and we are definitely going to be friends. I don't know if this will happen again between us or not. Let me see how this weekend goes with Tony and when I get back, we will get together and I will tell you everything! I really need to get going because he is coming to pick me up in a couple of hours," Susi said as she opened her purse to get her car keys out. She was feeling very confused and emotional; she wanted to cry. As she fumbled for her car keys, she tried to bite her lip so she wouldn't cry. She also noticed the half crumpled card she had taken from Tony's apartment. She pulled it out of her purse and stared at it thinking about Tony, Maria, and all that had happened to her in such a short time. Then she looked up at Maria, who was just waiting for her to cry. "Maria, can I ask you a favor?"

"Sure. What is it?" Maria replied curious to know what the card in Susi's hand was.

Susi handed Maria the card and Maria looked at it quizzically. "I found this card in my boyfriend's kitchen. It is obviously some prostitute he has been with at some point. I was going to call her to see how well she knew Tony, but I chickened out. So do you think you could call her and find out how well she knows Tony Salerno?"

"Sure, I can do that for you," Maria replied thinking that the name Tony Salerno sounded familiar though she couldn't place it exactly. Maria looked at the card and noticed the small dark brown spot on the back. For some reason, the note that

Felix had left her when he had committed suicide flashed into her mind. She felt a cold shudder go through her body. She thought about how Felix had slept with other men and it made her feel sick to her stomach even though she had just slept with a woman. She looked up at her friend who had now composed herself and was getting ready to leave. She wondered why such a lovely person would be getting involved with a man who slept with prostitutes. She was more naïve than Maria had thought she was. She wanted to talk to her and find out more about this guy. Susi was very sweet and deserved a lot better than that. Susi was standing up ready to leave and there wasn't time to talk to her. "Susi, I will take the card to one of the detectives and find out everything I can about this girl and your Tony Salerno if you like?"

"Ok, that would be good. Really, thanks for everything," said Susi.

"Call me as soon as you get back from Vegas."

"I will." Susi hugged Maria, but felt sort of stupid for giving the card to Maria because that let her know that her boyfriend slept with prostitutes.

Susi looked at her cell phone as she drove back to her apartment; Tony had left 3 messages for her. She called him back and could tell he was worried. She told him she had spent Thanksgiving with her friend and had spent the night there. She said the battery had run out on her phone. Tony was going to pick her up in an hour. When she got back to her apartment, she hurriedly packed her things and decided to take a quick shower. She almost fell asleep in the shower, but the sound of the doorbell brought her out of her dreamy state of mind. She quickly put a towel around herself and went to the door knowing it was Tony. She was very tired and just wanted to sleep.

## Chapter 15

Tony arrived at 4 PM as they had planned. He had a dozen roses hidden behind his back when she opened the door.

"Hi, sweetie," Tony said with a big grin on his face, as he handed her the roses.

She smiled, reaching out for the roses, but then Tony grabbed the end of the towel and pulled it off her. She was naked in the doorway. Susi scowled at him and dropped the roses as she grabbed the towel and quickly put it back around her. "What are you doing!" she asked in an angry voice, as she scurried back inside.

Tony picked up the roses and brought them inside. "I'm sorry, sweetie. I just couldn't resist seeing you naked!" Tony said with a smile. He felt aroused now and hoped they could go to bed before they headed to Las Vegas.

Susi ran into her room and locked the door. She wanted to cry again, but held back the tears. She composed herself and started to get ready, but Tony tried to get in the locked door. "No Tony. You can't come in. I am getting dressed. Go find a vase in the kitchen and put the flowers in it for me. I will be ready in a minute," Susi said.

"Ok," Tony said and he obediently went into the kitchen to look for a vase for the flowers. He found one and set the flowers on the kitchen table. He sat down and stared at the flowers. He saw a newspaper and picked it up, but it was in Korean and he wondered how anyone could read that language! A few minutes later, Susi came out dressed with her suitcase in hand ready to go.

The drive from Los Angeles to Las Vegas took about four hours. They talked on the way. Tony was curious about what Susi had done on Thanksgiving so Susi told him about her experience though she left out the intimate details about her and Maria. The whole conversation made her think about the night before with Maria. At some point she fell asleep with a smile on her face from thinking about the previous night. She woke up when Tony turned up the volume on some annoying rock song he was listening to. When she looked outside it was dark and they were only about a half hour from Vegas. Tony pointed out the lights on the horizon.

"We are almost there now! This is going to be like our little honeymoon!" Tony said anticipating the nights he would have with her.

"Are you asking me to marry you?" Susi replied. She wondered what he had really meant.

Tony laughed nervously and regretted blurting out what he had said. "Well...not right now, sweetie." Susi was starting to dislike the sound of "Sweetie" and wished he would stop using it. "I mean that we can pretend like we are married."

The last line Susi liked because that meant he really was thinking about her in a serious manner. She leaned over and gave him a little kiss on the cheek. Tony could feel himself getting aroused. He sped up wanting to get to the hotel as soon as possible.

Driving into Las Vegas at night is like entering a fantasy world of bright neon lights, sort of like a perpetual huge Christmas tree luring you into the waiting arms of sinful excitement. After hours on the road, everyone driving in is anxious to reach their destinations, but then the traffic slows to a crawl. It is frustrating because even though you can see your hotel from the elevated freeway, you are going at a torturously slow pace. Like everyone else, Tony became frustrated with the traffic and complained by banging his fist on the dashboard and swearing. Susi didn't like seeing him act like that. It scared her.

When they finally arrived at the Tropicana Hotel and Casino, Tony let out a sigh of relief. He had waited all week to be with his new girlfriend and he had refrained from any self-gratification the whole week. He wanted to get her into the room. Tony refused the bellhop and carried both of their bags to the elevator after they checked in. Tony loved the Tropicana mainly because of the pool. It was the best pool area in Vegas as far as he was concerned. He had reserved a room overlooking the tropical pool area.

Susi loved the room and especially the view. The green and blue flowered furnishings reminded her of a place she had stayed in Korea with her family. Tony immediately opened his bag and pulled out a large thermos of rum and coke that he had mixed at home. He poured them both a drink and they sat in the rattan chairs around the small glass table looking out at the pool area. It was a warm evening for the time of year and Tony imagined that the next day he would see girls in bikinis lounging around the pool from his window.

"Wow, you like to come prepared," Susi commented, as she held her drink. She didn't want to drink after what had happened the night before, but figured one drink wouldn't hurt. She was looking forward to taking a long hot bath, going to a nice dinner, and then maybe playing a little in the casino. Tony had other plans for them.

"Well, I have stayed here before and I know how expensive it is and how long it takes to order drinks to your room so I decided to bring my own!" Tony replied as he eyed her breasts through her blouse, which was wet from perspiration from the long ride. She had on a knee length steely blue dress and he could see her thigh from the slit on the side of the dress. He couldn't wait any longer so he leaned over and put his hand on her exposed leg. "God, I have missed you."

Susi smiled and enjoyed the touch, "I have missed you too Tony." She really did miss him, but hoped he would only tease her a bit and wait until later because she was tired from last night's sex and the long ride to Las Vegas.

"I have thought about this all week," he said as he moved his hand up her inner thigh and roughly tugged at her panties. Susi instantly felt the difference between Maria's soft touch and Tony's rough hands. She shuddered because she didn't like the way he was touching her and trying to force her to be excited. She didn't like it, but didn't resist because she still liked him and didn't want to be a lesbian. Her future could be with him and her future meant more to her than anything else. Tony moved off the chair to his knees and spread her legs. He aggressively started to stroke her crotch. Susi wanted to stop him, but didn't. She tried to think of the night before with Maria, but she couldn't do that either. She started to feel sick to her stomach.

Tony picked her up and kissed her passionately. At least the kiss felt better than the way he had been touching her. He then picked her up and threw her on the bed. He feverishly pulled her dress and panties, throwing them to the floor. He hurriedly took his clothes off and she could see he was fully erect. Susi tried to kiss him hoping they would continue to kiss for a while and maybe snuggle like she and Maria had, but Tony pulled away from the kiss. He didn't stop. He forced himself on her and penetrated her even though she was not wet enough. Susi let out a small cry because of the pain, but Tony misinterpreted the cry and thought she just wanted him even more. He pounded her and Susi started to have tears from the pain. She tried to relax, but it was useless. He was thrusting in and out and faster and faster. She just wanted him to finish, but it seemed he would go forever. A few minutes seemed like hours to her. She had visions of him doing the same thing to the prostitute he had been with and she felt even more sick to her stomach. He wasn't making love to her the way she wanted to make love. He was just being a brutal beast and using her. She tried to block that thought out of her mind and she told herself that things would change. It was just because they hadn't seen each other for a whole week. He grabbed her wrists and forcefully held her hands down. It was just pure lust and sexual desire. She felt her pelvis getting bruised from the force and her wrists started to hurt because he was holding them with such force. The more she moaned in pain the harder he thrust, thinking she liked it. She prayed he would finish so he would get off her. He then let out a long moan and went limp, hugging her like a child. She could feel the wet heat squirting inside of her and she knew he had finished. He lay there on top of her panting for what seemed like an eternity and then rolled off her to the side of the bed. He put his hands behind his head and stared up at the ceiling with a large grin on his face. She stared at him and for the first time, she just saw him as a forty-year-old man with wrinkles and scars on his face. He looked ugly to her, like a sick animal. She noticed how his cologne blended with his male smell. She thought of a dead animal she had once smelled when she was a child.

He turned and kissed her softly on the cheek, "That was so good. I waited all week to be with you," he said proudly. It was as if waiting all week was some kind of big accomplishment for him. Susi wondered if that meant he usually slept with some prostitute instead of waiting for her. She tried to smile back at him, but she couldn't make her facial muscles smile. Her face just sort of twitched in a sickly manner. Tony didn't notice. He followed up with, "I think I could fall in love with you Susi." Again her face twitched as she thought to herself, "Could? You aren't in love with me yet, but you just basically raped me!" Tony let out a sigh and turned over so his back was facing her. "I think I'm going to take a little nap before we go for dinner. That was a really long drive."

Susi rolled off the other side of the bed. Her pelvis bone hurt and she felt dizzy. She made her way to the bathroom and locked the door. She let the water run for a bath, but then went to the toilet and threw up. She cried, but tried not to make any noise so he wouldn't hear. She went in the bath and the tears continued to flow. The warm water felt so good. She closed her eyes and as the warm water caressed her body, she once again was able to think of Maria. She fell asleep in the water hoping that when she woke up, everything had just been a bad dream and she would wake up back in Maria's apartment.

When she woke the water had cooled off so she got out of the bath and dried herself off. She put on her robe and left the bathroom. Tony was still asleep. She got dressed and sat down at the little table waiting for him to wake up. She wondered if she was doing the right thing being with him. She played over how they had met and what had happened to bring her to this point in time. She tried to convince herself that she really did like him. It just seemed that the night she had spent with Maria had made her change her views on her relationship with Tony. She wondered if what had happened with Maria had changed how she felt, but couldn't decide. Maybe she should stop thinking that she needed him to support her and take care of her. She wondered if the new freedom that she felt since breaking up with her old fiancé was really worth anything. Also, would she be giving up that freedom if she continued her relationship with Tony?

Tony woke up and stretched in the bed. He noticed Susi was sitting at the table already dressed. "What time is it?" he asked in a low sleepy tone.

Susi looked at him and noticed he seemed like a different person now. It seemed like his aggression had faded away with the sleep and he was now calm. Susi looked at her watch. "It is almost 11 PM," she said very calmly.

"Wow, I really slept. Let me take a quick shower and then we can go to dinner," Tony said as he got out of bed and headed for the bathroom.

Susi waited calmly while he showered. She thought of calling Maria, but decided against it. She didn't want to bother her with the tales of her problems. Not to mention Tony might hear her talking on the phone.

They went down to the casino and the excitement made Susi forget about her problems for the moment. They went to a Mexican restaurant inside the casino. Tony drank two more rum and cokes during the meal, but Susi refused to drink any alcohol. She started to wonder if he had a problem because he drank every time they did anything. Tony was very calm and loving toward her during the meal. He asked her a lot of questions about her goals with school and Susi liked that. He then told her stories about other trips he had when he went to Vegas. The stories were about his gambling exploits and how he had won money. She sort of wondered how much he was exaggerating because she knew most people that gambled a lot tended to end up losing.

After dinner they went hand and hand into the casino. Tony wanted to play blackjack. He felt pretty good about himself now and he enjoyed having his lovely young Korean girlfriend next to him. Susi stood next to Tony as he sat down at a table. He was having fun, but then got on a losing streak and blamed it on the fact that he wasn't concentrating because of Susi. He pulled his wallet out and handed her two one hundred dollar bills. Susi looked surprised. "Here, Susi. Why don't you go play the slot machines?" he said as he handed her the money.

"Oh, I don't want to gamble with your money!" Susi replied as she tried to hand the money back to him.

"Take the money. Maybe you will get lucky!" he replied, refusing to take the money back from her. "Go have fun. I owe you anyway after all you have done for me!" He then winked at her.

Susi felt embarrassed when he said that in front of the other people at his table. She took the money and walked over to slot machines that were nearby. She wondered if he just thought of her as another prostitute and again she felt sad. At the same time, she was happy she had the money in her hand. She decided to save one of the bills and play with the other one. She looked back at Tony before she put the money in the machine and saw that he was ordering another drink. After a few minutes, a cocktail waitress brought her a rum and coke. She turned and saw Tony wink at her and hold his glass up. "This is from your husband," she said handing her the drink.

Susi smiled back at Tony and then turned around to begin playing the slot machine. She started to have fun and smiled because she was happy he had called her "wife." She thought to herself that maybe everything was going to work out fine. Tony did like her and he would help her go to college. When the drink hit her, she felt very tired; she hadn't had much sleep over the past few days. She thought about Maria and it just seemed so far in the past. She won a little and then lost a little. When her $100 went down to $50, she cashed out the machine. When she turned to leave, she didn't see Tony at the blackjack table anymore. She put her hands on her hips and scowled. Her emotions went up and down with this guy; it was crazy she thought to herself. She reached into her purse to get her cell phone and call him, but she couldn't find her phone! At first she thought she had left it in the room, but then she remembered that she had left it on her dresser back at her apartment. Now she was mad, frustrated, and even more tired. She looked around briefly for him and then went to the cashier to turn in her coins. She walked around the casino trying to find him, but gave up and went up to the room.

Tony had left the blackjack table in a hurry. He was mad and frustrated because he had lost $400 in less than an hour. He got up from the table and looked over at Susi who had her back turned and seemed to be having fun. He thought about going over and telling her he was going to another table, but then he saw the roulette table where two blonde women had just sat down. He decided he had better not tell Susi he was leaving. He sat down at the roulette table and instantly started hitting his numbers. The blonde women were from Chicago. Tony started up a conversation with them and ordered more drinks. They were laughing and making jokes. He had almost won his $400 back so he played slowly now. He was starting to have a very good time. Every half hour or so, more drinks came. The two blonde women were married, but were in Vegas on their own. They were about his age and one had a great set of knockers that Tony just couldn't stop looking at. All at once, the table started to spin and Tony knew he was totally sloshed. He scooped up his chips, handed his phone number to the hot blonde, and then went to the cashier. He cashed in around $700 so he felt good. He looked at his watch and saw it was nearly 3 AM so he headed back to the room.

Susi was fast asleep with the TV still on. Tony crawled into the bed next to her and passed out drunk.

Susi woke at 9 AM and saw Tony was in bed next to her. He was partially clothed and smelled like stale rum and cokes. She couldn't believe he would go to bed without taking a shower. Susi slid out of bed quietly and dressed quickly. She felt alone, unhappy, angry, and disappointed. What was supposed to be a romantic weekend had become a nightmare. She wondered if he had slept with another prostitute last night before he had returned to the room. She left Tony sleeping and went down to the lobby's coffee shop to kill time and think about her life.

## Chapter 16

Saturday

Maria went to work at the request of her boss to catch up on some paperwork. She knew MacIntosh was really just asking her in his own way if she wanted to get in some overtime. There really wouldn't be much paperwork to do. She liked earning the overtime pay and she could use it now that she was on her own with the boys. She had the card that Susi had given her and thought about giving it to her boss to investigate. Then she thought better of asking him for the favor. She sat at her desk and answered a few important calls.

Tim had also come to work on Saturday. Last night he and his wife had made love for the first time in a while and he felt good about it. They were starting to get back the flame because they were both making the effort. He had never told her about his escapade with Maria and never would because he knew that would only make things worse.

The investigation of the three murdered gang members seemed futile. There was no evidence leading anywhere. The media had stopped asking questions when there had been no subsequent killings. Tim hoped it would stay that way. Tim would continue with the case, but knew from experience that the chances of solving it were slim.

It was around 5 PM and Maria was getting to leave for the day when she remembered the card She quickly called Tim, planning to leave the card on his desk in an envelope. She was surprised when he picked up his extension on the first ring because she hadn't expected him to be working on a Saturday. "Oh, hi. I didn't know you were in. I was going to leave a message," Maria said quickly.

"I am just catching up on some work," Tim replied.

"Tim, I need to ask you for a favor," Maria blurted out.

"What, Maria?" Tim wasn't sure he could comply if it was something personal.

"Can you run a background check on someone for me?" Maria asked.

"Sure, who is it?" Tim replied with a bit of relief that it was not something personal. He realized at that moment that Maria didn't want him...that she never would. His ego took a blow. He looked at the picture of his wife and daughter on his desk and smiled at his own stupidity wondering if he would ever learn.

"It has nothing to do with me. My girlfriend gave me someone's business card and I promised her I would do this favor for her. Is that okay with you?"

"Sure Maria. Bring it over," Tim replied.

They hung up the phones. Maria gathered her stuff and walked down the stairs to the big office.

"Here," Maria said as she reached out to Tim with the card. "My girlfriend found this at her boyfriend's place. It is the name of some hooker. She just wants to know if her boyfriend is a regular."

"Ok, I can call her and try, but she might not tell me anything. Why don't I just do a background check on her boyfriend?" Tim asked. He turned over the card and noticed a brown spot. It could possibly be blood. He tried to look at it closer. Tim had plenty of experience with dried blood spots.

"His name is Tony...Tony something. I don't remember his last name. They are in Vegas for the weekend."

"Maria, this is blood. You need to call your friend and get Tony's last name so I can check both of them at once." Tim pointed to the spot on the card and put it into a little plastic evidence bag.

Maria took out her cell phone and dialed her friend's number. There was no answer so she left a message asking her to call back. "I have to get going Tim. My boys are at their grandparents and I need to pick them up. When she calls back I will get his name and call you," Maria said. It was uncomfortable being around Tim, but she knew it was necessary if she wanted to continue with her job. She turned quickly to leave and called out, "Thank you, Tim."

Tim sat at his desk and looked at the card again. "Cici." he thought to himself. That sounded familiar. He dialed the number on the card and got her answering service so he left his number. Then it dawned on him. He opened the file drawer and pulled out the file on the woman's body that had been discovered in Malibu. The prints had had come in from the cadaver and it was a Cecilia Jorgenson from Long Beach. He typed in her name on his computer search and her rap sheet came up. She had a few arrests and it said she was also known as Cici. Her last arrest had been two years prior in Anaheim for shoplifting. Otherwise she didn't have much of a record. She had never been picked up for prostitution. Tim looked at the spot on the back of the card and then called forensics. He took the card in the plastic evidence bag to the forensic department. He asked them to run the blood and to check the card for fingerprints. He wrote a quick report on his computer and sent it to homicide, which was handling the case of the dead prostitute. He then dialed Maria's number. Her answering machine picked up so he asked for her to call him as soon as she got the message.

When Susi came back from eating her breakfast, Tony was in the shower. She thought about just leaving for the day, but that would create drama and she didn't want him to be upset. Instead, she sat at the little table and looked out the window waiting for him to finish showering. He came out soon enough with a towel wrapped around his waist. His eyes were bloodshot from drinking the night before. "Well good morning, my little angel. Where have you been all night!" Tony said. He knew she had been in bed, but just wanted to make her feel a little guilty so she wouldn't say too much about his behavior.

"I woke up early and went to have breakfast. Tony, you really smelled like alcohol when you finally came back to the room last night," Susi replied with a sad look on her face.

"Yeah, I think I drank a little too much, but I had fun and won some money!" Tony replied as he started to get dressed.

Susi felt uncomfortable and trapped. This was supposed to be a weekend of fun and romance. Her plans of moving in with him seemed distant and she no longer welcomed the idea. It made her feel depressed and tired. She wished time would just pass and she could go back home, but she had to go through one more night with Tony. She stared at him getting dressed and then blurted out, "What happened to you last night? You left me alone. I looked all over for you and then just came up to the room because I couldn't find you."

"I looked for you also!" Tony lied. "I even called your cell phone, but you didn't answer!" That part was true and now he had put the burden of proof back on her. The whole conversation felt childish to him and he was hung-over. He needed food and relaxation for a while rather than a jealous woman asking him questions. "Look, I was in the casino. I just moved to a different table."

"I think I left my cell phone back in Los Angeles," replied Susi knowing it was her own fault though it was not a reason for him to desert her. Susi saw no point in arguing with him because she knew she couldn't win anyway. She just wanted the weekend to end. Her desire to be taken care of had blinded her view of Tony. Yes, he had been very romantic in the beginning, but now she could see what he was really like and she could never endure a relationship with him. The whole situation made her feel sad and depressed.

After Tony dressed, he came over and gave Susi a kiss on the cheek. He could see that she was unhappy so he decided to cure that the only way he knew how. He sat down opposite her at the table and put his wallet down. He opened it and pulled out three brand new one hundred dollar bills. "Look, I did pretty well last night." He held up the money for her to see. "I think I won over five hundred dollars. Here. Take this and go down to the outlet center. It is right next to the casino. Why don't you buy yourself a new bikini and meet me down by the pool in a few hours? I need to get something to eat."

Susi was surprised again at his offer of money. She immediately smiled and her mind shifted again. She thought that maybe things were not as bad as they appeared. She definitely would not gamble any of the money and there was no way she would spend it all on clothes. She smiled and took the money. "Wow. Thanks Tony! Ok, I will go buy a new bikini, but when I get back I don't want to have to look all over for you." She stood up and walked out to the patio. "Let's pick a spot down there by the pool where we can meet in two hours." Tony stood up and followed her out to the patio. He could see people starting to lie out by the pool. He put his arm around her waist and then slid his hand down lower and squeezed her. They picked a spot to meet and then he pulled her toward him and kissed her. She could still smell the alcohol from the night before. Tony started to pull up her skirt and probe with his hands, but Susi grabbed his hand and stopped him. "Not now Tony. Not out here...people might see us!"

"That would make it more exciting!" Tony said softly still trying to touch her.

"No, stop it!" Susi replied trying to pull away from him. "Let's wait until tonight." Susi pushed him away and made her way back into the room. Tony followed her inside.

"I though you would like some excitement here in Vegas," Tony said with a smile.

"Tony, I am not an exhibitionist!" Susi replied. She wondered if he really did think of her as some kind of whore. This was just getting way too crazy she thought to herself.

"Ok, I'm sorry. I'm going to get something to eat. I will meet you by the pool in a few hours." He gave her a kiss on the cheek and then headed out of the room.

Susi sat back down at the little table and tried to think, but her mind went blank so she picked up her purse and headed down to the outlet center.

Shopping made everything better and the fact that she had over four hundred dollars made things a bit sweeter. She told herself to be positive for the rest of the weekend and she ended up finding a nice bathing suit for a good price. She walked around, found a few other items that she wanted, but only bought a couple of them. She still had plenty of money left that she could save. She had never met a man that had been so generous with his money. She thought to herself that maybe she could put up with his other problems as long as he kept giving her money. When she returned to her room, she changed into her bikini and looked at herself in the mirror. She liked the way she looked and how the top made her breasts look bigger. She went out on the patio to see if Tony was waiting for her down by the pool. When she looked down to the spot where they were supposed to meet, she saw he was there. She wanted to yell down, but it was too far away and would draw attention so she just watched him. He was lying on a lounge chair with a drink in his hand. She observed him for a few minutes. Like every other guy, he watched the girls as they walked past in there bikinis. Then two tall blonde women walked straight up to him and stopped. They started to talk to him. She saw Tony motion for them to sit down. He even got up and grabbed another lounge chair so the three of them could sit next to each other. They were talking and acting like they were old friends. One of the women even gave him a little kiss on his cheek after he pulled the lounge chair over! Susi could feel the anger welling up inside of her. She quickly went back inside and kicked one of the chairs over. She pulled her dress over her bikini and quickly headed down to the pool.

As Susi was walking up to them, she could see they were laughing and that there were numerous drinks on the table. Susi walked up slowly and planted herself directly behind Tony. The two ladies took their eyes off Tony and stared at Susi. This made Tony turn his head around and he saw Susi standing behind him with a scowl on her face.

"Hi Susi," he said drawing out her name as if he wanted it to almost become a question. "How was your shopping?" he added, hoping her scowl would go away.

"I'm fine," Susi replied. There was nowhere for her to sit and she almost turned around thinking she should just go back to the hotel room. She then flung open her robe so the ladies and Tony could see her new turquoise bikini. "Here is the bikini I bought with the money you gave me!" she said sarcastically. She wanted to show off her body in front of the older women, but she realized that maybe she just sounded like a hooker!

She was hoping the two women would just get up and leave, but instead they whispered something to each other and started to giggle.

"Wow, it looks really great on you!" Tony replied with a big grin. She looked very hot and he loved it! "Oh, I'm sorry. This is Alice and Carrie." He waved toward the two blonde women next to him. "We met last night at the roulette table."

"Hi," Susi said throwing a quick glance and fake smile at the two women.

"Hi," replied the two women in unison. They looked at each other and giggled again.

Susi still had nowhere to sit, but Tony realized it and quickly jumped up out of his lounge chair so Susi could take it. Susi took off the robe and spread herself out in the chair in an attempt to not make eye contact with the two women. Tony went to find another lounge chair.

"We didn't know Tony had an Oriental girlfriend," Carrie said directly to Susi, who now had her eyes closed hoping the whole weekend would somehow just end.

Susi sat up quickly and looked directly at the woman who had addressed her so rudely. "Actually, I am Korean and most of us prefer to be called Asian; not Oriental."

The two women could feel the tension and had no intentions of letting her spoil their fun. "Really, I didn't know that! Asian or Oriental, there is no difference to me! Anyway we were just leaving. We just wanted to say hello to Tony. We both had a really fun time with him last night. We didn't know he had a girlfriend!" Alice and Carrie quickly gathered their things, but just at that moment Tony returned with another lounge chair.

"Oh Tony, we really need to get going. Call me sometime when you get back to Los Angeles," Alice said with a sensual tone and coy smile. She went over and gave Tony a hug like he was an old friend.

Tony smiled and replied, "The two of you don't have to leave. You are more than welcome to stay here with us. At least finish your drinks."

"No, we really have to get going," Carrie said. She was feeling a lot more uncomfortable than her friend and didn't want to cause any trouble in public. Carrie pulled Alice by the hand away from Tony.

"Bye," Susi said to the two blonde women as they started to walk away. Under her breath, loud enough for Tony to hear, she muttered "Bitches."

"They were just two women I met last night," Tony said. He leaned over and gave Susi a little kiss on her cheek, but she turned her head away.

After a minute or so of tense silence, Susi asked in a soft mean tone, "So how did you meet them?"

"I told you already. I met them at the roulette table last night," Tony replied. He was annoyed that Susi seemed so jealous. He liked her and definitely wanted to have a serious relationship with her, but he didn't want to see her jealous all the time. "We were all having fun and winning too! They were nothing more than friends. They came up to me at the pool." That was sort of a lie, but he knew he had to say it.

"You told me this morning that when you left the blackjack table you went to another table. Not that you played roulette and met two women," Susi replied. She wondered if he was telling her the truth at all about the two women. For all she knew, he had gone to their room and had sex with one or both of them. At this point, she wouldn't put it past him and it didn't really matter too much what he said because she didn't trust him. "Well you came back very late no matter what you did and I was waiting for you in the room."

Tony knew he had to appease her and smooth things out if they were going to have any fun at all together their last day in Vegas. "Susi, you don't have to be concerned. You are the only woman in my life and I don't want anyone else. I just joked around with them and played roulette. That is all we did and then I went back to the room. Look at how sexy you are in that bikini you bought. Do you really think I would want anyone else out here?"

"What does that mean? Do you only like me because I am young and have a nice body?" Susi fired back.

"No really. I didn't mean that. I just mean that you are what I want in a woman; not just your body, but everything else about you." Tony was trying as hard as he could to get her to calm down.

Susi didn't believe a word he was saying to her. The only good thing in her life right now was the fact that the sun felt warm and caressing on her body. She was concerned about the fact that he may have slept with that woman last night especially because he wasn't using condoms with her. She was on birth control and she hadn't even asked him to use condoms. God, that was stupid she thought to herself. She was mad at herself for being so naïve.

"Guess what? I bought us tickets to a really great show tonight. It is the longest running show in Vegas." Tony was doing everything he could to get back on her good side. He was lying about the tickets, but it didn't matter because he could get them. He was annoyed because she should understand that he was just having fun last night.

"Really, well I just hope your two blonde friends aren't coming along with us!" Susi replied still not convinced that he hadn't slept with one of them.

"Oh come on Susi. Of course they are not coming with us. Remember we are supposed to be pretending this is our honeymoon!" Tony smiled at her even though she had her eyes closed and couldn't see him.

Susi sat up and looked him directly in the eyes. "Oh really? Well, if we are pretending this is our honeymoon then why don't you start acting like it!"

Tony looked down at the ground sheepishly and the conversation pretty much ended. Susi lay back down and tried to just think about the warm sunshine on her body. Tony lay back also and thought about the situation he had created. He realized now that Susi was not the subservient Asian woman he thought she was. She had a temper and like most foreign women he had dated, she had become Americanized. Still, he really liked her and even when she showed anger, she was cute. He could tell she didn't want to be angry. He liked her and wanted to stay with her. He had told himself before he had come to Vegas that he was going to stop drinking so much. It was just that he was in Vegas and it was so easy to get a drink. He actually wanted another drink now he thought to himself. Drinking and gambling just went together and right now he wanted to do both. He knew if he got up and left her though he would be in serious trouble so he tried to relax and not think about anything.

They hung out at the pool for another hour or so until the winter sun dipped behind the buildings and the air turned crisp. They had both fallen asleep and the cold air woke them up so they went back up to their room. Once in the room, Tony felt fairly refreshed and he looked at Susi. She was lying down on the bed with her robe partially open and he wanted to have sex with her. Susi pushed his hand away and tried to avoid his advances. She wasn't ready yet to make up with him. The TV was on and Tony dozed off again. Susi went to the bathroom and showered. The noise woke Tony up and he remembered that he needed to get the tickets for the show. He quickly put on some clothes and went downstairs to buy the tickets. Fortunately, he got back to the room before Susi had finished her shower. When she came out, he held up the tickets and then went and showered himself. Tony planned out the evening with her while he was in the shower. He had already won money from the night before so he told himself he didn't need to gamble anymore. When he got out of the shower, he told her they were going to dinner at a nice Japanese restaurant and then they would go to the show. Susi was happy at least that he was taking her out and not going down to the casino to gamble. Again, her mind wavered back to thinking that maybe he wasn't really that bad and things would work out. Definitely though, he had to stop drinking so much.

The evening started off perfectly for Susi because Tony was treating her like a goddess. He was being gentle and kind.

They stopped in the gift shop and he bought her some earrings before dinner. He was acting very sweet and very romantic by offering her little compliments and not looking around at the other women while they walked together. Susi softened her attitude toward him and started to enjoy herself. It felt more like the first few dates they had gone on and she liked it.

The food at the Japanese restaurant was delicious. Tony had dressed nicely and he looked very handsome. He reminded her more than once that this was their honeymoon. At one point, Susi told him that if they ever did get married that she wanted a real honeymoon. Tony assured her that if they ever did get married that they would have a much better honeymoon than this one. They were enjoying each other's company. Susi started to think that this was the real Tony and that it had just been the excitement and fun of being in Vegas that had made him do the things she didn't like.

After the show, Susi thought for sure that Tony would want to go into the casino and gamble again, but he didn't even suggest it. Instead, they went back up to their room and he called room service. He ordered a bottle of champagne, the first alcohol he had ordered all night. They sat and sipped the champagne and this time when Tony leaned over to kiss her, she responded and enjoyed it. Susi had completely forgiven him now. Tony felt proud of himself knowing that he had made an effort to devote the evening to her and that she had responded. He liked the fact that she was so easy to please and that she was not demanding or interested in expensive things. When they had gone to buy the earrings, she had picked out a pair that did not cost too much. The little things were adding up and he even thought to himself that maybe he would let her move in with him. Susi had decided that maybe his bad qualities were not that bad. She would just have to watch him carefully and make sure he didn't try to sleep with any prostitutes. They made love and then fell asleep feeling satisfied and content with each other.

## Chapter 17

Maria did not get back home Saturday night until after 9 PM. She had stayed at her parents' house with her sons. When they returned to the apartment, the boys immediately went to their room to play videogames. Maria made sure that her parents didn't have any videogames because it just seemed like the kids were too obsessed with the games. She wanted to make sure they did other activities when they were at her parents' house.

Maria sat down in the kitchen and saw she had a missed call from Tim so she played the message. "Maria, this is Tim. It is a shortly after 6 PM and I wanted to let you know I found out some information on the woman from that card you gave me earlier today. I think it is important you call me right away. I will be here in the office for another hour or so. If I'm not here call me on my cell." Maria could hear the anxiety in his voice. She felt a chill go down her spine. Something serious was going on.

Maria called Tim and unexpectedly it was a woman's voice that answered the phone. "Hello."

"Oh hi. This is Maria Sanchez. I work with Tim and he asked me to call him," Maria said in her best business tone.

"Oh, thank God you called! He has been very concerned. Just a minute...he is getting out of the shower. Hold on and I will get him for you," Linda replied.

Maria realized that was the first time she had ever talked to Tim's wife, the wife of the man she had slept with. It seemed very strange, but she was comfortable with it. Maria felt bad because the woman sounded so nice. Maria shuddered again and felt a cold chill.

"Maria?" Tim asked as his wife had handed him the cell phone.

"Yes, it's me, Tim. I just got your message. I'm sorry I was at my parents' house and had my phone in my purse. I didn't notice when you called before. What's going on?" Maria asked.

"Well, it is not a good situation, Maria. I am going to need your help with this. I know you have your two boys there so I just want to make sure you remain calm before I start."

"Remain calm about what?" Maria said back. She was annoyed that he was treating her like some little kid. God, didn't he know that she had just lost her husband? Who did he think she was?

"Ok, Maria. The card you gave me...the one that said Cici on it...well her real name is Cecilia Jorgenson. Her body was found last week in the Malibu hills. She was the one that had been hit over the head and killed. The card had a drop of blood on it and it is being analyzed in the lab," Tim said.

"What?" Maria asked.

"Yes, it appears this woman was murdered," Tim said.

"Oh my God. My friend is with this guy in Vegas right now!" Maria now understood why Tim had warned her to remain calm. Maria's mind went blank. She had been through so much lately and now her friend was with a potential murderer. Maria broke down and started to weep. She could hear Tim trying to say something on the other end of the phone, but she couldn't focus on his words. She had cried very little when her husband had died, but now the tears just flowed. She had been with Susi just a few days ago. They had slept together and now she was in danger! After a minute or so, she was able to compose herself and hear Tim again on the phone.

"Maria, are you okay? Everything is going to be fine."

"Yes, I'm fine. I'm just so shocked and scared," replied Maria.

"Maria, I need you to work with me on this. I need you to give me the name of your friend's boyfriend."

"Tony, Tony umm, God...what is his last name? I think she told me. Oh my God. I can't remember his last name. She has a roommate though and she would know I think," Maria replied.

"Well, what is your friend's name and what is her phone number?" Tim grabbed a notepad and a pen.

"Her name is Susi and her boyfriend is Tony. God, I don't know their last names. I never asked!" Maria felt guilty that she didn't know. If anything happened to Susi she wouldn't be able to bear it. Maria started to cry again suddenly thinking that it was all her fault.

"Maria, please try to calm down," Tony repeated as Maria continued to weep.

"I don't know their last names!" Maria mumbled through her tears. She grabbed her purse and started to look for Susi's phone number. She found it quickly and composed herself enough to tell Tim the phone number.

"Ok, great. Let me try to call her and I will call you right back. Try and compose yourself and try to help me on this. I am sure everything is going to be fine." Tim hung up and quickly dialed the phone number. He tried three times and each time he got her answering service. That was not a good sign. He called Maria back and she picked up on the first ring.

"What did she say?" Maria asked right away.

"I only got her answering service. Maybe she is busy. Don't worry. I will keep trying," Tim said.

Maria visualized Susi dead in her room in Vegas. She couldn't talk.

"Maria, I am coming over there now. It will take about thirty minutes. See if you can find any more information or if you can remember their last names. Call me if you find anything." Tim hung up again and told his wife the situation. He dressed quickly and headed over to Maria's apartment.

Maria put her head in her hands and saw her two sons were running up to her. "Mommy, mommy, we heard you crying." Maria comforted her sons and told them that everything was going to be fine. She took them back to their room, let them play a game with her, and then told them that a friend was coming over. Julio asked if it was a man from work and when she said yes, he asked if he could see his gun. The boys assumed everyone from the police station had a gun and liked to ask their mom why she didn't have a gun. Maria always replied that God protected her and she didn't need a gun. The boys went back to their videogames and Maria went to the kitchen to start a pot of coffee. She had her friend's cell number and home number, but she could not remember any last names. Maybe she never asked she kept thinking to herself as she made the coffee. She tried Susi's cell phone again and got no answer, but she left a message for her to call her as soon as she got the message. She then dialed the phone at her apartment, but no one answered so she left the same message.

Tim arrived around 10 PM. They sat down in the kitchen and Tim took out a clipboard and a pen. Maria's boys snuck out of their room and asked Tim if they could see his gun, but Maria intercepted them, put them back in their room, and told them to go to sleep. They begged her to let them stay up longer because it was Saturday. She agreed, but told them to play their games. She explained that they could not come out and bother her and her friend.

Finally settled at the kitchen table, Maria was nervous. She didn't want to be alone with Tim and worse she didn't remember the last names. Tim had a "situation." He needed information. He was over Maria and knew there could be other women in his life, but he could never do it again with someone from work. That was stupid to have slept with a co-worker. He could like Maria, but only as a friend. Still, she did look nice, he thought to himself.

"Maria, listen. We work together. For how much longer, we don't know. So for now, we are friends."

Maria fumbled with a napkin she had been staring at and playing with in her lap. She didn't want to have to look Tim in the eyes. She heard him now. "Yes." She looked up for the first time since they had sat at the table. "We will be friends, but Tim, I don't remember their last names! I have the phone number for her apartment, but she is not answering that either." Maria took the pen and wrote it on the notebook on the table. Afterward, she looked up at Tim and smiled. It was the same smile when they had played their little flirting game the day they had met, but this time she could see from his reaction that he would only accept her as a friend.

"Do you know where they are staying in Vegas," asked Tim.

"No, Tim. I am telling you all I have are the phone numbers," Maria replied. She started to tear up thinking that her friend was with some killer.

"Does she live with anyone?" Tim asked.

"Yes, she has a roommate, but I don't know her name. I just called both numbers a short while ago and didn't get any answer.

"Well, that's a start; we will call again and see if we can reach her. Listen Maria, this may not mean anything; there may not be any connection between this guy and the card. I will get the blood type back shortly and we can go from there," Tim said trying to calm Maria down. He took out his cell phone and dialed the apartment phone number.

"Hello," said the roommate.

"Hello, this is Detective Sloan with the LA Police Department. May I speak with Susi?"

"Susi is not here. She is in Las Vegas with her boyfriend. Why are you calling? Did she do something wrong?" the roommate asked.

"No, I don't think your roommate did anything wrong. It would be helpful if you could answer a few questions. What is your name?" Tim asked bluntly.

"Ellen Wong," she replied. "But, how do I know you are a cop? Maybe this is just some prank call?" Ellen blurted out. She was illegal and really didn't need the cops around.

"Ellen, if you like I can come over right now and show you my badge." Tim put his hand over the receiver and whispered to Maria, "Do you know where she lives?" Maria nodded yes and Tim felt relieved that he at least had something to work from in case this girl hung up on him.

"Hum, no. Well ok. I believe you then," said Ellen. "That is good," Tim replied as he reached out for a pen to start taking notes. He needed to get as much out of this roommate as possible and fast. "Listen Ellen. The guy with your roommate may have committed a serious crime so please be helpful."

Now both Maria and Ellen were scared. Tim asked Ellen a bunch of questions and wrote down the answers on the little notepad. Unfortunately, the roommate did not know the last name or even the phone number of the boyfriend. She gave a fairly good physical description of him and Tim noted that he would need to call the sketch artist. Ellen also said he drove an older car, maybe a Mustang. Tim told Ellen to look around the room, see if she could find any information, and call him back.

Maria got up and went to check on her boys who had both fallen asleep. When she came back, Tim hung up the phone.

"Maria, I talked with the roommate and she is going to look around and see if she can find anything on the boyfriend. I'm sorry Maria. It doesn't seem we can do much about anything until they get back from Vegas," said Tim.

"God, I hope Susi is safe. I wish I knew her boyfriend's last name. When will you know about the blood on the card?" asked Maria as she sat back down at the table.

"Let me call. They should have the results in by now." Tim dialed the lab number and asked for the results. He quickly clicked his phone shut while Maria stared at him with a frightened look on her face. "The blood type is a match. They will check the DNA, but that will take a few days. As for now we can assume it was the victim's blood on the card. Do you by chance have any idea where your friend found the card in her boyfriend's apartment?"

"No, she didn't tell me!" Maria felt bad enough that there was nothing she could do to help her friend. The thought that there was even a possibility that she was in danger was overwhelming. Tim was not being comforting, but he did not know how close she and Susi had become as friends. "So, there is nothing we can do but wait until tomorrow?"

Tim wanted to comfort her. He felt bad for Maria. "Really Maria, I think everything is going to be fine. There is a good possibility the blood just got there because this girl cut herself or something. We have no way of connecting this guy to anything until we question him." He reached across the table and put his hand on top of hers. It felt awkward to both of them so after just a few seconds, he pulled his hand back. "Listen I will go over to her apartment and station a car there just in case they come home early."

"I won't be able to sleep until I know she is safe," Maria said.

"Don't worry. Your friend is going to be fine," Tim said knowing that there was a good chance she wasn't. He needed to leave because he had work to do. "I will talk with her roommate in the morning and we will be there when your friend Susi and this guy get back. I need to get going now. Try and get some rest. I'll call you first thing in the morning and free free to call me if you need anything." Tim got up from the table and put his notebook under his arm. He wanted to give Maria a hug, but he had to be professional. He let himself out. On the way home, he made mental notes on what he had to do.

After Tim left, Maria felt very depressed. She almost wished Tim had stayed with her just so she could have a man around. She cried thinking to herself that she had never felt secure in any relationship and now she would be alone. At least her boys were growing up. She took a long shower and then went to bed still feeling sad.

On his drive home, Tim called the department and notified them of the situation. He arranged to have two officers in an unmarked car wait outside Susi's apartment in the morning. He knew since they did not know this guy's last name or address that they would have to run his license plate number as soon as he and Susi returned from Vegas. They would follow him back to his house and get a search warrant to enter his house. Tim didn't want him to run or know that he was being investigated so it would be best to question Susi as soon as he left. He would go personally and talk with the roommate in the morning before Susi and Tony returned from

Vegas. He made mental notes on exactly how he wanted to proceed and hoped all would go according to his plan even though that never happened. It would be another Sunday that he spent working. He would not be able to be with his family, but there wasn't much he could do about that now. He thought to himself that he had to seriously think about a new career.

## Chapter 18

Susi and Tony woke up around 10 AM Sunday morning. The night before had been perfect for Susi. She snuggled up against Tony and they made love again. It was noon before they checked out of the hotel. They stopped about a half hour outside of Vegas at Border Town and ate a leisurely lunch. Susi was very happy. What had started out as a miserable trip was ending just how she had hoped. She knew now that she wanted to move in with Tony. She had come to the conclusion that despite his ups and downs it would probably work out fine in the long run. She was hoping he would ask her to move in with him, but even if he didn't, she was sure he would agree to it.

It was 1:30 when they finally got back on the road for the long drive across the desert. Tony usually left Vegas a lot earlier on Sunday to avoid traffic, but the traffic didn't seem that bad today. He put in some of his favorite tapes and began to sing along with them. In between songs he would tell Susi stories about the bands. He was an encyclopedia of trivia information. Susi had never heard most of the music and she didn't like it that much, but she acted like she did to make him happy.

Susi dozed off and Tony turned the music down. She only slept for about half an hour and they stopped to get gas and a few snacks. She decided she would go ahead and ask him about her moving in with him on the final part of the drive back. They were in Barstow so it would take another two hours to get back. When they were back on the road, Susi leaned over, turned the music down low, and smiled at Tony. Tony looked at her like she was crazy because he didn't like anyone messing with his music, but he smiled back anyway.

"Tony, I need to talk to you now!" Susi said

"Oh no, don't tell me your pregnant?" Tony replied, laughing.

"No, of course not. But, I want to talk to you about something," Susi replied feeling a little hesitant about bringing up the subject of moving in with him. She was still willing to try though because she had made up her mind that he was not that bad and it would be her quickest opportunity to pursue her dream of going to college.

"Yes, of course we can talk, sweetie. I was just joking around," Tony replied. He was feeling very good about himself. Things were going well with her and he liked that. Plus, he had won money in Vegas and that had not happened in quite a while. She was good luck for him he thought to himself.

"Tony, I am totally in love with you," Susi said. Tony instantly had a big grin on his face so Susi continued. "I don't want to have to wait another week to see you and we just live too far from each other to go back and forth during the weekdays."

"Yeah, we do live sort of far from each other. So you are really in love with me now? You were pretty mad at me on Saturday at the pool," Tony replied.

"I know. I was mad, but I'm not mad now and I do really love you. You are the best thing that has ever happened to me!" Susi replied. Tony smiled again feeling very good about the situation.

"Well I'm in love with you also, sweetie," he said sincerely. He looked over at her and could see that her skirt had bunched up from sitting so long. He could almost see her panties. He reached over and started to rub her thigh. He wanted to stop the car and make love to her again. He didn't want her to talk anymore. He just wanted her to go down on him in the car while he was driving. Oh, that would be exciting he thought to himself. The car swerved because he was distracted, but he quickly brought it back under control. He wanted to pull her toward him, but remembered the incident they had on the patio and decided against it. "I don't think I can wait another week to make love with you. That is for sure!"

Susi knew he was horny and also knew that if they kept talking that he might ask her to move in with him. Either way she was sure that if she asked he would agree now. "So what can we do Tony?" she asked coyly.

"Well, I think you'll just have to stay at my place more often!" Tony said right on cue.

"So does that mean that you want me to move in with you?" Susi replied knowing she was getting him excited. She leaned toward him and put her hand on his thigh this time and made sure her skirt climbed up a little higher. Tony turned toward her and could now see her panties. The car swerved again, but he quickly pulled the wheel back to get the car in line. Susi was smiling at him, waiting for an answer.

Tony wanted to pull off the road somewhere but they were coming into Victorville and there was nowhere to pull off the road. For a second, he thought of maybe getting a hotel in Victorville. "Yes, you can definitely move in with me. I would like that!" Tony blurted out. He didn't even know what he was saying, but didn't really care. He was happy as long as he could have sex with her again and soon. He knew he didn't have anything to lose anyway.

Susi was ecstatic because this meant she could probably go to the university. "Oh Tony, I am so excited. I promise I will cook for you everyday and you will be really happy with me. I will keep the place clean and you will have everything you want."

Tony didn't care about any of that, but it made him smile. "Really Susi, you don't have to do all that. I just like being with you!" He knew he would be thrilled to have her in his bed every night! They drove on without talking for a while. They were thinking about living with each other. The traffic was getting heavier as they passed through Victorville and over the mountain pass that led down into the outer LA County suburbs. Tony had to concentrate on his driving.

Tony broke the silence. "Susi, maybe it would be better if you moved in a little at a time."

Susi looked at him, trying to discern what was on his mind. She had no idea. "What do you mean?

Tony could see she looked sad. She also pulled her skirt down. He had only said that because he wondered if she really did want to live with him. He knew he was a lot older and that he could be moody, but somehow she had put up with it all to this point. "Oh, no. I just mean that if you wanted to take your time moving your things into my apartment that that would be ok."

"Well, I really don't have that many things anyway," Susi replied still confused.

"I guess what is really on my mind is just the fact that I haven't had a woman living with me for quite some time! It might take me a while to get used to it, but I really like the idea of you living with me. I just hope you can put up with me."

Susi smiled, leaned over, and kissed Tony on the cheek. She was happy. He had played right into her hand and this made her feel very good about herself. "I promise that I will take very good care of you!"

"I know you will," Tony replied, wondering if he had made the right decision.

Susi was also wondering if she was making the right decision, but she knew she had little to lose. "If I do move in with you Tony, then you have to promise me one thing."

"What is that?" Tony asked, curious as to what kind of conditions she was going to make.

Susi knew she shouldn't say what she was going to say, but it had been on her mind constantly and she just knew she had to say something. "You have to promise me that you won't sleep with any more prostitutes." She regretted saying it and when she glanced at Tony's face, she could see his expression was sour.

Tony's eyes narrowed and his grip tightened on the steering wheel. He turned to face her. "What makes you think I sleep with prostitutes?" Susi knew she had opened a bad can of worms, but she couldn't go back now. "Why did you say that?"

"It's nothing really Tony. I just ..." Susi didn't know what to say now and she could see he was angry.

Tony's mind flashed back to the incident with the girl who had hit her head in his kitchen. He hadn't thought at all about the killings over the past few days. "It is something and I will stop this car right now and we can sit here until you tell me why you said that!"

Susi could think of nothing to say but the truth. "Ok, I will be honest with you. Last weekend when I was cooking breakfast, I found a business card with a lady's name and number on it. Her name was Cici."

Tony's mind started to race. "Where in my kitchen did you find that card?" he asked.

"It was in your kitchen drawer," Susi replied feeling a bit scared because of the stern look Tony was giving her.

Tony stared at the road and tried to take some deep breaths and relax. He needed to think. The card must have flown out of that prostitute's purse when she fell. It was the only way it could have ended up in his kitchen drawer. What a fluke he thought to himself. Tony felt strange like he was a different person. He had spent the whole weekend not thinking at all about the past month and now his mind was racing a mile a minute. He needed to get that card back from his girlfriend no matter what. The damn hooker slips and falls in his kitchen and now she is coming back to give him problems. His bad luck was returning and he didn't like the feeling. He formulated a plan in his mind.

"I am not sure what you are talking about. I have never heard of anyone named Cici. Yes, I did sleep with one prostitute, but that was over six months ago. Let me see the card," Tony said calmly. He needed that card back. He would toss it out the window and be done with it. It had been a good weekend so far and he really did not want to think or talk about this anymore.

Susi was happy he had calmed down and she could see his face looked normal now also. Maybe he was sincere she thought to herself. "I don't have it," she replied.

"What? What do you mean you don't have it?" Tony's mind went blank. He could feel the anger swelling up inside of him.

"I just threw it away," Susi said, knowing she was lying. She wasn't too concerned because there was no way she would tell him she had given it to Maria. She knew Tony would go off the deep end if she told him the truth.

Instantly, Tony calmed back down and felt a sense of relief. His hands relaxed on the wheel and he turned and smiled. "Oh, that's good," he said in a calm voice. Listen Susi. I promise I will not sleep with any prostitutes when you are living with me. Really, you have me wrong. I am going to be very devoted to you!"

Susi smiled back at him and felt a sense of relief also. She wanted to trust him mainly for her own future. "Ok then, I'll trust you," she said smiling at him. She felt he was telling the truth and even if he did sleep with that girl once, so what? It couldn't happen again if she kept him satisfied. That is just how relationships worked and she knew it.

They were now within an hour or so of Los Angeles. The sun was starting to set behind the hills in front of them. Tony turned up his music and they drove on.

The same day at 7:30 AM, Tim had called Susi's roommate, Ms. Wong. He had explained to her that he would be coming around noon to ask some questions. The unmarked police car with two plainly dressed officers in it had been waiting across the street from Susi's apartment since 8 AM. Tim had been to Vegas enough times to know that if you left Sunday morning it usually took a good six hours to make the drive back. Still, it was a good precaution in case they had left late last night. Tim predicted they would arrive in the late afternoon.

Tim showed up at Susi's apartment just before noon. He went over to the car with the two officers and had a brief discussion with them. He called for another car to come to relieve them at 3 PM and then went up to the apartment. The roommate opened the door and he gave her his credentials.

Tony looked around and asked quickly if anyone was there with her. She looked very scared when she told him she was alone. She was rubbing her hands together in a way that made Tim think she was very concerned. They sat down in the living room of the small apartment. She went into the kitchen and brought out a small ceramic pot of steaming tea and a small plate of cookies. Tim saw the blanket on the chair by the couch and guessed that one of the roommates slept on the couch.

"I am really sorry to impose, but I need to ask you a few questions." Tim started off the conversation trying to make her feel more comfortable.

"Oh, you are not imposing! I am really worried about Susi!" Ellen replied as she poured tea for them.

"Well, to follow up on our conversation last night...did you find anymore information on her boyfriend?" Tim asked.

Ellen started to tear up, "No. I'm sorry Detective Sloan. Really, I looked through her things and couldn't find anything. She has a black address book, but I am guessing she has it with her."

"How long would you say she has known this guy?" Tim asked. He was glancing around the apartment and was amazed at how neat and orderly it was for such a small place. It was fairly obvious that this girl and her roommate were decent people and were not involved in anything. He had been a detective long enough that he could tell what people were like by how they lived.

"I am sure it has only been a month or so. She was engaged up until a month ago to someone else. Well, it is sort of hard to explain. She is Korean and it was more or less an arranged marriage. Susi just didn't like the guy so she called it off. Anyway, I think it has been about a month or so that she has known Tony. I never liked him from the first time I met him. He just had those eyes that were always flirting with me if I was here. I felt uncomfortable." Ellen wanted to start asking her own questions, but thought better of it at this point.

"Are you sure they actually went to Las Vegas and that they are coming back today?" Tony asked.

"Yes, I am sure they went to Las Vegas. She talked about it for days because she had never been there. I am not a hundred percent sure they are coming back today, but I do know she always works on Monday and I don't think she would miss work. Detective Sloan, I am scared for her and worried. I don't know why, but I have a bad feeling. Can you tell me what is going on?" She had to ask, but it felt awkward.

"No, I really don't think your roommate is in any danger. We just need to question her boyfriend," Tony replied very calmly.

"Well, I don't mean to be smart or anything, but if you don't even know his last name...how do you know it is him that you need to question?" Ellen said.

Tim smiled at her and she smiled back. "You actually might make a good detective!" They both laughed and Ellen felt a lot more comfortable. Tim realized she was an intelligent young woman.

"Oh, yes. Now I know. You asked me last night to describe him to you!" Ellen said.

Tim knew she was trying to be as helpful as she could, but the fact was he didn't know that much himself. Of course that was not something he could let her know. He knew the best way to work with a person like her was to be as honest as possible. "Ellen, the truth is that your roommate gave a business card to someone who works in our office that she found in her boyfriend's apartment. The business card is a piece of evidence and we need to question Tony and maybe even search where he lives for more evidence."

"Evidence for what? What kind of crime did he commit?" Ellen asked.

"Well, we are not even sure he committed any crime yet, but let's just say it is a serious matter and we do need to talk to him," Tim replied.

"In other words, you don't want to scare me, right?" Ellen asked.

"Yes, something similar to that." Tim smiled back at her and he could tell she was at least comfortable with him now.

It was always difficult interviewing people in this type of situation because fear clouded their minds. The problem was he needed information and it appeared that she had nothing to offer.

"You don't have to be that worried. I do need to have you do a few things though if you can. I am going to have an officer come here and wait with you until they get back or at least until 6 PM. You don't have to stay here if you need to do things, but I need your permission to have an officer wait here." Ellen nodded her head in agreement. "I will come back around 4 PM and if you can think of the guy's last name or find out anything else please call me immediately." Tim stood up and handed her his business card. She walked with him to the door and thanked him for coming. Once outside, Tim walked around the building. He wanted to make sure that if Tony returned with Susi and just dropped her off without going up to the apartment that there wouldn't be any other place than the front of the building to drop her off. Then he went back to the unmarked police car that was on the other side of the street and asked one of the officers to go up and wait in the apartment. He could see that Ellen was standing near the living room window and watching them. He waved at her, letting her know that one of the officers in the car would be coming up to wait with her. He then went back to his car and called his office to find out if they had enough probable cause to detain Tony when he showed up to drop off Susi. He got the go ahead to have him arrested so he called for another unmarked car with two more officers to come and wait in case there was any trouble. Now all he had to do was wait. He leaned back and closed his eyes thinking he should take a nap. Suddenly, it dawned on him that he had promised to call Maria. He quickly dialed her number. Maria answered after the first ring.

"Hi Maria. I'm sorry I didn't call earlier," Tim said feeling a bit guilty that he had totally forgotten to call her.

"What's going Tim? I'm so worried. I barely slept at all last night. Did they come back yet?" Maria asked hurriedly.

"No, they are not back yet. I just finished talking with the roommate and I am waiting outside on the street. The roommate didn't know his last name so we still have no idea who this guy is. We are going to detain him when he gets here and take him in for questioning. I am confident everything will go smoothly and I am sure your friend will be fine. I expect them to get back here no later than 5 PM if they left Vegas today. If not, then we will just have to think of something else."

Maria felt a bit relieved. At least he had called her and told her what was going on. She felt confident in him so she told herself not to worry. "Ok Tim. Well please call me again when you can and let me know what is going on."

Tim went back to waiting and actually fell asleep. At 4:15 PM, he got out of his car and headed back up to the apartment as he had promised Ellen. He knew they should arrive anytime now. She was studying at the kitchen table and he relieved the officer he had sent up. The officer left and went back to the unmarked car while Tim sat on the couch and waited.

Tony and Susi were almost out of gas. Once they had made it to the greater LA basin he thought he would go as far as he could without getting gas, but now he knew he had to stop. They pulled off the freeway. Susi knew exactly where they were because she had stopped at the exact same gas station when she had gone to see Maria. Maria lived just around the corner. Susi used the bathroom in the gas station while Tony was getting gas and then decided to call Maria quickly just to tell her she was back in LA. It had been a bummer she had left her cell phone at home. Otherwise she would have called Maria before and told her about her trip as well as the news about her moving in with Tony. It was the Korean part of her, the coincidence of being in the same gas station that made her want to call Maria also. It was good luck and she knew she had good luck now because Tony had asked her to move in! So, she used the pay phone and dialed Maria's number. Tony watched her as he was pumping the gas and wondered whom the hell she was calling now.

"Hello, Tim," Maria answered her phone.

"Hi Maria. It's me Susi!" Susi said, sounding tired but cheerful.

Maria couldn't help herself. She blurted out, "Oh my God, Susi. Thank God you're safe!"

Susi didn't know what was going on and the tone of Maria's voice scared her. Maybe there had been some disaster in Las Vegas after they had left or something. "Of course I'm safe! Actually, guess what? I am at a gas station just a few blocks from your house! We had to stop here because we almost ran out of gas!"

"What?" Maria gasped.

"We are getting gas! We had a really great time in Vegas." Now that she was secure about moving in with Tony, she felt she really had a great time. "Tony is putting the gas in the car and since I was so close I decided to call you! He asked me to move in with him!" There was silence on the other end from Maria and Susi was feeling a bit weird. Maybe she had called her at a bad time she thought to herself.

Maria's jaw had dropped on the other end of the line and she didn't know what to say. Here was her friend just a few blocks away and the stupid girl had no clue that she was with a potential murderer! She wanted to warn her, but at the same time she knew if she did then she would totally freak her out. "Susi, so you had a good time in Vegas?" Maria had to buy time to think.

"Yeah, we had a really good time. I will call you when we get to his place. Oh. He is waving at me now to hurry up so I have to go," Susi replied. She saw that Tony was motioning for her to get off the phone and get back to the car.

Maria panicked for second and didn't know what to do. "Wait Susi. Don't go back to his place now!" Maria knew that Tim was waiting at Susi's apartment and she needed to make sure that Susi was getting dropped off there. If Susi went to her boyfriend's place, that would be a disaster.

"I don't understand? Why Maria? What's going on?" Suddenly Susi felt the fear from Maria and she shivered. Tony was getting out of the car and looked like he was coming over to the phone booth.

Maria didn't know what to say, but she definitely couldn't let her go back to Tony's apartment; her friend might end up the next murder victim! "Listen, Susi. You are so close to my place. Have him drop you off here and I can tell you what is going on. It is about that card you gave me." Maria thought she would just call Tim and then he could come over and talk with Susi and get all the information he needed. Plus, Susi would be safe. Tim could then go and arrest Tony at his apartment and Susi would be safe until it was over.

Now Susi was instantly scared. Maybe it was something more than the fact that he had slept with the prostitute. Why in the world would this happen now just after she decided she really liked the guy and wanted to move in with him? Tony was almost at the phone booth and she couldn't start asking Maria questions now. "Ok, I'll have him drop me off at your apartment." She then hurriedly hung up the phone just as Tony got there.

"Jesus, who the hell were you talking to? Couldn't you wait until we got home?" Tony said sternly. He grabbed her by the hand and took her back toward the car.

Susi saw his anger and jealously again. It was evil, just like she had seen it in Las Vegas. She didn't like that side of him. "How could he be so loving and sweet and then instantly change into someone else?" she thought to herself as they got into the car.

"Well, who were you talking to?" Tony asked again more calmly now, as he started the engine.

"I was talking to my friend Maria and you shouldn't be so angry," Susi said. She was trying to stay calm even though she was completely confused as to what was going on. "She just lives a few blocks away."

"Maria is the one you spent Thanksgiving with?" Tony asked as he pulled the car out of the gas station and back onto the road.

"Yes, that's right. Tony, could you drop me off at her house now? She said she needs to talk to me about something and anyway I need to pick up a few things that I left at her place," Susi said hurriedly, seeing that they were heading away from Maria's place and back toward the freeway.

Tony looked at her and tried to see what she had in mind because he had been hoping to take her back to his place and at least have a nice session in bed before he took her back to her apartment. Besides he had told her that she could move in with him and he wanted to talk to her more about that. "Sure, we can go by there and you can get your things. I can wait in the car."

Susi was nervous, but didn't want Tony to know it. "Really, it is going to take some time. You know how girls can talk! I can have her give me a ride home and I'll call you when I get back to my place," Susi said wondering how he would react.

Tony didn't like not getting his way, but saw no point in pushing it with her. He was tired from the long drive anyway. "Ok, that's fine. Where does she live?"

Susi told him they had to turn around and Tony let out a distracting moan when he did a U-turn. Maria's apartment complex was in the same neighborhood where he had shot that low-life drug dealer. What the heck was he doing back in this area? Always something to please a woman he thought.

After Maria had hung up the phone with Susi, she immediately called Tim. He was waiting in Susi's apartment with the roommate expecting Tony and Susi to show up at anytime.

"Tim, it's Maria. Susi just called me and she is coming over to my place. They are just getting in from Vegas and he is going to drop her off here," Maria said hurriedly. Meanwhile, she looked out the window of her kitchen so she would be able to see when they arrived.

"What? Why? Maria, what are you talking about? If she called you then you should have just had him drop her off at her apartment. We are here waiting for them!" Tony said annoyed.

"I know. I'm sorry Tim. It just happened that way. There was nothing I could do. She was in a gas station just a few blocks from here and she called me. Her phone is back at her apartment. She forgot to take it to Vegas. I think she was planning to go back to his place. On the spur of the moment I just told her to come here. I didn't want to scare her and I couldn't talk to her over the phone," Maria said.

"Ok, I am on my way now. Make sure the guy just drops her off and leaves. I'll be there in about 20 minutes. Whatever you do don't let the guy inside, but try to get the make of his car. We will get the information on him from Susi and then I can call the office and get a search warrant for his place. We will arrest him there if we need to. Hold on a second." Tim stood up and quickly told Ellen that he had to leave and that Susi was safe. He headed out the door. "Ok, Maria. I am on way now."

"Good, she will be here any minute. I am sure. Wait, yes, they're pulling up now. It is an old Mustang, sort of yellow with a lot of patches. He is kissing her goodbye. She is getting out. Ok, he is pulling away now."

"Great, have her sit down and don't tell her too much. Wait until I get there. I will call you back in five minutes," Tim said. He turned on his siren and sped down the road with the two officers in the unmarked car following him.

Maria continued to watch as the old Mustang headed down the road and Susi walked up the stairs to Maria's second floor apartment. Susi knocked on the door and Maria moved away from her kitchen window to answer the door.

Maria quickly opened the door and pulled Susi into her arms instinctively giving her a long hug. "What is going on?" asked Susi as she pulled away from the hug.

"God, I am just so glad you are here!" Maria said smiling.

The two boys peeked out of their room and saw it was Susi. They waved and then went back to their games, closing the door behind them. Maria went to the couch and fell back onto it with relief. She motioned for Susi to sit down. Maria knew it was over now and her friend was safe. Tim would be here in a few minutes and she felt completely relieved. Susi sat down next to Maria and looked at her directly in the eyes.

"Maria, are you going to tell me what is going on now?" Susi said forcefully.

Maria smiled and admired her youthful face. She recalled the night they spent with each other and a smile crept onto her face. She wanted to kiss her again. It was a selfish thought at a bad time and she knew it. Susi just felt annoyed, but when she saw Maria smile, she smiled back in a quizzical way and she too felt the feelings of the night they had spent together. She felt embarrassed. She asked again, but this time in a softer and calmer tone of voice, "Maria, what is going on?"

As Tony was turning the corner to leave Maria's place, he noticed that Susi had left her purse on the seat next to him. He turned around to take it back to her.

"Ok, Susi. I will tell you what is going on," Maria finally said. "Lets go in the kitchen where the boys won't hear us." Maria was trying to buy some time until Tim arrived. She didn't need Susi freaking out in front of the boys. They had been through enough. They headed into the kitchen and Maria pulled the blinds shut before sitting down at the table with her friend.

"You have me totally scared, Maria." Susi sat down at the kitchen table. "It is about that card I gave you, right? You already said that on the phone. I just want to know the details."

Tony had gone up the stairs and passed in front of the kitchen window just at that instant and heard Susi ask the question. He froze and stood there trying to hear more. "What the hell is going on?" he thought to himself. Susi had lied to him. She never destroyed that business card; she had given it to her friend!" His ears perked up and he continued to listen from outside the window.

"Yes, Susi. It is about the card," Maria said slowly. "Do you want something to drink?" Again, she was trying to waste time hoping Tim would hurry up.

"No, I don't want anything to drink! I want to know what is going on. What about the card?" Susi was getting nervous and impatient. There was definitely something wrong and she needed to know what it was. She was planning to move in with Tony and so what if he slept with a prostitute? He wouldn't do it again if he was with her and she knew that. She was tired from the long weekend and now her friend was trying to avoid telling her what the problem was.

Maria had to say something or Susi was just going to become more agitated. Maria took a deep breath and decided she would say as little as possible. "Susi, I called the number on the card you gave me and the lady's real name was Cecelia Jorgenson."

"What do you mean her name was Cecelia Jorgenson? Did she change her name? Really, I don't understand what is going on here," Susi said feeling confused and angry.

Tony overheard the conversation and he had heard enough. He went to the front door and knocked loudly. He was pissed off and his anger was getting stronger by the second. The woman he thought he loved had lied to him and now he wasn't sure what was going to happen.

Maria heard the knock and thought for sure it was Tim. She got up from the kitchen table and hurried into the living room to open the door. When she reached the door it dawned on her that there was no way Tim could have driven here this fast. There was a second knock and this one was louder than the first. "Who is there?" Maria asked from behind the door.

"It is Tony. I have Susi's purse. She left it in the car."

At the sound of Tony's voice, Susi got up from her chair in the kitchen and went to the front door where Maria had taken a step back. Maria was frozen like a statue. She shuddered and felt cold. She did not want this man in her apartment. "Just a second please," Maria said as Susi came up to her. Maria grabbed Susi by the hand, pulled her close, and hurriedly whispered in her ear. "Trust me; please do not let him in the apartment... Just open the door and take your purse. Tell him anything, but don't let him in."

"Ok, ok. I will do that, but you have to tell me everything after he leaves!" Susi whispered back to her. Maria nodded her head in agreement.

Maria ran into her bedroom and dialed Tim on her cell phone.

Susi was getting very nervous and was also starting to get seriously pissed off at Maria. Maria was just acting weird and she did not like being treated like she was some little kid.

Susi opened the door and stood directly in front of Tony with a fake smile on her face. "God, what an airhead I am! Thanks for bringing it back to me." She reached out to take her purse from Tony's hand, but Tony pulled the purse back so she couldn't get it. Then he forcefully grabbed her arm and twisted it. He forced her back into the apartment and closed the door behind him.

Tim answered the phone on the first ring. He knew it was Maria. "Is she there yet?" he asked.

"Yes, she is here, but she left her purse in his car and now he is at my door!"

"Well, don't keep him there. Get the purse and send him on his way," Tim replied.

"Yes, that is what I told Susi to do. I am in my bedroom. I am sure he is gone by now," Maria said. Just as her words left her mouth, she heard voices in the living room.

She went over to her door and cracked it open. She saw Tony was inside and was pulling Susi over to the couch. He looked directly at her as she was peering at him from the bedroom. Maria ducked back in her bedroom and closed the door. "Shit, Tim. He is inside. Please get here as soon as you can!"

"Maria, that is your name right? Get your ass off that phone right now and get out here with your friend!" Tony yelled. Maria didn't know what to do. She wanted to lock herself in the bedroom, but her two boys were in the other bedroom and her friend was in danger. She dropped her phone on the ground and walked into the living room. Tony motioned for her to sit on the couch next to Susi. Maria glanced at the boys' room and could see one of them was peeking out to see what the commotion was. Luckily, Tony had not noticed them yet.

The two women sat on the couch holding hands. Tony sat across from them and glared at them. He needed to find out what was going on and what exactly had happened to that card.

"Tony, what are you doing? Why are you acting like this?" pleaded Susi.

"Listen, everything is going to be fine. I just need to know why you lied to me. You said you threw that card away, but you didn't throw it away. You gave it to your friend Maria here. Isn't that right Maria?" Tony glared at Maria.

All Maria could think about was when Tim would get here. She knew the two boys were in their room and were probably scared, but at least they were being quiet. She had to do something to get herself out of this situation and protect her children. She looked at Tony defiantly. "Yes. She gave me the card. So what? What is your problem?" Tony glared back at her, gave her a sick grin, and then looked at her legs. Maria realized instantly that she had taken the wrong approach with him and really started to feel scared. "I called the number on the card."

"So? What did you find out Maria?" Tony asked.

Maria knew she had to play stupid and just buy time until Tim arrived, but at the same time she was getting the feeling this guy really did kill the prostitute and she had a feeling that was only part of it. Who knew what else he had done? "I just called and her roommate answered. She gave me her real name."

Tony took a deep breath. He felt relieved, but he still wanted that card back. "So where is the card now?"

"I threw it away the other day," Maria replied.

"See, Tony. I told you it was thrown away!" Susi said. Susi was feeling hurt from being forced to sit on the couch. This whole incident reminded her of how he had treated her in bed that first night in Las Vegas. She felt disgusted with him and with herself. It was all because she wanted to be taken care of and go to school. Her desires had blinded her from the reality around her.

Tony shook his head. "I just don't understand why you had to lie to me in the car and tell me it was you who threw away the card. You never told me you gave it to your friend."

"Well, I just didn't want you to know that Maria was involved. That's all," Susi said.

"Look, I told you I only saw that girl once and that was a long time ago," Tony said directly to Susi.

Maria was happy the conversation had calmed down and that they were just eating up time. Tim would arrive soon. Maybe she could even get Tony to leave now. Maria wanted to go to the boys' room and check on them, but at the same time she didn't want Tony to know they were in the house because so far the boys had remained quiet. Maria stood up, "I need to go to bathroom." At the same instant, there was a loud knock on the door.

"LA Police!" Tim said loudly. "Open this door immediately."

Tony jumped up and acted instinctively. He knew it was over for him. He looked at Susi and she blankly stared back at him with her mouth open. He really did love her, but it was over. Everything was over. Maria jumped up to run to the door, but Tony got up at the same time and motioned with his hand for her to sit down. Tony knew she had given the card to the police for whatever reason and he also knew they wanted to question him. He reached inside his jacket, pulled out his 38 revolver, and held it in front of him. Susi yelled out, "Tony, what are you doing?"

Again, Tim knocked loudly on the door. He had two officers with him. They all had their guns pulled and were ready to force in the door. Another squad car had just pulled up and more were on the way.

Tony backed his way toward the door keeping his eyes on the two girls sitting on the couch. He turned quickly and yelled out loudly toward the door. "I've got a gun and I am not opening the door. Back away from the door and go down the stairs or I am going to shoot someone." Susi started to weep in Maria's arms. Maria glanced quickly toward the bedroom where the boys were. The door was cracked open, but she didn't see them. She prayed they were hiding in the closet.

"Tony, we are just here to talk with you. Why don't you put the gun down and let us in? That would be the best thing you could do," Tim yelled back as he motioned for one of the officers to move down the hall toward the kitchen window.

"This is the last time I tell you. Get away from the door and go down the stairs now or I start shooting!" Tony yelled back.

Suddenly, Susi jumped up off the couch and came at Tony with open arms. "Tony, Tony! What are you doing?" Tears were streaming down her face.

"Sit back down you lying bitch." Tony pointed the gun at her, but she kept coming toward him. Tony moved toward her and pushed her back onto the couch where she fell into Maria's arms. The two women held onto each other shaking with fear.

Tim and the officers went down the stairs. Tim dialed Maria's cell phone, but it just kept ringing because she had dropped it when Tony had entered the apartment. Tim and the other officers waited for the SWAT team.

Tony walked over to the window near the door and peeked out. He saw that all the officers were now downstairs so he went back to his chair across from the two women. He sat down with the gun in his lap, but couldn't think clearly. He really wanted a drink.

He looked up at Susi. "I never told you Susi, but I work as a traffic cop so trust me...I know what I am doing now. I know exactly what they are doing outside right now. I know I don't have any chance, but honestly I don't really care." Maria stared hard at him when she heard him say he was a traffic cop. She knew his face had looked familiar. She must have seen him at some point, but couldn't remember. She wanted to look back at the boys' room, but knew he had his eyes on her. The last thing she wanted was for him to figure out that the boys were in there. Tony continued talking in a low tone while staring at the women with his dark cold eyes, which were void of emotion. "I just want you to know Susi; I did not kill that prostitute. She slipped in my kitchen and hit her head on the floor."

Susi's eyes widened and her jaw dropped. Now she finally understood what was going on. Maria had found out that the card had belonged to someone who was dead and the police suspected Tony of killing her. She felt sick to her stomach. Her face cringed with the realization of the situation at hand. She felt like she was going to faint.

Tony continued, "I'm telling you both the truth. I don't have any reason to lie now because it is all over for me. She tried to steal from me and we struggled when I tried to take her purse from her. She just slipped and hit her head really hard on the floor. I didn't kill her. Don't look at me like I am some kind of crazed serial killer. It was just an accident. Yeah, I wanted to kill her because she stole from me, but she just slipped!"

"Then why are you holding us here as hostages?" Maria asked calmly through her tears.

"Why? I'll tell you why. Because it is over for me now. I took her body and dumped it in the Malibu hills. When they search my apartment they are bound to find matching fibers, hair, or even blood. Even if I say it was not intentional I still go down for manslaughter and get the maximum because I tried to cover it up. What? You think because I am a cop I will get a break? I don't think so. Plus, what if they find out about the other ones!" As soon as the last words came out, Tony knew he should have never said them. No one would ever know about the other killings, but the words just slipped out. "Shit."

He banged his gun on his head as if to punish himself for saying what he should have never said.

"What other ones?" Maria asked calmly. She started to feel like she wasn't even there anymore. She suddenly realized she was clutching her teeth. Her jaw was firm and hard, her temples pulsed. There was no more control. She tried to blink, but the tears blurred her vision. Then the teeth. Everywhere teeth. It felt like someone else was doing the talking for her. She blinked her eyes because she thought she saw a butterfly like the one she had seen at the Lake Gardens dancing behind Tony.

Nothing mattered to Tony now. The fact was that he had just told a total stranger that he had committed other killings. That meant he had had only dug a deeper grave for himself. He knew he had only one choice to make and that was to stick the gun in his mouth and end his life. He didn't feel any emotion and didn't even feel scared to do it. His life would be screwed if he lived and he knew it. There was no chance of getting away or getting off in a trial. He would be convicted and he would have to serve a long sentence. He wasn't going to let his life end in jail. Being a cop and going to jail was the same as dying and he knew that. He looked back and forth at the two women. He didn't feel any anger toward them and he didn't want to scare them anymore. It was over for him. "Lets just put it this way. I would never kill two decent people like you so you have nothing to worry about. I think the best thing right now is that both of you get up and walk into the bedroom over there." He held up his gun and pointed it toward the direction of Maria's bedroom. He didn't want them to witness him putting the gun in his mouth and pulling trigger. He didn't have much time before the SWAT team broke into the apartment.

Julio and Leo had been hiding in their bedroom closet. Julio had pulled out his father's handgun that he had been hiding inside a box of old toys that they never used. Leo's eyes widened at the sight of the gun in his older brother's hands. "Is that a real gun? Where did you get it?" he whispered to his brother.

"It is a real gun. It used to be Dad's gun, but he said I should have it if anything ever happened to him so it's mine now," whispered Julio.

"Does Mom know you have it?" Leo said quietly.

"Of course she knows I have it. That's why I have it to protect her. You wait here and I am going to sneak over to the door and see what is going on," Julio told his little brother.

Julio crawled on his hands and knees toward the bedroom door that was cracked open. He peered out and saw that the man was now holding his gun and pointing to Maria's bedroom. Julio's mom and her friend were getting up from the couch and starting to walk slowly toward the bedroom. Julio had watched enough movies to know what that meant. The man was making his mom go to her bedroom so he could hurt her or kill her. He lay down on his stomach and thought about himself like a sniper in one of his videogames. He slowly took the safety switch off and aimed the gun at the man's back. He squeezed the trigger. The flash and recoil from the gun was tremendous and he started to scream.

Tony crumpled to the floor and dropped his gun. The bullet hit his back and went directly through his heart. Blood started to gush out of him. The two women ran toward the boys' bedroom and scooped up the two boys. The smoking gun lay on the floor. The SWAT officers knocked down the door with their guns drawn and Tim came in behind them. Tony tried to move, but he couldn't feel anything. He knew he had been shot. He cried out his last words, "Susi," and then his head fell back down to the floor in the pool of blood.

When Tony's apartment was searched, they found over fifty guns, mostly handguns, all unregistered. Most likely he had confiscated them from people he had stopped as a traffic cop. Carpet fibers matched the carpet fibers that had covered the prostitute's body and they also found blood evidence. The other killings he had committed remained unsolved.

Susi told her roommate what happened and made her swear to never tell anyone. Susi felt very ashamed and embarrassed by the whole incident. She did not want to date anyone for a long time and vowed not to get married for a long time either. Her and Maria remained friends, but they both felt completely different toward each other. There was no closeness or even compassion. There was sympathy, but not compassion. Susi talked constantly with Maria on the phone for days afterward trying to convince her that she would never date a guy like that again. She was never going to date any guy again at least until she got her degree from a college. Maria really couldn't care less because Maria had softened where she had been hard. She opened herself now to her spiritual side and embraced whatever dreams came to her. Fortunately, she felt a calm wave slowly settle into her each and every moment. What had been a routine and structured life had changed to a loving and creative life. Even things at work had changed. She started to talk with more people at work and share her stories. She started to see what the beat officers went through on a daily basis and related to their work on a very realistic level. She started to think about going back to school and studying to become a psychologist.

Maria moved in with her parents and never went anywhere near her old apartment. She immediately put both of the boys into trauma counseling, which the police department provided. She went to private counseling and started to talk about her feelings. She put the money they had collected for her into an account and thought about buying a condo in a better neighborhood. The mundane life went on and she was grateful for that. At first, she had felt scared at every turn. It was hard to even go back and forth to work, but it was getting easier. Her sons had spent so much time at their grandparents' home before that they adapted even faster than Maria. She went back to doing her workouts at the police gym three times a week. Life seemed to be going back to normal and that felt very good.

The End.

## Chapter 19

It was Saturday and the end of November, nearly one month after Tony had been shot. Maria was sitting at the dinner table with her parents and her two sons eating dinner. "Mom, can you take us to the new 'Lord of the Rings' movie? It is really good I heard," said Leo.

"Well, I don't think it is in theaters yet," Maria's father said.

"It starts on Wednesday. Can you take us after school on Wednesday?" pleaded Julio.

"Sure. We can all go after school on Wednesday and you both can bring a friend if you want and I will pay for them," said Maria with a smile.

"Wow, thanks Mom. You are the best mom in the whole world!" said Julio.

Maria excused herself from the table and went outside. The winter sun was setting and the sky was filled with pastel colors. There was something on her mind, something she wanted to remember, but it just wouldn't come to the surface. She knew it was a peaceful thought. Then she smiled and remembered. "The Writer." They were supposed to meet again the following Monday.

On Monday, Maria told her boss that she needed a few extra hours at lunch to take care of some personal matters. She left at 11:30 AM and headed toward the Pacific Palisades to the Lake Shrine to meet the man she had met before. Brent, the guy, who said he was the "Writer" for that day. The thought made her smile. They had promised to meet again so she wanted to fulfill her end of the promise. If he didn't show up, she would sit and relax for a while, and then get some lunch on the way back to her office.

As she headed onto the path that surrounded the lake, she could see him sitting in the distance. He was at the same bench where she had met Tim. She smiled to herself at the funny coincidence of it all as she walked toward him. He stood up and waved to her when he saw her coming. Maria waved back as she continued walking along the flower-lined path at the edge of the small lake. Maria was dressed in a black pantsuit for work, but she had let her hair down in the car on the drive over. For some reason, as she walked, all she could think about was how good the warm gentle breeze felt as it blew through her hair. The feeling brought a smile to her face and she almost giggled, but contained herself and tried to wipe the smile off of her face just in case he got the wrong impression. When they both said "Hi" simultaneously, the smile instantly came back to her face.

"I didn't know if you would remember and show up, but I am glad you are you are here!" Brent said.

"Honestly, you are lucky. I almost completely forgot!" Maria replied as they stood facing each other. "Now first off, you told me that when we met this time you would tell me your full name. So, I am not sitting down here to talk with you until you do!" Maria said directly with her best Latina attitude and little headshake.

"That I did. My name is Brent Townsend," the man said as he extended his hand out to her.

Maria took his hand, "Nice to meet you once again, Brent Townsend."

They sat down on the small concrete bench overlooking the lake. Maria put her purse in her lap. She looked at Brent and expected him to speak because the last time they had met he had spoken a lot, but he didn't say anything. He looked out at the lake and then turned and looked at Maria. His eyes seemed to see inside her and for a second she felt sort of embarrassed.

"So Brent, you promised to tell me about yourself this time, remember?" Maria said softly. Maria looked at his face. He was at least 45 years old and had a very peaceful face.

"Well, I am not that good at talking about myself. But, I did promise so I will try. I guess I can start with the basic data that most people want to know. I'll try not to sound like an advertisement in a dating service because obviously you can see what I look like. I am 52 years old." Maria's eyebrows went up. She would never have guessed he was that old. "I was born in Malibu. I grew up as your typical Malibu surfer kid. As a teenager I was fairly wild. I wasn't the type to get in fights or anything like that. I loved the beach and surfing. I went to college in Santa Barbara and played on the volleyball team there. I have worked most of my life and actually I have written most of my life, but only recently have I tried to publish some of the things I have written. I worked for a long time after college as a personal trainer. I invented a few personal training devices and had them patented. I was surprised at how well things turned out, but I actually became fairly wealthy. I married a woman from Florida who was a sort of famous model at the time. I have a son who is 18 years old. He has lived with me for the past three years. I have been divorced now for 5 years and my ex still lives in Florida. That is the brief history of me!" Brent smiled at Maria and waited for her reaction, but instead she just smiled back at him so he continued talking. "I love to read and I love to take care of my garden. I come here on and off just to enjoy the serenity. I actually live within walking distance of here." Brent turned and looked at Maria and saw that she was starting to get tears in her eyes. He was puzzled as to why? "Maria, are you okay? Is it something I said?"

"No, no. It is not anything you said. I have just been through so much in the past few months and for some reason my mind just wanders sometimes. I start to recall some of the things that happened. It is very complicated. I'm sorry." Maria wiped her tears away with a tissue from her purse. "I am 32 years old and I just lived a nice normal boring life and then it all of a sudden changed! It just has been crazy. I guess I really came back here today because this is a place where I feel at peace with myself. The last time I met you here we had a conversation about much deeper issues than most people usually talk about," Maria said clutching her tissue.

"Its fine. We can talk about anything you like," said Brent. He tried to comfort her by putting his hand on her shoulder, but he only left it there for second because it felt awkward.

Maria enjoyed the brief touch of his hand, but wasn't sure if now was the right time to be close to anyone. Her thoughts couldn't stop her emotions and she started to talk really fast.

"I don't really know how to say it, but I guess sometimes I feel very sad because life just seems to have little meaning for me now. First, I have an affair with a guy from my work. We had been so attracted to each other for so many years, but afterward it just screwed up our friendship. Then my husband committed suicide because he was gay and found out he has AIDS. Then I met a woman that I really, really liked and we spent an unbelievable night together. Then she went off to Las Vegas with some guy she met who turned out to be a murderer. He took us hostage in my apartment and the whole thing ended when my oldest son snuck out of his room and shot the guy in the back killing him. Seriously Brent, this is all the truth. You don't have to believe me, but I am just scared the craziness won't stop. What is in store for me next? What is my destiny?" Maria started to sob and she turned her head away from her new friend.

"Wow! That is a lot to go through for sure," Brent replied with a look of astonishment.

"I just hope my boys can grow up and be happy people after going through all of this." Maria couldn't believe she had let all that out at once to a man that she barely knew.

"We all want a happy future for our children," Brent replied trying to sound comforting.

They sat next to each other in silence for few minutes looking out at the lake. Then Brent reached over and took Maria's hand and held it with both of his hands. He turned and looked into her eyes and held her eyes in a compassionate gaze.

"Maria there is meaning in life. There is love. The purest love in life is the love between a parent and their child and you are fortunate to have that." Maria smiled at him and then they let go of each other's hands.

"Thank you. That made me feel better. I understand what you are saying." Maria spoke softly and felt light headed. "You know, I have tried all my life to be a good person but I never really knew if being a good person made that much difference. Now though, after all that I have gone through recently I can see that being a good person does make a difference. Just as well I can see that not being a selfish person makes an even bigger difference."

"That is a very wise thing to say Maria. You have learned from your experiences," Brent replied also in a gentle tone.

"Oh, trust me. I am still learning and I am sure I have a long ways to go." Maria was glad she had come and talked with this man.

"Yes, we all have a long ways to go. Life is a never-ending process of learning from our mistakes. Darwin's theory of evolution is based on that concept. Life really is the survival of the fittest," Brent said.

"Especially in LA!" Maria replied and then they both laughed, Maria through her tears.

"So now that we have met twice would you like to become friends?" Brent asked.

Maria turned to him and this time she reached out and took his hands in hers. She looked deeply into his eyes. She smiled at him and thought for a second about kissing him, but then she noticed a butterfly dancing in the background. "I hope we can be friends forever!.

She closed her eyes and briefly saw the blood and the flash of her past, but when she opened them, the butterflies danced behind her new friend. The sun felt good on her skin and she saw his lips approaching hers.
The end.

CPSIA information can be obtained at www.ICGtesting.com
Printed in the USA
LVOW011634020112

262047LV00008B/209/P

9 781456 327361